THE MONSTROUS DEATHS AT THE CIRCADI INN

Linden Larson

For all the kids who love the monsters

- 1 -

A big black shape moved through the tree line. Quinn gasped and dove into their tent.

Inside, their classmate Izzy tore her eyes away from her equipment to gawk at them.

"I see him!" Quinn cried. "He's here!"

Izzy gasped and started reaching for her things. Camera lenses and microphones clattered as she dug through her bag.

Quinn sat next to her and grabbed their notebook, shoving their glasses up their nose. Their sleeping bag was surrounded with magazine and newspaper cutouts showing blurry bipedal apes, giant moths, and long-necked water serpents.

Just as they were about to leave the tent, the dark shape

lumbered closer. They both froze.

The animal outside grunted softly and sniffed around the tent, then heaved up on broad hind legs to paw at the bundle of food they had tied to a tree branch.

"Quinn!" Izzy hissed. "That's not Bigfoot! It's a bear!"

Quinn froze. "Really?" they whispered.

"Yes!"

They were silent for a moment.

"Well, this is *way* better!"

"*What?*"

"Black bears can swim *and* climb trees, and they're twice as strong as lions! Can Bigfoot do all that?"

Izzy looked at them like they had just said they had an elephant in their pocket.

Quinn watched in awe as the huge silhouette swiped at their food pack. Unable to tear through it, the bear eventually lost interest and shuffled away.

When the noises faded, Quinn and Izzy looked at each other.

"That was so scary," Izzy breathed.

"I know!" Quinn shook their head in amazement. "I've never seen a bear that close. I got some photos, but they're not that good." They held up their phone. A few shaky pictures showed the bear's outline through the tent fabric.

"Hmm. We could always say that's Bigfoot, I guess," Izzy said with a shrug. "But that's not why we're here. We want real evidence!"

"Yeah!" Quinn got to their feet. "I'm gonna get some clearer shots."

"Not of the bear, dude! Of Bigfoot!"

"Yeah, yeah, I know. I just want to check it out. I'll be right back." They climbed out of the tent.

"Quinn!" Izzy cried.

They smiled at her over their shoulder, trying to reassure her. It didn't work.

Looking around, Quinn quickly spotted the bear, walking away from them along the ridge where the two had pitched their tent. They smiled as their feet sank into the bear's round footprints, imagining these feet carrying the bear through forests and meadows. They could almost see the claws ripping through tree branches and squirming fish.

The ridge was tall and the decline in front of them was very steep. They scooted over to the edge, angling their phone to take some pictures.

They couldn't understand why Izzy didn't care. This was a black bear! One of the most interesting animals in the region! To Quinn, animals that were documented were just as fascinating as those that weren't. The Eyewitness Books and National Geographic articles they devoured as a kid were full of birds and bugs, not mythical creatures. But cryptids represented a field of endless possibility to study new species. Izzy wanted to document and report on these creatures, but Quinn wanted to write about the metamorphosis of the Loveland Frogman and track the migration patterns of the Jersey Devil.

They leaned over the ridge's edge a little. The view was much better! They could zoom in and see details on the bear's body: big teeth, shining eyes, twitching ears. This was the coolest thing they had ever seen.

They leaned farther over, putting their weight against a young tree. They took a few more photos.

The tree began to bend and Quinn tried to move away.

They were too slow.

The tree snapped.

Izzy screamed.

The bear huffed in fear and ran away.

Quinn toppled over the edge.

~~~

So maybe following the bear wasn't the best idea, Quinn thought the following week as they studied the bandage on their arm. They shifted their weight on the hot concrete of the bus depot as flocks of whining students and listless commuters flowed around them and their parents. The afternoon sun stung their eyes and spread the scent of heated garbage.

The fall down the ridge wasn't as bad as they expected. Quinn's body was badly bruised and their wrist was sprained, but Izzy's panicked 911 call turned out to be unnecessary. The visit with the doctor lasted less than an hour.

They pulled out their notebook and pencil and flipped to the page titled Sprained wrist June 26. The page read, *Pain 8/10. Extends up arm when touched. Flesh feels squishy(?). Hurts most when touched from a 30 degree angle. 4 or 5 layers of gauze, scratchy, smells like plastic. Small spot of blood.* They poked the pencil's eraser end against their wrist, gently at first and then harder, then updated the pain rating
~~~

to a 3/10.

"Doesn't that hurt?" their mom asked.

Quinn nodded. "Yep."

"That doesn't need to go in your diary, honey. Stop hurting yourself."

She put a hand over Quinn's to stop them. Quinn shut the notebook and slid it into their pocket. Their mom nervously undid her bun, ran her hands through her hair, and redid it. Quinn had inherited her thick and frizzy black hair along with her amber skin and short, broad frame, and for a brief moment they looked alike. Then she twisted her hair back up and the resemblance faded.

"Remember," her mom said once every hair was in place. "Don't see this as a punishment. It's an opportunity."

Their dad nodded. Quinn shared his sharp nose, thin lips, and the deep-set gray eyes that made them both look perpetually tired.

"An opportunity for misery, right?" Quinn said. "Because this is totally a punishment." They resettled the heavy bag on their shoulders, which their parents had packed full of organization tools, self-help texts, and other supplies for the study of prosociality. The summer program at a nearby town's community college was supposed to teach teens leadership and "people skills," which as far as Quinn was concerned were the consolation prize for not having any real skills.

"You've got to learn to be more careful," their dad said. "That ridge is so tall. It could have been…"

"Don't talk that way, Sam," their mom cut in.

He cleared his throat. "Uh– right. So… we want this camp to be a fresh start for you. A chance to grow in a welcoming, safe–"

At that moment a reporting crew walked past them. "...later to-night," the announcer was saying. "In other news, another body was discovered outside the city, in a neighborhood just north of Cardiff Community College. There were no visible injuries apart from a small piercing wound on the chest. We are at the site where the last body was found, only the latest in a string of similar incidents…"

Quinn laughed bitterly. "Are you serious? The exact place where you're sending me? Good choice."

Their dad and mom looked anxiously at each other, then back at them. "It's a coincidence," their mom finally said. "You'll still be safer out there than you are in Syracuse. And it will be a good environment to help you mature."

"Ew. What?"

"Honey, you know we're proud of how smart you are. And you've got a wonderful imagination. But you're a little… intense, sometimes. Remember when you dissected frogs in school and you tried to take home the organs?"

"And that prank you pulled on your art teacher," their dad reminded them.

"That wasn't a prank. The assignment was about things we love. How would I know she's afraid of tarantulas?"

"The point is," he said, "that some structure will help you. You could even make some friends. People who understand you."

"Well, why can't you understand?" Quinn asked, their voice catching unexpectedly. They hated how vulnerable that sounded.

"We're trying, honey," their mom said.

"No you're not!" Quinn's eyes stung and they swiped at them

angrily. "You're just trying to avoid me."

"Quinn," their dad said authoritatively. "This will be good for you."

"How do you know that?" Their breathing quickened and their chest ached. They wished they could calm down. "Maybe it'll be worse! Maybe they'll think I'm even weirder out there. And I'll be even lonelier. You don't know!"

"Just give it a chance, Quinn," their dad cut them off. "This has been a stressful time for us all. Why don't we just see how it goes? Maybe this summer will surprise you."

Before they could respond, Quinn's mom said, "Look, there's your bus. We should go."

Anger and anxiety simmered in Quinn's chest as they received a stiff hug from each of their parents. With a few final words of encouragement, they ushered Quinn towards their bus and retreated to their nearby car.

"Good luck, honey," their dad called from the open window. "Call us when you're settled in." There was something soft in his voice they didn't recognize. Regret?

Quinn nodded. "Okay."

He nodded back and drove away. The city quickly swallowed them.

With a sigh, Quinn summoned all the courage they could, then walked towards the bus to their leadership camp.

And kept walking.

And passed it.

The bus their parents wanted them to take pulled away, and Quinn searched the depot for the one they had really come here for. Pretending to give in to this summer-camp idea had given them time to hatch a real plan. They had researched their extended relatives in search of one who lived somewhere with trees, and found an uncle, Jasper, who they hadn't spoken to in a while. He ran a small inn deep in the woods– a little dreary, maybe, but a much better option than the camp. At least out there, Quinn could run around the woods in peace. Their parents didn't like Jasper, but they didn't like anyone cool so it didn't bother them. The worst that could happen was probably spending a summer changing bed-sheets.

They found their bus and climbed on. As Quinn stepped inside and the musty doors folded shut behind them, they hoped this was the start to a new chapter for them. A chance to trade in their lone-liness for exploration and adventure.

They had no idea how horribly correct they were.

- 2 -

That evening, Quinn fidgeted and stared out the bus window as maple trees and exposed rocks whipped by. Their bag, which they had emptied when their parents weren't looking and refilled with important items, knocked between their knees with each bump in the road.

The bus was nearly empty. Only a few others were traveling through the Finger Lakes with them after they boarded alone in Syracuse: at one stop, an old woman heaving a very large dog crate aboard with her; at the next, a young couple now dozing on each other's shoulders; at the next, a round man in a suit with a bristly gray-brown beard. The forest rose up around them, growing darker and denser as the sun set.

They were getting close to Jasper's inn. Quinn didn't see him often, so they knew little about him and less about this place. There was barely anything about it online, and when they called he didn't offer many more details. The excitement in his voice when they asked to join him was worth the guilt of lying about their parents giving permission.

A part-time employee who lived there was supposed to meet them when they arrived. All they knew about him was his name was Ashwan and he was fourteen, a year younger than Quinn. They briefly wondered what happened to get him sent out here.

They wondered what he was like. Him and a friend named Ciara, people Jasper had decided to live in the woods with in favor of his family. Were they kind? Were they weird? Would they think Quinn was weird? Did they like animals?

The bus rattled to a halt. This was their stop. In place of a station, the small town near Jasper's inn had a snow-beaten sign in front of a taxidermist's shop listing routes to Buffalo and Harrisburg. Quinn was surprised to see the bearded man climb out after them.

The bus pulled away and left them shivering in the dark. They were most of the way there, they reassured themself. All they had to do now was to find their way to the inn. They meant to walk the rest of the way, but in the dark the town looked complex and daunting. They glanced at the bearded man and quickly looked away, much too nervous to ask him for directions.

"Excuse me," the man said. They winced.

Quinn tried an awkward smile. "Yeah?"

"I'm looking for the Circadi Inn," he pronounced carefully. Quinn startled at the mention of their uncle's inn. "Do you know how I can get there?"

"Oh– uh…" They shook their head. "Sorry. I'm trying to get there too, actually."

He squinted at another bus approaching from the opposite direction. "Could that be…"

"That one's going south, I think," Quinn said. "We want to go north."

"Ah."

The bus came and went, dropping off a couple of passengers who were chatting over a map.

"It's up the hill," one of them said. Despite the mild evening he was covered up head to toe, with a scarf wrapped around his face and a flat cap pulled low over his eyes. He was small, maybe half the height of his companion, a bald man who stumbled forward with a dazed look in his pale eyes. "I called someone who's already going up there to take us. He should be waiting." He pointed towards a van parked out front of the taxidermist's shop.

The bald man dropped his bag, spilling clothes across the sidewalk. "Slow down, Tim," his friend teased him as he and Quinn helped him pick his things up. "You can do that as much as you want once you get your room."

Quinn paused. "Are you guys going to the Circadi Inn?"

The two passengers stared at them in surprise. "Yes…?" the overdressed one said slowly.

"May we join you?" the bearded man in the suit asked them.

The gazes of the two strangers shifted over to him before softening in recognition. The tension broke. "Of course, Mr. Fenris," the bald man said respectfully.

Quinn turned to examine Fenris. Was he someone important around here? The wrapped-up figure looked at him for a long moment but didn't argue as he led the others to the van.

The engine rumbled to life when the driver saw them. The doors unlocked with a click and one headlight lit up, the other long-shattered and hosting a family of spiders.

Quinn froze when they saw the inside of the van. Aglow with the beady eyes of cameras and monitors, the walls were plastered with maps and printouts of pale trailcam photos. Large nets, traps, and hunting knives were strapped to the ceiling and under the seats. Quinn slowly climbed in after the others, suddenly very self conscious, and tried not to sit down too loudly. Fenris sat beside them in the back row and the other two sat in the middle.

"Hey there Tosk," the driver said, twisting around to smile at them. He was wiry and sunburnt and smelled of cigarettes. "Am I seeing double?" He was wiry and strong-looking, with a patchy beard.

"They're going to the inn too," Tosk said. "Asked to come along. Is that okay, George?"

"Fine by me," George said, sounding puzzled. His eyes flicked between Quinn and Fenris before widening in recognition. He nodded to himself and sat back in his seat.

The man in the passenger seat turned to look back at them too. He looked like a younger, broader version of George. He clenched his jaw when he saw Fenris and leaned over to whisper to George. Quinn couldn't hear what he said, but he sounded angry. He smacked his palm for emphasis against the back of their bench seat, which Quinn noticed had three macramé seat covers on it.

The middle one sat empty.

"Because, Hector," George hissed in response. "You don't mess with a man like him, no matter what he is." His voice dropped below their hearing.

The four passengers waited awkwardly as George and Hector continued their whispered argument. If being discussed this way bothered Fenris, he didn't show a hint of it. Quinn glanced at their seatmate from the corner of their eye in bewilderment. Who was this man, whose name alone opened doors but whose presence was so chilling?

Tosk fidgeted absently with the fringe of his scarf. "Anyone want some clove gum?" he asked, clearing his throat. They all shook their heads.

Finally the argument subsided. George laughed uneasily as he pulled the van out onto the street. "Sorry about that, folks. Siblings— you know how it is." Hector glared out the window, arms folded.

They turned onto an unlit road fringed by shaggy firs. George turned the high beams on, flushing the trees with cold white light. "So, uh," he said, trying to take on a lighter tone. "Mr. Fenris. What brings you and your, uh…" He glanced at Quinn in confusion. "…friend here?"

"Family business," Fenris said curtly. "And the two of us just took the same bus here."

"Ah." The others reassessed Quinn with new eyes now that they were no longer Fenris's companion.

"What kind of family business?" Tosk asked, but was quickly distracted when the bald man knocked his head against the window at a bend in the road. "Woah! Be careful there!"

"And what about you?" George asked Quinn.

"Oh—um— I'm Quinn. The owner is my uncle. I'm staying with him for a little while."

"Jasper?" George asked in surprise. "That guy has family? Did you know that, Tosk?"

"Not at all," Tosk said. "He never brings them up. I just assumed he was born out of an extra-large magnolia pod or something."

Quinn chewed their lip, hoping they weren't making a big mistake. The truth was their mom and her brother-in-law hadn't spoken in years. He was married to her brother, Lev, who dragged him to holiday gatherings in an effort to keep the family talking to each other. Jasper's awkwardness distanced him from the adults, and he and Quinn often bumped into each other on separate quests to escape from the rest of the family. As a kid they were fascinated by him. He sketched elaborate monsters on napkins and carried little homemade inventions in his pockets, and the fact that their parents didn't like him made him even more exciting. But they never saw him outside of those gatherings, and when Lev died three years ago they stopped seeing him at all. The inn had been Lev's dream and they were surprised to learn Jasper was keeping it open. Maybe they didn't know as much about him as they thought.

The road twisted in sharp zigzags up a small hill and suddenly the Circadi Inn emerged.

The big Victorian structure was almost easy to miss despite its size, its wooden shingles blending in with the shaggy bark of the surrounding cedar trees. The only light came from a small lamp

14

over the door and the gentle glow of the windows. If Quinn had come across it on their own, they wouldn't have known they were looking at a hotel. There wasn't even a sign displaying the place's name.

George pulled around the back and they all piled out. Tosk pulled Tim aside to speak with him in a low voice. George and Hector hopped out to check on a rattling noise under the van's hood while Fenris stayed in the backseat to take a call. It looked like they would be going in alone.

Grabbing their backpack, Quinn walked around to the front of the inn, where an elaborate metal grille of branches and stars covered the door. Doubt flooded their body for a moment. The extent of their plan's craziness suddenly sank in. They hadn't seen Jasper in years, and everyone else in this inn was a total stranger. They didn't know anything about this place or what it would take to fit in here. Was this all a big mistake?

At this point it didn't matter, they figured. The bus that brought them here was long gone. It was too late to change their mind.

Here goes nothing, they thought. They pushed the door open and stepped inside.

Quinn glanced around the lobby, breathing in the earthy scents of pine and vetiver. The place looked old but well-loved. A twisting chandelier hung from the tall ceiling, its light vainly grasping for the corners of the room. The dark wood forming the doors, front desk, and ceiling carvings was carefully dusted and polished, its edges rounding with age, and the delicate gold pattern on the dulling wallpaper was filled in by hand where it chipped. A large fireplace crackled gently on one wall with a few curved sofas of crimson velvet gathering around its warmth. Quinn's feet sank a little into the thick rust-colored carpet. The clerk at the front desk looked at them with bleary eyes and said nothing.

"Hey!"

Startled, Quinn spun around. A boy their age appeared at their left, seemingly out of nowhere. He was tall and lean, his loose tee shirt and jeans almost hanging off him, with light brown skin and fluffy black hair peeking out from a beanie pulled over his ears.

"You're Quinn, right? I'm Ash." His smile lit up his eyes, making their color look almost orange. "It's so great to meet you! Me and the owners are the only ones who stay at the hotel full-time. I can't wait to have someone my age around."

Quinn smiled hesitantly. He seemed nice, but that didn't make meeting new people any less scary. "Yeah. Nice to meet you too."

"I didn't scare you, did I? I can be pretty quiet. Ciara says I should wear a bell."

"It's okay. I mean— you did, kind of." They both laughed a little, the quiet reflexive laugh of tension breaking between strangers.

"Sorry. Want some help with your bag?"

"Sure." They handed him their suitcase and followed him across the lobby.

"How was the drive? You came here from Syracuse, right?"

"Yeah." Quinn sighed, quickly coming up with a believable story. "My parents want me to learn some *responsibility*. Is that why you're here too?"

"Nope. I've lived here since I was little, actually. I used to live in Rochester with a doctor until he couldn't take care of me anymore."

"Oh– sorry."

"It's alright. I like it here. I bet you will too. You get to meet all sorts of cool people."

Quinn winced. "People aren't really my thing. What about the forest?"

"The forest is nice. Jasper likes it a lot. It's kind of spooky, though."

"Even better!" Quinn perked up. "Is there a lot of wildlife?" This whole situation seemed awfully boring, but if they could see some cool animals it might be worth it.

"Sure, we've got birds, frogs, squirrels…"

"Anything I can't see back home? Like a mountain lion?"

He hummed uncertainly. "I've never seen one of those. But I bet there's one around here somewhere."

Disappointed, they tried again. "Is there anything else to do here? What's the town like?"

"Oh, the town is great! We have a grocery store, and a school, and even a fire department."

They looked at him. He seemed totally serious. "Oh," they said, because they couldn't think of anything else.

Along one wall were several photos of Uncle Jasper and a few other people. Quinn stopped to look at them. They could tell how old each photo was from Jasper's appearance– haircuts, pre- and post- top surgery and hormone therapy, the slow spread of tattoos over his deep brown skin. The earliest one was of him and Uncle Lev sometime in their twenties, on a mountaintop surrounded by autumn trees. Lev's frizzy hair went in all directions and his tan skin was pocked with acne scars- he was definitely related to

Quinn. There was another with just the two of them on a city street, then a small redheaded woman appeared in the next one. They were all standing in front of the inn, but the metal grille on the door was gone, replaced by a porch and a mailbox. The three looked like they had just escaped a bar fight, with their faces bruised and cut and the woman's hair falling out of its braid. A big part of the house's exterior was burned. In the next photo, the three were posed in the same spot as the previous one but the house had fallen into disrepair and a worn FOR SALE sign hung off one rusted nail. Jasper was holding a toolbox and Lev was proudly showing the camera a set of new house keys. The woman didn't look any different from the last photo despite the obvious passage of years. In the next one, a young boy stood beside the three in the inn's lobby. Quinn could tell the boy was Ash from his fluffy hair and wide grin. The final picture was the only one without Lev. Jasper's eyes didn't show the same raw joy as in the others, but he held his friends close and gave the camera his best smile.

Behind them Ash let out a frightened yelp. Quinn turned to look at him. He was holding a small shoebox that had tumbled out of their bag. The box was stuffed with cotton balls, each one skewered with a pin displaying a shiny dead insect.

"What's wrong?" they asked.

"This box is full of creepy bugs!" he cried.

They shrugged. "It's my beetle box."

"Your *beetle* box?!"

"Yeah. I find lots of dead bugs and molted exoskeletons on the ground, and I pin them in that box to save them. Pretty cool, right?"

Ash shivered. He looked a little frightened of them now.

"What's wrong?" they asked. "Are you afraid of insects?"

He nodded. "I don't like bugs. They creep me out."

"I've got bad news for you, dude. Insects are around 80 percent of the world's species."

"What?" He went pale. "I don't want to know that!"

"Yeah, actually they think there are more undiscovered insect species than named ones."

"Aaagh! No!"

"Isn't that amazing? There are around 200 million insects for every human in the world!"

"Okay, okay! I don't want any more bug facts!"

Quinn paused. Why didn't he want any more bug facts? That didn't make sense. Still, if he wanted them to stop they would. "Sorry." They shoved the box back into their bag.

"How about I show you around?" Ash said to change the subject. Quinn nodded. After handing their bag to the clerk he pressed the button for the elevator, and the doors opened with an exhausted sigh. The decrepit car shuddered as it dragged them to the second floor, a labyrinth of burgundy doors, round yellow wall lamps, and geometric carpeting. It was almost silent with an occasional whisper or snore escaping under the doors as they passed. The third floor looked identical but was surprisingly loud for this time of night, with conversation and laughter coming from almost every room. A few barks and bird calls were audible too. Pets must be popular here, Quinn guessed. They realized, after passing by the elevator for the third time, that this place was incredibly easy to get lost in. They were glad they weren't alone right now, but from the way Ash stopped to read the room numbers at every turn, he didn't seem to be doing much better.

The fourth floor was for staff only, but as Ash explained to them, they needed to be added to some kind of system or they would set off an alarm. They didn't really understand but they nodded and followed him back to the lobby.

"Jasper's around here somewhere," Ash said. "He must be in the lounge. Over there." He pointed to the doorway on the right. "Guests hang out here, and we get a lot of locals too." He opened the door and loud chatter and soft light spilled out. Quinn peered in, curious about what types of people stayed in a place like this. In the dim lighting, not much more was visible than a lot of silhouettes of varying shapes and sizes.

They were about to turn away when a loud groan came from deep underground. The guests stilled and looked around in surprise and worry as the floor trembled. The overhead lamp shook violently and the filament burst. "I'll get it!" a familiar voice shouted.

Out of the crowd Uncle Jasper emerged. He wasn't as tall as they remembered- still a big guy, but like furniture in a childhood bedroom he shrunk a little as they grew. Besides the flecks of silver in his tight coils of hair, he looked mostly the same as he had three years ago: paint-streaked clothing, dark eyes that were thoughtful yet guarded, and a laugh that was equal parts playful and delighted with a little touch of crazy. Quinn heard that laugh now as the figures at his side chatted and teased him. They pulled a chair out in front of him and he stepped onto it, rolling up the sleeves of his hoodie and reaching towards the lamp. He waited a moment, a determined squint crinkling his face, and the tattoos on his arms slowly began to emit a cool blue glow. Quinn gasped. A small ball of light grew between his fingertips and he gently nudged it under the lampshade. The guests cheered and he hopped down from the chair and walked towards the door.

Behind him two of the guests chatted and drifted into the light. One of them was a tall creature covered in silky black hair that swayed as it walked, and the other was a brown wood frog about half the size of a human wearing a linen suit. The front door swung open as Tosk and Tim ran inside. Tim headed for the stairs and Tosk waved to the tall creature and the frog and moved to join them. He freed himself of his scarf and hat before bounding over. Quinn was shocked to see red tufted ears and a fluffy tail spring up. A giant pine squirrel! Their jaw hung open.

Jasper ducked through the doorway and almost ran straight into Ash and Quinn. He jumped back at the last second and stumbled. The stone beads around his wrists and neck clacked together. "Quinn!" he gasped. "Hi!"

Quinn was lost for words, unsure whether to scream at him about the magic or the monsters first.

The hairy creature, the frog, and Tosk waved goodbye to Jasper and moved past them towards the stairs. Quinn made up their mind and ran after them.

"You guys-" they gasped, catching up to them, "are *so* cool!"

The hairy creature stared at them blankly. "Er… thank you," the frog said.

"Are you wearing costumes or is that real?"

The creature frowned and said sarcastically, "I don't know. Are *you* wearing a costume?"

"I don't think so." Quinn tugged at their scalp just to be sure.

The creature rolled its three eyes and trudged away with the two animals trailing behind. Quinn sheepishly watched them go. Jasper covered a quiet laugh with his fist. "I love the excitement. But go easy on our guests, okay?"

They gawked at him. "Jasper! What's going on?"

"Nice to see you too."

"This place is amazing! Why didn't you ever tell me?!"

He smiled nervously. "Your parents already don't like me. They'd never let you stay here if they knew."

"I wouldn't have told them!"

"I didn't want to take chances. They already think I'm a bad influence. And… they're kind of right."

"You're not a bad influence!" Ash said. "I learn so much from you. Like how to identify mushroom species. And how to cook mushrooms. And how to treat the symptoms from eating poisonous mushrooms."

"We like to offer a full employee education," Jasper said. "Listen, I have to check out what made that noise. Here's your room key, Quinn." He dug a key out of his pocket and gave it to them. His hands were warm and weathered. "See ya!"

He walked over to the front desk and pulled out a large toolbox, the same one he was holding in the old photo. Then he disappeared down the stairs.

Ash looked at Quinn carefully. "Are you okay?" he asked. "Jasper said this might be a lot for you to handle. I was gonna tell you slowly… I had PowerPoint slides…"

22

"Nah, don't worry about me," Quinn said quietly. "I'm just having my whole understanding of the world scrambled like an egg."

"Do you want to sit down?"

Before they could answer, a small woman with long red hair burst out of the lounge. She was very pale and freckled all over, like someone had flicked a paintbrush at her.

"Jasper!" she bellowed. "Where are you? I've done something stupid again."

Quinn glanced back at the photos on the wall and realized this was the woman in the pictures. The rough sound of her voice didn't match her young face.

Her green eyes lit up when she saw them. "Ah, Ash! And… would you happen to be Quinn?"

Quinn nodded.

"Fantastic." She pulled a bottle opener from her pocket and held it out towards them. "Be a dear and wrench this cap out of my teeth?"

She opened her mouth wide and Quinn gasped. Her teeth were long and pointed and very, very sharp. Lodged between two of them was a twisted metal bottle cap.

"What's wrong?" the woman asked when she heard Quinn gasp. "You look like you've seen a ghost. Or a vampire." She cackled.

"Ciara, how did you do this?" Ash asked, taking the bottle opener from her. "Were you trying another dangerous bartending trick?"

"Another *cool and impressive* bartending trick, thank you very much. It's not my fault they make these things out of wet cardboard. It should have popped right off."

"What were you saying about a vampire?" Quinn asked.

"You should be careful," Ash reminded her. "Remember when you ripped the front door off its hinges because you forgot it was a push door?"

"Hey! The vampire thing!" Quinn cried. "We're not glossing over that!"

"What about the vampire thing?" Ciara asked disinterestedly. She opened her mouth wide and Ash yanked at the cap with the bottle opener. It didn't budge.

"Well– are– are you one?" Quinn stammered.

"Oh. Yes." Ash yanked again. The cap still didn't move. Quinn watched them in stunned silence.

"What? Do you want proof?" Ciara pulled down the collar of her knit sweater to reveal a gnarled bite mark, presenting it with a flourish of her hand as if it was the prize on a game show. The skin was twisted and discolored like a third-degree burn scar. Quinn gasped.

"Is that enough? Or would you like me to bite you to demonstrate?" she offered.

Quinn thought about it for a moment. "Not now," they decided. "I need my blood right now." They paused, curiosity quickly overtaking fear. "Can I see your teeth again?"

"Even better, take a crack at this cap and you can see them up close," Ciara said. Ash passed them the bottle opener and they leaned in, fighting the survival instinct which begged them to move their hands away.

They positioned the tool over the bottle cap and gave a slow twist. "Oh, go on," Ciara said. "Harder than that. I've been burnt at the stake, I can take it."

Quinn frowned and wrenched again, a little harder. Still no movement. "How old are you?"

"Oh… abaw sebeh hundeh yeh."

Quinn took their hands out of her mouth. "Sorry."

"About seven hundred years," Ciara repeated.

"*Seven hundred?!*" Quinn gasped. That was older than their favorite tree.

"I *am* quite amazing, I must say. But I'm hardly the oldest vampire around. We've been making ourselves a nuisance since *Homo habilis,* or so I'm told! Then again, it was a vampire who told me, so he was probably lying."

Quinn shrugged and yanked harder at the cap. It moved a little. They tried again, harder, and the cap flew free. Something came with it and landed on the carpet. A tooth, Quinn realized with a jolt.

Ciara shrugged when she saw it. "Keep it. They grow back."

Quinn picked up the tooth and examined its cruel shape for a moment. They tucked it into their pocket, careful to point it away from their thigh.

Just then a horrible noise roared through the inn, the scream of grinding metal meshed with the bellow of shifting wood. The floors shivered gently.

"Well that doesn't sound good," Ciara said quietly.

Ash paled. "Is that thing in the basement still happening? I thought Jasper was fixing it."

"So did I." Ciara shrugged. "Looks like we're going to the

basement, daywalkers."

Ash fidgeted. "I don't want to go down there! I hate the basement."

"Why not?" Ciara said. "The basement keeps things exciting! It adds spice to our lives."

"Spice?" Quinn repeated. "It's a basement. How spicy can it be?"

"I don't need any more spice!" Ash protested. "I prefer my current level of spice!"

"Let's just go," Quinn interrupted.

The three hurried downstairs to the basement. It took a few moments for Quinn's senses to adjust to the dark, musty space. A long table strewn with paint, scraps of metal, and dried herbs stood along one wall. Quinn recognized it as Japer's space as soon as they saw the giant burned spot on the floor. It lay in the middle of a chalk circle, surrounded by smeared remnants of words and symbols. So this was what Jasper had been up to all these years. Watching him draw as a kid used to feel like a window into his life, but now they realized that window was more like a keyhole. And the room it led into was vaster and weirder than they had ever imagined.

Jasper called out to them from below. As they continued downwards the passageway became more dark and cramped with every step. It was very warm down here and strangely humid. The smell was organic but alien, like the soft crumbling wood of a rotting log mixed with the lively tang of animal body odor.

At the bottom Quinn gasped. A huge wooden mass in the shape of a stomach took up the opposite wall. A large brass door lay in the middle, moist heat escaping around the edges, and a dense network of wooden blood vessels sprouted out around it and disappeared into the walls.

They turned to the others, their eyes wide. "Whoa! You guys! Is this real?"

The others nodded. Ciara looked bored and Ash looked nauseous. Jasper patted the stomach affectionately. "Yup. This baby heats the whole building."

Quinn put their ear against a vein and heard some type of liquid sloshing inside. "Oh my god," they breathed. "Is this place...alive?"

"That's right."

"Nobody's ever seen the rest of it," Ciara added. "But if you listen close, when it's completely silent…" She grinned. "You can hear a heartbeat somewhere deep in the earth."

Quinn snatched their hand away from the vein. Waves of fear and revulsion rolled through their body, simultaneously repelling them and drawing them in.

"See? This is why I don't like the basement," Ash grumbled.

"Is it… safe?" Quinn asked slowly.

Jasper and Ciara looked at each other and shrugged. "We've been here a while," Jasper said. "If the house was dangerous, it would have killed us already."

"Yes," Ciara added, "It's friendly! Probably friendly. It may not even be aware we're here!"

As if that settled it, she turned away and rolled up her sleeves. She gripped the handle of the brass door and heaved it open. A wave of heat immediately hit everyone's faces. Inside it was too dark to see anything, but Quinn could hear the soft roar of distant fire and the creak of shifting wood and metal.

"Are you sure something's in there?" Ash asked nervously. "Maybe we should just leave it alone."

"I'm sure," Jasper said. "The ground shaking is a bad sign. I think it's trying to throw something up."

"Well, if we let it keep trying, maybe it'll get it out! Right?"

Ciara shook her head. "Not worth the risk. Sorry, Ash, but you know you're the only one who can do this."

He groaned again, looking unhappily into the stomach. Ciara grabbed his hand and helped him pull himself onto the rim of the opening.

"Wait, you're making him go in there?" Quinn asked. "Are you serious?"

"Hey. Technically, we've never explored far enough to run into anything dangerous," Jasper pointed out. "So the stomach *could* be perfectly safe."

"Then one of you should go in!"

"I can't go in there," Ciara said. "Do you know what that fire would do to my pores? Not to mention a grotesque if spectacular second death. And I'm not throwing my current favorite human in there either."

"But Ash could die!" Quinn protested. "You guys are his care-takers, right? You should be protecting him! Not putting him in more   danger!"

"Ash will be fine," Jasper said calmly. "Right, buddy?"

Ash frowned uneasily. "Um…"

The stomach rattled loudly. Whatever was in there, it sounded big. The whole basement shook.

28

Ash turned to look in again, and Ciara gave him a pat on the back that turned into a small push. "There you go, friend! We're counting on you."

He sighed. "Alright." He climbed into the stomach. Quinn screamed as the darkness swallowed him.

A few tense moments went by. Quinn covered their ears. They had never thought about what it might sound like when someone burned to death. They had never wanted to find out.

Eventually there was a metallic clang. "Guys, something is stuck in here!" Ash cried.

Quinn was shocked. They hadn't expected to hear his voice again, except for maybe a scream of pain.

"What is it?" Jasper shouted back.

"No idea! There's something smooth that wasn't here last time. I'm gonna try to pull it out."

Quinn stared at Jasper and Ciara, their eyes wide. "What's going on? Is this a trick?"

Jasper shook his head. "No tricks." He nodded at Ciara. "*She* wanted to pull a trick on you but I vetoed it. You're welcome."

"What's wrong with a little hazing?" Ciara said.

"I got it!" Ash called. He climbed out of the stomach and hopped down to the floor with something round tucked under his arm. Quinn was amazed to see that, despite the singed edges of his clothes, he was completely unhurt.

"Whoa! Dude!" they cried. "What happened? How are you okay?"

He smiled. "I dunno."

Quinn stared at him, then at Jasper and Ciara.

"He doesn't burn," Jasper said. "He's fireproof."

"How did you find that out? Did you set him on fire?" Quinn asked.

"Only once!" Ciara said. "Well– once intentionally."

"It was awesome," Ash added. "And scary. And awesome."

"Well…" Quinn stammered, turning to Ash, "Fine! If you're fireproof, what was the problem?"

"It's not the fire." He shivered. "It's the dark."

Quinn paused, their mind reeling as it tried to catch up. "Oh– you're… afraid of the dark."

He nodded.

"And he was very brave!" Ciara added. "Well done, Ash. What was in there?"

Ash took the object from under his arm and lifted it into the light. It was a long animal skull.

He dropped it like it was radioactive. "Ew! Ewewew!"

"Well, now we know what type of fuel this place runs on," Jasper said.

Quinn picked the skull up and admired it. "Wow, an eastern coyote! This thing is beautiful."

"You can tell the species?" Jasper asked, impressed. He elbowed Ciara playfully. "Maybe if you spent less time listening to those murder reports you could do something like that."

She elbowed him back. "So when I identify something by smell it's disgusting, but when they do it by sight it's cool? Besides, I'm keeping aware of danger. We're not very far from the city."

"Right, like someone's gonna travel out into the middle of the woods to get us."

"You never know. What's to stop them from leaving town while the attention blows over?"

"Wait!" Quinn gasped.

"What?"

They looked carefully at the skull. "This isn't an eastern coyote. This is a gray fox."

"Can we go back upstairs?" Ash whined. "I hate it down here."

"Yeah, let's go," Jasper said. They all turned away from the stomach. "And Quinn," he added, looking at them meaningfully. "You'll be staying with us for a while. That means you have a responsibility to protect us by keeping us a secret. If word gets out, there are some very dangerous people who could start sniffing around here."

"Right," Ciara added. "Our existence depends on each of us doing our part to protect the others."

"Of course. I understand." Quinn spun the skull gently in their hands. It was warm.

Ciara gripped the door to the stomach and began to push it shut. Ash gasped, remembering something. "Wait!"

"What is it?"

"Quinn needs to go into the system! So they won't set off the staff alarms."

"Oh, yeah," Jasper said. Before Quinn could react he leaned in, plucked out a few strands of their hair, and tossed them into the stomach. A burst of blue flame lit their faces for a moment and died down.

"There you go! Welcome to the Circadi Inn, Quinn."

The walls shifted gently in agreement.

- 3 -

The bucket overflowed with a loud splash and Quinn blinked. How long had they been zoning out?

It was the next day. Outside the cold wind buffeted the tree branches like a restless animal. They were on the second floor, helping Ash prepare a room for a new guest. Making accommodations to rooms was a big part of his job because the guests here came from all sorts of environments and their needs varied just as much. Earlier that day they had prepared rooms for a couple of trolls and a giant scorpion. This room belonged to a riverbeast named Delta and her young daughter Brooke. She lingered by the heating vent with her child on her right hip and watched them work. Delta was very tall and wore a long black dress and no shoes on her webbed feet. She had tough green skin, tangled hair, and eyes like mother-of-pearl, and her sharp teeth poked out of her gums at conflicting angles. She looked beautiful and fearsome, but she responded to most of Quinn's questions about how her biology worked with a shrug. Quinn had to admit they didn't know their own blood pH either so they couldn't blame her.

Quinn turned off the tap and grabbed the bucket, carrying it out into the bedroom. Delta dipped a clawed finger into the water and nodded. "That's good. Go ahead."

Quinn looked down at the bucket for a long moment. When they decided to come here, they imagined changing sheets, cleaning rooms. Their guess had been just slightly off.

They took a deep breath and poured the water all over the bed.

When the mattress and sheets were thoroughly soaked, Delta gently lay her daughter in the middle and tucked her in. Brooke looked a lot like her mother when her face was visible, but as she snuggled down into the sheets, her long hair fell over her and she began to look more like a clump of seaweed. She raised one small hand into the air without lifting her head, waiting. Delta searched under the bed for a moment, pulled out a large plush sturgeon, and handed it to her, and Brooke's body silently folded around it. Her breathing soon slowed.

Ash shuffled up behind them with another bucket. "A little more and we should be all set– oops!"

He tripped over his foot, falling forward and flinging the bucket into the air. Brooke opened her eyes to peer at him and didn't flinch when the wave of water hit her. She yawned and went back to sleep.

34

"Whoa! Are you okay?" Quinn cried, running over to him.

Ash shook himself like a dog drying its fur. "Yeah, I'm fine. My bad!"

Quinn slowly helped him to his feet. They were beginning to realize what a talent for clumsiness Ash had. Just that day, he had leaned against a meat slicer, fallen down a flight of stairs, given himself several paper cuts, and now scraped both knees and elbows. Despite all that he was still as cheerful as when he greeted them that morning. (A *morning person!* That scared Quinn more than the injuries.) They wanted badly to know what made him so indestructible, but this felt like the wrong time to ask.

"Is there any way you can heat this place up?" Delta said, shivering. "We need a warm, wet environment. That's why we're here." She gently stroked her daughter's hair. "Brooke isn't feeling well. Heavy storms are coming and she won't survive if we stay at home."

"Absolutely," Ash assured her. He glanced around with a thoughtful hum and seemed to get an idea. Kneeling, he unlatched the cover on the heating vent and set it on the floor, allowing hot, moist air to pour out of the opening. "There you go. The heating vents connect to the house's stomach. So it should keep you comfy."

"Thank you." Delta lifted her chin, enjoying the warmth and humidity. "I think I'll follow Brooke's lead. We could both use a nap." She turned away and stepped into the bathroom. In one smooth movement, she threw herself into the tub, her body softening and dissolving into a murky liquid. She landed with a splash.

Leaving Delta and her daughter in their room, Quinn followed

Ash downstairs to the lobby. Jasper was at the front desk tinkering with a small invention he had shown them yesterday, a radio which he rewired to record and play back messages. A pale-skinned human man with heavily gelled blond hair stood in front of him, watching. The smell of his body spray was strong enough to reach them from the stairwell.

"But I don't just want to be known as the landlord's son, you know?" the man was saying. "I'm trying to get out of my old man's shadow. I used to work for a company selling cheap knives, but that was a giant scam. This time I'm gonna be in charge. I've been working on a few businesses of my own." He counted the fingers on his left hand. "Haunted dishware, fur-bearing-trout wool, energy supplements, curse removers, curse enhancers. I also trade crypto."

Jasper stifled a yawn. "That's great."

"I was just at this conference last weekend, where all these speakers were sharing their secrets to success. The key is mindset, they said. If you have the right mindset, the rest will follow. Isn't that incredible?"

"Hi kids," Jasper said when he saw them, desperate to change the topic. "This is Ryan. He's doing an inspection for his dad."

Quinn mumbled a shy hello as Ryan energetically shook their hand. It felt like he had practiced the movement many times.

"Yep," Ryan said. "I'm just gonna take a look around the inn and surrounding land, then I'll be out of your hair."

"Do you have the ground lease?" Jasper asked. "It's about time to renew, isn't it?"

Ryan's smile faltered. "Actually, my dad hasn't made a decision about that yet."

"What?"

"He's considering renewing your ground lease," Ryan stammered. He laughed anxiously. "He's also, uh… considering… selling it." The last two words came out in a quiet rush.

Jasper stared at him for a long moment, his face not moving. Then he turned away and strode towards the lounge. "Ciara!"

"The one and only," she said, appearing in the doorway.

"They want to sell our lease."

"That hasn't been decided yet!" Ryan cried, hurrying after him.

"To whom?" Ciara asked.

"He might not be selling at all…"

"To *whom*?" she repeated firmly.

Ryan swallowed. "Peter Fenris," he whimpered.

Her lips drew tight. "How convenient. Mr Fenris is here now. Why don't we have a chat with him?"

The three of them walked into the lounge. Ash and Quinn glanced at each other, shrugged, and awkwardly followed them at a distance.

The unpapered walls and eclectic mix of old chairs and tables made this space feel less finished than the lobby and more intimate. Messy amateur portraits hung on all sides and a gangly pothos plant spilled up one wall and across the ceiling, its veins pulsing with a soft green light. Some of the inn's guests were clustered at tables and tucked into corner booths.

Jasper called Fenris's name and the hairy man stood up. He snarled in annoyance at being disturbed and long, hooked canines slid out from between his lips. Quinn winced. They hadn't noticed those teeth before.

Suddenly sharp talons flashed in Quinn's face. They yelled out in shock. A flapping mess of black and white feathers and jasmine perfume landed on the chair nearby, rocking back and forth in cruel laughter. Quinn gasped for breath, their heart racing. The beast that had jumped at them was twice their size. Her broad wings shone with an oily iridescence and her jagged blue beak was studded with tiny teeth. Her brown eyes were uncomfortably human.

A metal coffee pot clanged against the creature's head and she squawked. "Sod off, Meena!" Ciara shouted. "They're new!"

Meena snatched up the pot and hurled it back at Ciara. She caught it before it could smash into the rows of bottles on the wall behind her and stuck out her tongue, then went back to talking with the three men.

Meena squinted her creepy eyes at Quinn and grinned. "So you're the new guy, huh? Nice form. Mind if I borrow it?"

She leapt off the chair. When she landed she was smaller, rounder, and featherless. She straightened up, dark hair sprouting from her head, fingers separating with a snap, and Quinn lurched back in surprise at seeing an exact copy of themself.

Meena cackled again at their reaction. The inside of her mouth was the same vivid blue as her beak had been. It was the only thing she hadn't copied perfectly. Even Quinn's acne scars and deep eye bags were the same.

"What–" Quinn stammered. "How can you do that?"

"How can you do that?" the creature parroted. The rough croak of her voice started to blend with Quinn's softer tones. She tried a few more times, improving the impression, until she sounded exactly like them.

"Stop it!" Quinn cried. The mix of discomfort and fascination they had felt at first seeing Meena was giving way to horror. Quinn could handle talking animals, eldritch houses and bloodthirsty monsters, but facing down their own appearance and voice? No way.

"That's enough!" Ciara leapt over the counter and nudged Meena back.

Quinn struggled to put their thoughts back in order. For once, they were too stunned to pepper the creature with questions. They would be avoiding mirrors for the rest of the day.

Meena hopped backwards into a chair, melting into a tall brown-skinned woman with silky black hair bobbed at her shoulders. Her blouse was the same shiny hue as her feathers a moment before, and when she smirked Quinn saw that she kept the tiny sharp teeth. "Relax new guy, I'm just messing with you. Never seen a starling before?"

"I would appreciate you keeping your nose out of my business," Fenris cried, pulling their attention back to him. Quinn followed his gaze towards the other end of the room, where Tosk was crouching over a neat stack of documents.

The squirrel tensed in surprise and leapt away. "It's not really *your* business when it affects all of us." he said when he landed on a nearby table. "You don't even care how many homes you're displacing with that development, do you?"

Fenris grunted. "I am not here on business and I do not wish to discuss it." His eyes drifted towards Jasper and Ciara. "The same goes for the purchase of your land. I'm simply here visiting my nephew, not that any of you need to know."

Meena leaned forward. "Wait, wait. *You're* the one putting up those offices? You're Peter Fenris?"

The hairy man huffed in annoyance. "I *said* I don't wish to discuss it."

"Listen, what are you doing to your workers?" Meena continued, ignoring him. "They show up at my office with horrible, poorly treated injuries. Takes me forever to fix. And they're not sleeping enough either. They can barely fill out their intake forms before passing out."

"The contractor handles occupational safety, not me," Fenris said with a contemptuous wave of his hand.

The squirrel leapt onto Meena's table. Pages of shorthand notes and typed articles crinkled in the pockets of his pants and collared shirt. He restlessly scratched his left cheek, smudging it with pen ink. "I've interviewed lots of families who got pushed out by this development. Lizards, rabbits, raccoons. Just like a werewolf to go after defenseless forest dwellers."

Fenris stiffened. "That's unfair, sir. You're implying I am connected to the werewolf packs who run organized crime rings to prey on the less-fortunate. My pack has nothing to do with those activities."

"That's not what I heard," Tosk grumbled.

"Well, if you'd like to discuss it further I can put you in touch with my lawyer. And you, doctor…" Fenris's eyes drifted over to Meena. She scowled. "The foreman who referred your patients will be happy to answer your safety questions."

Tosk and Meena glared at him for a tense moment. He stared calmly back at them.

The tension burst as Delta leaned into the doorway and looked around. "Have any of you seen Brooke?" she asked, puzzled.

"No. You were both napping upstairs, weren't you?" Quinn asked.

"That's the thing. I can't find her anywhere." Unease began to spread across her face. "She should be fast asleep. I gave her some valerian root. None of you have seen her?"

They all shook their heads. Delta ground her sharp teeth nervously as she glanced between them.

"Let's go look for her," Jasper suggested. "We'll find her in no time."

"I'll help you," Meena offered.

"Me too," Tosk added.

"I suppose I can help," Fenris grumbled.

"Great. Everyone meet back at the front desk in half an hour," Jasper said.

They all dispersed to look for the little girl. Jasper and Ciara searched the maintenance areas while Ash and Quinn checked the supply closets on each floor and the guests checked their rooms and walked through the halls. Tosk offered to look outside and scurried out the lobby's back door before anyone could respond. As Ash leaned on the doorframe to watch him run up the wall, the door shut and crushed his fingers. He let out a quiet squeak and shook his hand gently.

"Are you okay?" Quinn asked.

"Yeah, I'm fine." He looked down at his hand. The fingers were pink but undamaged.

Quinn awkwardly cleared their throat. "Hey. Not to be rude, but… what's your deal? How come you're not hurt by anything?"

"Well, I can be hurt by some things. Words, for example." Ash opened the door to the supply closet behind the front desk. Inside they could see stacks of buckets and piles of rags and spray bottles but no little green girl. "But yeah, I am pretty tough I guess. I've had plenty of tests but nothing conclusive came back. We don't know why I'm like this. Or even what I am."

"Do you have any other abilities?"

He chewed his lip, thinking. "Well, my skin is kind of rocky." He held out his hand and Quinn touched it. His skin felt like very fine pumice. "The old layer peels off when I grow. Oh! And I can do this!"

He rubbed his hands together the way Quinn did to warm them up in the cold. Bright orange sparks sprung from them and fell onto the closet door.

"That's awesome!" Quinn gasped. "But be careful of the wood."

"It's keratin, actually."

"Huh?"

"Nothing in here is made of wood."

Quinn glanced around them, trying hard to suppress their gag reflex. "Oh."

Finding nothing in the closet, they decided to move on and go up the staff staircase. Ash dug through his pockets for his keys and sighed when he realized he had left them in his room. He opened a drawer in the front desk and picked up Jasper's ledger, then froze with a worried frown.

"What's wrong?" Quinn asked.

"The spare set of keys should be under here," Ash said slowly. "You didn't move them, right?"

"Nope." Quinn pulled out their own set. "But we'll be fine. You gave me these yesterday, remember?"

His face brightened. "Oh yeah! I did."

The staff staircase in the center of the inn was much more plain and cramped than the public ones at either end of the building. The finely carved trim was absent here and the same round wall-mounted lamps from the hallways lit the space, rather than the dusty chandeliers which presided over the public staircases. As they climbed Ash scribbled a note on his hand to ask about the spare keys. The smell of his pen's ink mingled with the muggy organic smell from below. These were the same stairs they took down to the stomach last night.

The smell wasn't the only thing which would take some getting used to. It was intimidating showing up in a place where everyone already knew each other. They had no clue where they would fit in, or if they would at all. But at the same time they couldn't ignore the feeling of hope warming their chest. For once, they didn't feel like they stood out so painfully. This could be a new start for them.

As they exited onto the third floor, one of the brothers from the van last night stepped out of his room. Today he wore a fleece vest and his hair was crushed flat under a red baseball cap. He crossed the hall to the stairwell and opened the door. At the same moment Meena opened it from the other side and almost ran into him.

The man stumbled back in surprise. Meena didn't seem to notice. "Hey, Hector, have you seen a little green girl, looks like this?" She twisted herself into an exact copy of Brooke. The man screamed.

"If I'd seen that, everyone would have heard about it by now," he cried. She shifted back into her humanoid form and doubled over laughing.

At that moment Fenris emerged from the stairwell and walked past them. He glanced warily at Meena and startled abruptly when he saw Hector. "You—" he began to say, but his voice died and he turned away. Hector's face soured as he watched the werewolf walk down the hall.

"What was that about?" Meena asked when she saw his expression. "Does he know you?"

Hector shook his head. "It's nothing."

She folded her arms. "Come on, let's hear it."

He glared at the floor. "That's a werewolf, little lady. You'd better stay away from them. These woods are full of horrible things." He shook his head as if trying to forget a bad dream. "You can't ever let down your guard."

He turned away, and Meena stared in confusion at the spot he had just occupied. She shouted after him and followed him into the stairwell.

Quinn swallowed as they began rifling through the supplies in the closet. They wondered how someone who didn't like monsters came to stay in a place like this. Jasper told them they didn't advertise for safety reasons. Maybe people like this man were the safety reason.

A few minutes later Hector ran back in through the same door, looking relieved to have lost Meena. He tugged absently at the hem of his shirt. When Fenris reappeared at the opposite end he let out a noise caught between a groan and a growl.

Fenris considered the man carefully. "You… I know you. Don't I?"

"You should," Hector scoffed. "After what your kind did to my brother."

Fenris frowned and opened his mouth, but before he could speak Fenris came out of his room just a couple doors down. Quinn and Hector both gasped in shock.

"Excuse me!" one of the Fenrises cried indignantly. The other one turned and fled, melting into an orange slime and flowing away. At the stairwell Meena reformed into her humanoid shape and ran.

They followed Fenris at a distance to the second floor, where they checked the closet there. Ash laughed nervously. "It's not usually like this."

"What, with everyone lying and threatening each other?" Quinn teased, pushing aside a row of brooms to peek behind them.

"Yeah. I mean… they don't mean it. Most of the time. They're just messing around. In an affectionate way."

"How do I know when it's affectionate?"

"Well, it's not always easy. You just kind of… know."

Quinn shrugged. To them, *just kind of knowing* was basically telepathy. It was hard enough when people just said what they meant.

Delta stepped out of her room, running her hands through her hair in distress. When she saw Fenris she stopped dead. Her eyes flashed with some kind of realization. "Wait," she said. "Aren't you—"

"Oh, don't start," Fenris snarled. "I'm helping you, aren't I? I'm sure whatever reason you've come up with to dislike me can wait."

Delta frowned, thinking. She opened her mouth to say something, then changed her mind and closed it. She shook her head and went back into her room.

"Come on. Let's keep looking." Ash started walking down the hall but Quinn lingered, replaying the interaction they had just seen in their mind. There was real anger in Fenris and Hector's voices, some emotion in Delta's eyes that they couldn't recognize, and it had shaken them.

"Hey, are you okay?" Ash asked nervously. "Ignore them. I don't know why everything is so tense today."

Quinn hesitated. "You go ahead. I want to, um… check the closet again. I'll catch up with you."

He shrugged. "Okay." He began walking away, glancing warily over his shoulder at them before continuing down the hall.

They needed a breather, a little time to think. They could feel something awful in the air between the guests today. The hostility felt cold and sharp, digging through their hopes of belonging. Was it going to stay this way? Were they making it worse by being here?

There had to be something they could do. Everyone seemed to be worried about the missing little girl, Quinn reasoned. Maybe when she was found everyone would relax. Yes, this always worked in the past. Quinn didn't always pick up on the subtle stuff but they could get people what they needed. They just had to find Brooke.

Delta came back out from her room and Quinn quickly

pretended they had been looking out the window instead of staring into space like a neurotic mannequin. They tried nervously to smile at her, and she returned it with a disturbed eyebrow raise and hurried away down the hall.

As she climbed the stairs her door swung slightly back on its hinge with a creak. Quinn considered the sliver of visible room for a half a second before moving towards it. The decision to step into that room was almost unconscious, the phrase *privacy violation* barely ghosting the corner of their mind. Delta wouldn't mind if it meant finding her daughter. And they would. Quinn was good at finding things. Besides, if they didn't find her, they would be out before Delta ever knew.

They ran their eyes over the things in the room and their hands soon unconsciously followed. Clothes, toys made of carved bone and shell, bottles of mineral supplements and pain medications, rolls of gauze. Quinn didn't know what to consider normal in this case. But none of it seemed to point in any clear direction.

They glanced at the bed, which was completely empty. The water had cooled and made the sheets feel clammy. Their gaze moved on, then stopped and dragged itself back. Completely empty.

The plush sturgeon was gone. Brooke must have wandered away on her own, taking it with her, or else it would still be there. Quinn wasn't sure who the medicine was for, but if Brooke was in pain, she probably hadn't gone far. But where?

A clattering sound from the window made them almost jump out of their skin. They whirled around to see Tosk scrambling to regain his balance on the sill as one of the papers from his pockets twirled in the wind. He grabbed the paper, smiled at them, and raised one paw in a shaky thumbs-up, then he skittered away as Quinn caught their breath.

Their eyes came to rest on the vent opening. It was warm in there. Warm and muggy. Cozy for a little riverbeast. She couldn't have… no, that was silly…

Just to be sure, Quinn knelt down. Just a quick peek, then they would go. Any minute now Delta could come back in here. They hoped Tosk wouldn't say anything to her.

Quinn leaned their head into the opening. It was too dark to see anything.

"Brooke?" they called softly. They could feel hot moisture clinging to their skin the longer they stayed there.

There was no answer. Of course not, it was a dumb idea, it–

Something fluttered in the flow of air from the vent. A little moss-green scrap of fabric caught in the vent opening. They carefully pulled it loose. A ribbon. A hair ribbon! Encouraged, they stuffed it into their pocket, leaned back into the opening, and called Brooke's name again.

A gentle rustling sound came from down the vent. The little girl raised her head, and her eyes glinted a bright aquamarine several feet away.

Quinn gasped in delight. They reached their arms out, beckoning Brooke to come closer. "Hey, Brooke. Come here. Your mom is looking for you."

Brooke looked at them for a long moment. She shook her head and lay back down.

"Please? We're worried. Come here."

She turned away, nestling her body tighter against the vent wall.

48

The shine of her eyes disappeared.

Quinn pulled their head out of the opening with a nervous sigh. They ran to the doorway and started calling Delta's name.

"What?" she finally answered from the floor above.

"I found her! I found Brooke!"

Delta didn't answer, but her running footsteps told them she had heard. Pride swelled up in Quinn's chest. They had found her. Everything would be okay now.

"You found her? Really?" Ash cried from down the hall.

"Yes!"

"Everyone come here!" Ash yelled. "To the second floor! Brooke is here!"

The sound of footsteps multiplied as the other guests hurried towards them.

"Where is she?" Delta gasped, appearing in the doorway.

"She climbed into the vent," Quinn said excitedly. "It's warm and humid in there. See, I saw the sturgeon was gone and I thought, maybe she wandered away–"

"Were you in my room?" Delta interrupted.

"Well-" Quinn stammered. "The– the door was open."

She glared. Quinn noticed her eyes were raw and red and she was trembling. This wasn't the time for excuses. "I'm sorry!" they cried quickly. "I won't do it again. She's in here."

Ash slipped in behind them as Delta followed Quinn across the room. When she stuck her head into the vent opening, the tension in Delta's body dissolved. She sobbed in relief. "Brooke! Come here, minnow."

Quinn opened the window and shouted for Tosk to come

inside. He bounded down the side of the wall and slipped in. Meena, Ryan, and Hector appeared in the doorway one by one.

"Brooke!" Delta called again. There was a small shuffling noise from the shaft as the little girl crawled towards her.

Ryan crossed the room and knelt next to her. "Is she in there?"

Delta shrank away from him. He peeked into the opening and called Brooke's name.

"I can handle it," Delta said quickly. "Don't touch her."

"I just want to help. Brooke!" he called again. The shuffling noise continued to get closer.

"Really," Delta said. "I've got it."

"Oh, I see her!" Ryan cried. The noise grew louder. Brooke's damp mop of hair appeared in the opening. Ryan held out his arms and Brooke peered at him for a careful moment, then slowly dragged herself out.

Delta snatched the girl up and held her close to her chest. She glared at Ryan.

"I'm just trying to help," he repeated, retreating with his hands up in a gesture of surrender.

"We don't need any help." Delta ran her hand over Brooke's hair and gently kissed her forehead. "Are you okay, minnow?"

Brooke nodded slowly and buried her face in her mother's chest, seeming to forget anyone else was in the room. Quinn noticed with a pang of satisfaction that she was clutching the plush sturgeon.

Awkward silence hung in the air. The others looked at each other and began drifting out the door. They dispersed until Quinn and Ash were left standing in the hall, unsure what to do with themselves.

Just then Ciara and Jasper stumbled down the hall towards them. Ciara's movements lacked the easy poise she had carried herself with earlier and Jasper nervously picked at his shirt collar. He looked up at them, then Ash, and he pressed his lips together. Something was wrong.

"Hey freaks," Ciara said.

Her smile looked tense and forced, and her green eyes darted nervously between them.

"Want to see a dead body?"

$$- 4 -$$

Quinn stood frozen in the doorway while Jasper and Ciara hovered around the body. Ash was outside, gathering wild-flowers to wrap up in the shroud. He had refused even to look inside the room. Whatever they were expecting, it wasn't this.

Fenris lay on the floor half-transformed. His face was knotted in an intense blend of pain, fear, and anger and his clothes were torn. Blotchy red marks peppered his face and arms. They matched the size of the heavy Turkish lamp which had been taken from the nightstand and now lay near his shoulder.

Quinn chewed their lip and stared at the body. They had found dead animals in the woods before, but that was nothing like this. Just minutes ago, Fenris had been walking, breathing, insulting the other guests. They had no idea how to process this.

Instinctively their hands went for their notebook and pencil.

Body lying on its side, facing door

Halfway between forms- limbs bent, skull and teeth lengthened, eyes human

Red marks on face and arms

Quinn leaned in for a better look. They were gripping their pencil so tight their fingers were growing pale and numb. The red marks were mostly visible under the thin layer of fur that had frozen mid-growth, but they would need to get closer to see better. Against a rising tide of dread they inched closer.

Jasper shot them a warning glance before returning to photographing the scene. "I don't want you kids in here."

"We're not kids," Quinn pointed out.

"You know what I mean. This could be dangerous." He knelt to examine the body. His solemn eyes ran down the length of the werewolf's frame and lifted in confusion. He quietly asked himself the same thing they were all thinking. "How did this happen?"

Quinn craned their neck inside to peek around the room. A bed, wardrobe, and nightstand, all made of the same dark material they preferred to believe was wood, were all free of blood or scuff marks. A desk in the corner held a messy stack of papers, some of which had fallen to the floor, and the chair had been pulled out at an unnatural angle. The window was open, letting in a stiff breeze that made them all shiver. Quinn quickly wrote it all down.

"The killer must have either broken in," Ciara suggested, "or he let them in. Someone he trusted?"

An especially strong breeze came in through the window and stirred the air in the room. The sour tang of stomach acid seeped in from the bathroom. "Vomit," the vampire murmured.

"Was he sick?" Quinn asked doubtfully. "He looked healthy the last time we saw him."

"What else do you smell?" Jasper asked Ciara.

She frowned as she sniffed the air. "Cheap cologne and… clove. Does that mean anything to you?" They all shrugged.

She pulled the sheet off the bed and Jasper helped her wrap the body up in it. The top of Fenris's chest flashed bare before it disappeared under the folds of cotton. Quinn frowned.

"Hey," they said. Distracted, they dropped their notebook and pointed. They tried to step inside the room and stepped right back out at the look they received from Jasper. "Was his shirt unbuttoned like that before?"

Ciara pulled back the sheet to check. The top two buttons of Fenris's shirt were indeed open. "I don't believe it was," she said thoughtfully.

"He had on a tie," Jasper added. He pulled aside the werewolf's jacket, and there they could see the tie hanging loose around his neck. He hummed thoughtfully. "Maybe he felt hot… or like he couldn't breathe."

He moved the tie to one side, revealing a small red dot on the werewolf's chest, almost hidden by his hair. "Whoa. This looks like an injection."

Quinn shivered. "Maybe it was part of his death. The question is, when did he get it?"

Ciara's lips pressed into a thin line as they stood up. "So are we telling the guests about this?"

"I think we have to," Jasper sighed. "They'll start asking where he went eventually."

"But what if one of them did it?" Quinn asked. They backed out the doorway to give the two some space to carry out the body.

"Maybe no one did it." He grimaced. "I'd prefer if no one did it. At least, no one staying with us. Either way, everyone should know."

"Hi!"

Quinn jumped and turned to see Ryan. He held out their notebook which they had dropped.

Behind them Ciara silently shut the door. Everyone should know— *except* him, they figured. The mysteriously dead man in that room had been about to buy the land they were living on. It looked bad, very *very* bad. Ryan and his father couldn't find out about this.

Ryan examined their anxious face curiously. "Hey, are you okay?" he asked.

"Uh— yeah. I'm fine." They winced, knowing they sounded tense and stilted.

"Are you sure? You look pretty scared. You were kind of staring into space..."

"Oh... I was just, uh..."

The door to Fenris's room opened again. Ciara marched out, holding a stack of towels from the bathroom. "Ryan!" she cried in mock surprise. "What an afternoon, eh? I wish I could say it's not always like this, but, well..." She handed the towels to Quinn with enough authority that they almost forgot what was really going on.

"Oh, I don't mind," Ryan said. "I'm just happy Delta's with her daughter. It wasn't that big a distraction. I just have to look at the surrounding land and hand out a customer survey, and then I'll be out of your hair.”

She shifted her weight to one side, subtly pulling Fenris’s door shut. “I’m not sure it’s a good day for that,” she said carefully. “Everyone’s in such a state after looking for Brooke. And, you know, the weather, the moon phases, Jupiter in retrograde…”

“Alright,” he said uncertainly. “I can do those things tomorrow, I guess. I should meet with my dad anyway.”

“Yes, go. Give him our best,” Ciara said cheerfully. Ryan gave her a confused look as he walked away.

They wrapped the body back up and brought it down to the lobby. Ciara threw on a tattered gray cloak and ran outside to search for scent traces in case anyone might have escaped through the woods. Behind the counter was a large walk-in freezer where furniture was kept cold for snow-dwelling creatures. Jasper pushed an armchair out of the way before sliding the body inside.

From her seat at the counter, Delta watched the body go by with frightened eyes. “Who is that?” she stammered.

Quinn frowned. Was it that obvious that the shape wrapped in the sheet was a dead body? They sighed, supposing she was going to find out anyway. “Uh… well…”

The other guests who had looked for Brooke looked up sharply as they realized who was missing. Meena and Tosk joined Delta at each side and Hector slowly stood up, his brow furrowed deeply. The wood frog Quinn had seen last night peered around, wondering what he had missed.

“It’s… it’s Fenris,” Quinn said quietly.

A collective nervous inhale made the room feel like a vacuum for a moment. The guests all glanced at each other.

56

"Hey," Tosk said in a shaky voice, "I didn't mean those things I was saying to him earlier. Well– I mean, I did… but I didn't want to hurt him. I swear. I'm not a violent guy."

"Me either," Delta added quickly. "I wasn't serious last night. I was only complaining about his company."

"What, when you said you'd rip his head off?" Meena teased her with a bitter laugh. "Not me. I meant what I said. It was his time."

Delta stared at her incredulously, but Hector made a movement blending a shrug and a nod. "So did I. The forest will be a safer place without him."

"Hey, wait," Quinn said desperately. "Slow down. We don't know if *anyone* killed him. He wasn't injured very badly."

"Yes, maybe he was sick," Tosk said hopefully. "Or had a heart attack."

"It probably wasn't any of us," Delta said.

"He looked awfully healthy when we saw him last," Meena said doubtfully.

"What happened to him?" Delta asked Jasper as he stepped out of the freezer.

He sighed. "We're not sure. Maybe nothing. I called a pathologist and she's coming tomorrow to take a look."

Ciara burst in, shedding the cloak and smoothing out her hair. Jasper lifted his eyebrows and she shook her head in response. "No scents," she said. "Nobody from here passed through the forest in the last hour." She looked around at the guests and smiled. "Hello, potential murderers."

The group erupted in frightened cries and defensive shouts.

"It's not so bad," Ash said, trying to lighten the mood. "It will be easy to find the murderer. We already know where they are. Right here."

Rather than calming them down, the words *right here* sent the group into hysterics. The guests began to accuse each other in raised voices, and Quinn even heard a few sobs. They shrank back, paralyzed by uncertainty about what to do.

Jasper clapped his hands loudly and the building rumbled in echo. The guests went silent.

"Everyone listen." Cold determination creased his face. "We'll handle this. We can all stay safe if we work together. I need to hear where everyone was during the last hour." He glanced at the others and his eyes landed on Quinn's notebook, which they were anxiously fiddling with. "Quinn, can you take notes?"

"Sure." They followed him to one of the tables and sat beside him.

"Okay," he began with a sigh. "Ciara, you were with me when we found the body. We weren't apart long enough for either of us to do it. Unless you've set a new record."

"I'm flattered, but no," Ciara said, leaning against the chair back. She playfully elbowed his arm. "Besides, you're no killer. You're too soft. I had to wrestle that manticore myself because you would rather have let it eat you than kill it."

He elbowed her back, allowing a smile to soften his face. "I was just letting you have your fun. You wanted to wrangle that thing as soon as you saw it."

She shrugged. "Maybe." Then she paused. "We're... not suspecting the kids, are we?"

58

"We shouldn't exclude anyone without making sure," Quinn said. "But me and Ash were together the whole time. We can vouch for each other."

"Not the whole time," Ash said. Quinn jumped. He had drifted over without making a sound and scared them just like when they first met.

"Oh yeah. There was a little while between when we split up and when everyone came into Delta's room." They tapped their pencil against their jaw, thinking. That wasn't enough time, was it? It didn't matter. Ash couldn't hurt a fly. Despite what they had just said, they couldn't bring themself to suspect him.

"I checked the lobby, then I came back up the stairs to see if you were feeling better," Ash said. "I was at the other end of the second floor when you started calling for Delta."

Quinn nodded and jotted down what he said. "And I was checking Delta's room," they said, flushing with embarrassment. "The... door was open and I looked around a little."

"Can anyone verify that?" Ciara asked.

They thought for a second. "Oh–yeah. Tosk tripped on the windowsill outside and he saw me."

Jasper called for Tosk to come over. He did so nervously, scratching at his ears and twisting his fingers in rapid jerky movements.

"You were looking for Brooke outside while we were all split up, right?" Jasper asked.

Tosk nodded uneasily.

"Did you see anyone else while you were looking?"

He twitched, thinking. "Um– yes. I saw Bertram through a

window as I passed by." He pointed at the wood frog. "He was asleep. After a while I stumbled on the windowsill of Delta's room and I saw Quinn in there. Pretty soon after that they found Brooke and I went back inside."

Quinn wrote it all down and read over their notes, nibbling on the end of the pencil. "Okay. There are a few time points we can check. But other than that, it seems like there's a lot of time when you were unaccounted for."

Tosk's eyes widened with fear. "I swear it wasn't me! I was running around the outside of the inn the whole time! Ask anyone who saw me!"

Jasper hummed in thought, watching Quinn write. "Meena, you're next. What did you do after we split up?"

Meena melted into the form of a snake, slid across the room and up onto a chair, and shifted back into her humanoid form, crossing her legs. She showed them a relaxed smile and said, "I looked around the lobby for a while, then I went upstairs where I bumped into him." She tossed a thumb over her right shoulder to point at Hector. "Scared him with my true form," she snickered. "Classic. Then I checked the third floor, didn't see the kid. So I went down to the basement."

"The staircase to the basement's supposed to be locked," Jasper said with a frown.

"Well, it wasn't when I got there." She smiled again. "She wasn't down there either. I went back up and I was on my way back to the second floor when Quinn started yelling."

Jasper sighed, pinching the bridge of his nose. "Fine. Did anyone else see you during that time?"

She shook her head.

"Alright, Hector, you're up. You talked to Meena in the hall?" he asked.

Hector trudged over, eyeing Meena suspiciously. "Yep. Gave me a heart attack."

"Okay. What were you doing the rest of the time?"

He grumbled something inaudible before answering. "Before that I was in my room reading. I went down to the lounge to get a coffee, but no one was there. So I went back to my room. That's when *she* decided to scare me."

"Did you see anyone else?"

Hector's face had been slowly turning a deeper and deeper red. Now he exploded. "Why am I being interrogated? I'm the least likely out of anyone to do it. Look at us, surrounded by freaks and monsters. Why would I–"

"Just answer the question, man," Jasper said in a bored voice. "Did you see anyone else or not?"

He glowered for a moment. "Yes. On the stairs when I was coming back from the lounge. I heard someone above me, and I looked up and saw her." He pointed his left thumb over his shoulder at Delta. She stiffened. "She was going up to the third floor. After that I didn't see anyone else. Am I done now?"

Quinn quickly wrote it down. Jasper called Delta's name, and she lingered at the other end of the room as if she hoped he'd change his mind. Finally she came over and sat down, resting Brooke on her right knee. The little girl yawned wide and shut her eyes.

"After we split up," she began in a shaky voice, "I checked the lobby, then my room again. When I came out I ran into–" she grimaced at having to say the dead man's name. "–Fenris. I realized I forgot something and went back into my room– oh." She paused, remembering. "You two were there." She waved her hand in Ash and Quinn's direction. "After that I went upstairs and worked my way down again. Then you started calling my name."

She squeezed her eyes shut and tilted her head back. "Listen," she said, opening her eyes again and focusing them on Quinn with a frigid intensity. "I'm not stupid. I know how bad this seems for me. But please, look closer. Don't let his innocent act fool you."

Quinn's restless fingers stopped tapping for a moment, taken aback. It was a bold, somewhat aggressive way to describe a murder victim. What was she implying about Fenris?

Delta let out a trembling breath. "That may sound harsh. I'm just on edge about Brooke. I'd do anything for her. She's already sick, and I just…" She gently ran her fingers through her daughter's hair, maneuvering carefully around her long, sharp fingernails.

"We understand. We'll do our best to keep everyone safe," Jasper assured her. "Okay. That's everyone." He leaned back and peered at Quinn's notebook page. "What do we have?"

Quinn skimmed over their notes and summarized. "Fenris was last seen alive by me, Ash, and Delta right after he talked to Hector. Bertram was asleep the whole time. Tosk was running around outside and he was seen a couple times, but in between he could have done it. Hector was seen once, with Meena and Fenris, and we only have his word about where he was after that. Delta was seen once when we last saw Fenris and once after, climbing the stairs toward his floor."

The room was deadly silent for a moment. Then everyone started talking at once, repeating their alibis and insisting they could not have done it. Quinn shrugged and closed their notebook.

"No one's being accused of anything yet," Jasper said in a raised voice. "We'll know more when the pathologist comes by."

"Are the police coming?" Delta asked, her voice shrill with fear.

He shook his head. "No way. We try to stay out of the public eye, and inviting a group of humans who've never seen a magical creature would be a disaster." She relaxed at his words. "Which reminds me– no one say a word about this to Ryan. Fenris was about to buy this land when he died. There's no way we can make that look good."

Quinn made the same mental note regarding their parents. At the first mention of danger, they knew their mom and dad would lock them up and they would never see this place again. Understandable, perhaps, but they couldn't leave now. They had met creatures whose existence should be impossible and seen things beyond their imagination. And just as they were trying to find a place here, it was all being put in danger. They had to stay, had to try to protect this bizarre new world.

Jasper seemed to be thinking the same thing. He leaned back, glancing over Quinn's notes, and he breathed a heavy sigh. "Your parents are gonna kill me," he murmured.

~~~

That evening Quinn crouched on the soft blue carpet, ignoring the worn sofa behind them as they studied their notes. They were
~~~

on the fourth floor in one of the unoccupied rooms converted to a common space. Below the description of Fenris's body they did their best to sketch a map of the room when they had found it. Logically, they knew it wouldn't help them to obsessively collect all this information. If Fenris had died naturally there was no point, and if he hadn't, then the last thing that could protect them from a werewolf-killer was this flimsy notebook. But it was comforting to take stock of everything they knew and carry it all around in their pocket. Doing it brought a sense of control that was as reassuring as it was false.

When there was nothing left to put on paper, Quinn flopped onto the sofa with a sigh. On the floor below two guests were talking with anger and fear in their muffled voices. Quinn picked at the fraying threads and numbly gazed at Jasper's paintings hanging on the opposite wall. There were three, all swirling with life and color like a psychedelic Where's Waldo. As their eyes traced dancing moths and leaping cats they thought they might have a dim memory of watching Jasper sketch this one as a kid. Their parents always called him *imaginative* when they were trying to be polite. Quinn wondered what they would have said after a visit here.

The sharp buzz of their phone jolted them out of their thoughts. Their mom was calling. Quinn froze, fear creeping from their stomach up into their throat, staring at the screen. They took a deep breath and answered.

"Hi honey," their mom said, too gently like she was tiptoeing around shards of broken glass. "How is camp?"

Quinn tried to conjure the pent-up frustration and betrayal they would be feeling if they had really ridden to camp with Izzy like they had told their parents. "Boring. The dorms are too hot."

She laughed uneasily. "Right. Are you and Izzy spending time together?"

"She has her own group. She's always with them." That part came easily. They didn't even need to make it up.

"Maybe she could invite you to join sometime."

"I don't think they like me." Quinn frowned at the loose thread they had been picking at. They hadn't expected to say that. Not that it wasn't true.

"Well, have you met anyone else there? You could make your own group."

Why was this turning into a counseling session? Quinn groaned inwardly but stopped themself from making the noise out loud. Instead they said truthfully, "There's a kid who lives on my hall. He seems okay."

"That's good," their mom said encouragingly.

"Are you telling him about bugs?" their dad joined in. "Don't start with bugs. Ask him about his hobbies."

This time they did groan aloud. "Dad, I can make friends on my own."

"Okay, okay."

"We just want to know you're doing alright," their mom said.

"I am," Quinn lied into the awkward pause that followed.

"Good," she said, relieved. "I know it's almost curfew over there. Goodnight, honey."

"Goodnight."

She hung up. Quinn sighed at the ceiling. They wondered how long they could keep this lie up. Murder or not, they didn't want to leave this place.

The call was just a reminder that Quinn was on borrowed time. Every moment here felt fragile and precious. With a huff, they pulled themself off the couch. While they were still here, they might as well explore. Their notebook slipped into their pocket in effortless habit as they headed outside.

They perked up a little as the cool air hit their lungs and ran over their skin like soothing water. The oak and maple trees were nearly bare, their leaves lying in a stiff carpet on the ground.

The woods surrounding the inn were dark and full of possibility. Probably full of danger, too, they thought as the shadows of trees stretched and lengthened overhead. But they may not have long to explore it. If this was their only chance to explore the woods, they would take it. Quinn nodded to themself and walked decisively around the side of the inn– and straight into a ladder.

They lurched back at the last second to avoid colliding with the ladder and looked up. Jasper was perched on top, holding an oddly curved set of shears. He looked down and waved when he heard them gasp.

"What are you doing?" Quinn asked.

"Just giving the inn a little maintenance," he answered. "It feels stressed." He lifted the shears towards one of the shingles on the wall and clipped it. The crescent of brown keratin fell to the ground and Quinn's stomach twisted.

"Does the inn know what's going on?" they asked.

"I like to think so," Jasper said with a shrug. He gave the keratin an affectionate scratch. With a wave of his hand the weeds growing against the wall rose up and wiggled gently, and the building made a low rumble not unlike a purr.

"How did you do that?" Quinn cried. Under his shirt the blue glow of his tattoos slowly faded.

"The earth and I have been friends for a long time," Jasper said. "It's the source of all magic. When you manipulate the funky energies the earth gives off and make them do what you want, that's magic. I've spent most of my life studying it."

"Can you teach me?" they asked eagerly.

He stroked his chin. "Maybe if you do some extra chores," he teased. "Carry lots of heavy suitcases, clean the gunk out of the pipes…"

"Come on," they groaned. He smiled and didn't answer.

A shrill chattering noise echoed down from the sky and Quinn looked up to see a massive winged shape with gleaming eyes sail overhead. They gasped and scrambled for their phone. It was useless; all the pictures they took came out a grainy mess.

"Ha! I knew it!" they cried anyway.

Jasper   looked   at   them.   "What?"

"Mothman! I used to go out all the time trying to find him. And, y'know, Bigfoot, UFOs, zombies…"

"Oh, zombies aren't real." He leaned forward and clipped another shingle.

They frowned. "What?"

"Zombies. They're not real."

"No way. But the rest of them are?"

"Yep."

"Are you serious? Mothman is real? Giant talking animals, river monsters, vampires, and werewolves? But not zombies?"

"Sorry."

"I don't believe this. You're messing with me."

He shrugged, smiling.

The sun was low in the sky now, painting everything in deep shadow. Mixed in with the usual symphony of nighttime insects were noises Quinn didn't recognize, whispers and chirps made by anatomies they could only imagine. They could also hear quiet song and conversation from the creatures in the trees.

"Did you always know about magic?" Quinn asked. They couldn't believe all this was hidden from them growing up. If they had known, they thought, maybe things would be different.

"Nope. I had to go out and find it. I loved to explore as a kid, run around in the woods, climb things I wasn't supposed to. Sometimes I even got Lev and your mom to join me."

"Really?" Quinn was shocked. They knew Jasper and their mom grew up near each other, but they never imagined the two playing together.

"Yeah. When I was twelve, I pushed my luck a little too far one day and the pile of rocks I was climbing crumbled. My whole right side was crushed." He shook his head at the memory. "I discovered magic by accident during recovery, trying to function with half my body working. I was so excited about this power, I wanted to share it with Lev and your mom. Lev caught on quickly. He was a natural. That man always had magic in him." He gazed off into the woods, forgetting himself for a moment.

Quinn nodded somberly, unsure what to say. "He seemed great," was the best they could come up with.

"He was. He was wonderful. I can't believe he's related to your mom." He snorted. "No offense."

"No, you're right. If you were all friends, why did she turn out so different from you and Lev?"

Jasper shook his head. "Erica liked the way things used to be between the three of us. She didn't want to accept that I was changing. That we were all changing. It scared her."

He splayed his hands, showing off his tattoos. "It scared me too, but once I saw what was out there– and what was inside me– there was no turning back. I made a promise to myself and I wrote it in ink across my body. The real ones stayed. Lev stayed. Erica didn't."

Quinn nodded mutely. Somehow they weren't too surprised to learn this about their mom. While they ran headfirst towards uncertainty, she avoided it at all costs. Maybe she didn't dislike Jasper because of who he was but what he forced her to see in herself.

"That's why I'm glad you're here," Jasper said.

They looked up at him. "Really? You are?"

"Sure. You don't have to keep magic in your life, but I want you to have that choice."

Quinn turned their head away, smiling to themself in the darkness. His words helped them feel like they could stay afloat when grief and fear threatened to pull them under.

"Okay," Jasper sighed, "you've got me all sentimental now. I'll teach you something."

"Yes!" Quinn cried. They helped him balance as he climbed down the ladder. He rubbed his hands together in thought.

"The first thing you need to know," he said, "is that using magic is just directing the earth's energies. You can do that in a few different ways. My tattoos do it using language. Some creatures have bodies that interact directly with magic- it's how starlings can shapeshift and how some animals like Tosk grow bigger and more intelligent. That kind of magic is strong but can be unpredictable. But every living thing has a little bit of that type inside, animating us."

Quinn nodded, their brain buzzing as they tried to absorb what he was saying.

"Let's start with something simple. Pretty simple, anyway. Do you have that notebook on you?"

"Always." They pulled it out along with their pencil.

"I'll have you copy some sigils I used to create my tattoos. These things are like road signs for magic to follow. Magic has an innate intelligence, but without guidance it's just a lot of potential energy waiting for direction. When you write sigils, you use symbols to describe where the energy should go, and how, and for what effect. You can combine them in new ways to do different things."

Quinn frowned. "That's so complicated. Can't I just wave a wand or something?"

"Actually, you can, but that would be a physical manipulation. The wand exerts force on the atomic linkages of each air molecule between you and your target, causing a chemical reaction which–"

"Okay, okay," they cut him off. "I'll try this."

They tore a page from their notebook and squinted at the forearm he was holding out. Beneath the twisting wyverns and grinning tigers were inked complex networks of shapes and connecting lines. They looked a little like hieroglyphs, a little like runes, and a lot like a bunch of angry caterpillars. Quinn squinted and tried their best to copy the symbols.

"We'll start small," Jasper said. "Let's make a gust of wind to move those weeds growing by the wall."

"Lame."

"Hey. You start with wind, and one day you can summon lightning or make the ground open up. One thing at a time. Now, this one's a spell initiation, this one amplifies force, and this one describes direction relative to you. Focus on them, let all your attention and energy pour into them, and when you're ready, give them a big mental push."

"How do I do that?" Quinn asked.

"You'll know. Give it a try."

Quinn stared at the sigils on the scrap of paper until they began to blur. They let their whole world narrow to just the paper, studying every bend and detail of the symbols, focusing with all their might and desire. Their mind went still. Subtly they could feel something there. Something struggling to wake itself up, beginning sluggishly to move and recall old patterns forgotten for years. The more they tried to focus, the more they could feel it. Encouraged, Quinn threw forward a big burst of willpower. *Move.*

For a fraction of a second nothing happened. They looked up at Jasper in confusion, and just then something big and solid thunked against their head. They stumbled.

A shingle from the inn's wall had fallen on them. Quinn and Jasper laughed awkwardly at the coincidence.

"Give it another try," he encouraged them. They did. They barely got three seconds in before another shingle fell onto their head.

"What—" Quinn began. Another shingle hit them.

Quinn covered their head with their arms and backed away. "What is that? What does it mean?"

He scratched his head. "I'm not sure. The house never does this."

Another shingle fell, bounced off the ground, and hit Quinn again in their new spot. "But it does to me?" they cried.

"Don't worry, Quinn. It's just playing around."

"Cool way to show it. Seems like the house doesn't want me here."

"It's probably just getting used to you," he assured them. "It doesn't mean anything."

Quinn sighed. They stared at the pile of shingles, feeling deeply alone.

Just then a window on the fourth floor groaned open. Ciara poked her head out and looked down at them.

"Evening, freaks!" she called. "Jasper, are we still going to the night market?"

"I forgot about that," Jasper said. "Yeah, unless we want the oven to explode we'd better."

"What's that?" Quinn asked.

"The night market happens in these woods every full moon," he told them. "They sell all sorts of unusual or enchanted things here. Stuff you never knew you wanted— and probably still don't want, after you see it."

Ciara ducked back inside and leaned out again, this time dangling Ash out by his shoulders.

"Hey– he's too big for that now–" Jasper tried to warn her.

"Catch!" she cried and dropped the boy.

Jasper had barely started running when Ash hit the ground. He bounced a little before springing upright. Ciara leapt out after him and landed precisely on her feet.

Quinn stuffed the spell note into their pocket, shivering. Ciara and Ash chatted excitedly as Jasper joined them. They hesitated for a moment and then, throwing one last glance back at the fallen shingles, Quinn followed the others down the dark and narrow path into the woods.

- 5 -

The earth was soft under their feet as the group walked through the forest. The path smelled like damp soil and decaying leaves. The waxy moonlight filtering through the branches wasn't quite enough to see, so Jasper floated a small ball of light between his fingers that illuminated their faces. Without the sun the air was already growing chilly.

Ciara held out her hand to display a few rocks in her palm. "Jasper, are these rocks cool enough?"

He picked through the stones and pointed at one. "This one for sure. Maybe this one."

Quinn gasped. "You have cool rocks? Can I see?"

Ciara held out the rocks toward them. "Here. After tonight, you can keep the ones Aspen doesn't want."

"Who's Aspen?"

"They're a human who sells jugs of their blood in exchange for cool rocks."

"That doesn't sound safe," Quinn said.

Ciara slipped the rocks into her pocket. "It's excellent blood, though."

The walk to the market passed by quickly. As the group approached a clearing in the woods, the roar of voices and laughter grew louder until it enveloped them. A maze of canvas tents, vibrant colors and smells, and quickly moving bodies emerged through the trees.

Ciara split off from the others immediately, waving to someone they couldn't see. Jasper paused at a tent selling seeds and Quinn and Ash stayed with him for a few minutes, trying to occupy themselves by reading descriptions of poison apples and sentient Venus fly traps. They quickly grew bored, however, and with a reminder from Jasper to stay together they went off exploring.

There was nearly too much here for their senses to take in. Rich spicy aromas, elaborate displays of colorful items, and the shouts of vendors commanded their attention from every direction. Quinn soon lost track of where they had entered from and where they were. They passed by a tent selling magic flowers that could be worn alive on the body in place of perfume, another where a hive of bees was selling their own honey in a spectrum of vibrant colors, and a third selling possessed dolls that waved and called out to the passing customers. Ryan had a booth too, overflowing with a variety of intensely branded items plus his remaining merchandise from his old knife company. He was energetically trying to sell off his dead stock to a group of leering werewolves, pulling out a block of wood and attempting to slice into it. The blade bent pitifully and the werewolves howled in laughter.

"Hey," Quinn said, stopping. "What's that one?"

They pointed to a barely-lit tent where a cloaked figure was sitting. Origami animals and sachets of chamomile and lavender hung from the bars of the tent, and several notebooks and pens lay on the table.

"Huh, I don't know. I don't remember that one," Ash said. "Let's check it out."

"Hello, young ones," the cloaked creature greeted them as they stepped closer. The vendor was barely visible under their thick purple cloak- in fact, the only thing Quinn could see of their face was the orange glow of what they assumed were eyes in the darkness of the hood. They were arranging pens into a neat line with translucent hands.

"Hi," Quinn said. "What do you do here?"

"I purchase unwanted dreams from the patrons of this market," the creature said softly. *"I will gladly take any which you are willing to part with."*

Quinn picked up one of the notebooks. It had a couple pages torn out but otherwise looked new. "What's this for?"

"Write down the dreams which you wish to trade, human, and give them to me. In exchange, you may request from me one item of equivalent emotional value. Alternatively, I can pay you in the currency of this realm."

They hummed. "What happens when we give the dreams to you? Do we forget all of them?"

The dealer's hood bobbed, and Quinn figured they were nodding. *"They will pass from your mind with no more than a gentle whisper."*

76

Quinn shrugged and grabbed one of the pens. "Sounds good to me."

Ash put a hand on her arm. "Wait. What do you do with them?" he asked the dealer.

"Oh, yeah. Some of my dreams are kind of embarrassing. I don't need strangers reading them," Quinn said.

"Or copying us," Ash added, nodding seriously.

The creature tapped their faded fingers together. *"The contents of your mind are the sweetest nectar… an invaluable delicacy like no other. With every dream I consume, I become more corporeal. More physical. More… real."*

"Oh, you're just gonna eat them?" Quinn clicked their pen. "Be my guest. Bon apetit!"

They both started to write. Quinn jotted down a few of their most embarrassing and unpleasant dreams, finished up after a few minutes and handed in their papers. The creature produced a few bills folded into stars and cranes and dropped them into their palm.

"Cool!" They looked over at Ash, who was still writing. "I saw a booth selling edible fire. Want to go there next?"

"Yeah. I might be a while though. Why don't you go on and I'll catch up?"

"Are you sure?" Quinn asked. He was writing fast, not taking his eyes off the page. They wondered what he was writing about.

"Yeah! I'll text you when I'm done." He paused to flash them a quick smile then went back to writing. Filling the last page, he shut his notebook and handed it to the creature. "Do you have any more paper?"

As Quinn walked away from the tent, their mind felt pleasantly warm and light but a heavy ominous feeling lurked in their stomach. They hoped Ash was okay. They would ask him about it later, they decided, when they were away from all these eyes and ears.

They slowed down to look into a tent where three humanoid women were making clothes. One wove fabric while another measured cut and the third sewed everything together. They each looked fragile enough to disintegrate in a strong breeze, with papery skin and thin limbs getting lost in the folds of their robes. Despite their appearance they worked at a spectacular speed, producing garments in a few effortless minutes to match each customer's anatomy.

Perched on the seamstress's shoulder was a bird the size of a robin, purplish-black with white speckles. It spoke with Meena's voice.

"It's not like I wanted him to die," she was saying to the tailor, watching the stitches fly by with detached interest. "He was just making my life a lot harder than it needed to be. Word got out that people were showing up to my office with strange injuries and rumors started flying about my treatments. I wasn't gonna act happy to see him."

Quinn groaned internally. They wondered how many others Meena had told. At this rate, soon everyone would know about Fenris's death. That only added pressure to find out what happened to him, especially before people started asking questions about the owners of the building he died in.

"Bill! I thought you were dead!" someone said behind them. Quinn resisted twisting around to look.

"I was, I think," came the response.

"What?"

"Yeah, fell down the stairs and broke my neck. It was all dark and quiet for a while. But I'm all right now."

"What do you mean, all right now?"

"I'm here, aren't I?"

"Well… how do you feel?"

The other voice hesitated for a minute. "Hungry."

"Hungry?"

"Yeah."

"...Okay. Let's eat then. Hey, watch out for–"

Bill stumbled and fell onto Quinn, knocking them over. They helped him get back up as his friend, a hunched bipedal creature covered in eyes, apologized repeatedly to them. Bill was a frizzy-haired human wearing a neck brace, his body spotted with bruises. He dragged his feet as he followed his friend away, bumping into a few other people before disappearing from sight.

Quinn shuddered and started walking again. A tent came into view where a tall copper-skinned woman stood behind a table overflowing with jars of salt, bundles of herbs, and carefully rolled scrolls of paper. As they came closer the braids of her hair raised their heads to gaze at them, and Quinn realized they weren't braids at all but dozens of tiny snakes. The sign behind her read *spells for every need by Madame Celeste.*

"Hello, my dear," Madame Celeste greeted them with a lilting accent Quinn didn't recognize. "What brings you to me?"

"I'm just looking around," Quinn said.

Celeste shook her head with a knowing smile. "If you're at my tent, you need something. Love? Comfort? Revenge?"

Nice sales tactic. "I'm okay. I don't want anything." Okay, that wasn't true. But they didn't want anything a stranger could hand them. Even if this woman could suddenly make Quinn good at talking to people or more confident in their appearance, it felt shamefully vulnerable to ask.

"Understanding," Celeste said.

Quinn frowned. "Huh?"

"You want understanding." She carefully ran her fingers over the little snakes on her head, stroking their backs. "The world is a frightening, confusing place for you. You think you would feel more secure if you understood why things happen the way they do. Particularly between people."

"I–" Quinn stammered. Was that true? They had always been curious about the world. Being unable to understand people did feel scary sometimes. And they certainly didn't feel safe now, knowing the inn they had just moved into was full of potential murderers. They crossed their arms defensively over their chest. "Not all the time. But I guess… right now, yeah," they conceded. "Something really scary has just happened. I need to find a solution fast."

"A murder in one's new home would make anyone feel destabilized," Celeste said.

Quinn groaned. "Did Meena tell you about that?"

"She wanted to know if I knew anything about Mr. Fenris's business dealings. I put two and two together."

Quinn sighed. "Fine. Some understanding right now would really help. You're right."

"I usually am." Celeste finally looked up, meeting Quinn's eyes.

"If you wish, I can perform a divination to help you find the information you seek."

"Really? You can do that?"

"Of course."

Quinn felt a stir of movement by their side. They turned to see Ash there, smiling cheerfully.

"Hey," they said. "Did you get a lot of money from that guy in the cloak?"

He sighed. "No. I chose the 'item of equivalent emotional value.'"

"What did you get?"

He pulled a jar of dull goo from his bag. They both looked at it for a moment. "Oh," Quinn said.

"Yeah," Ash said. "I have no idea what it is. I guess the emotional value doesn't have to be mine."

He held it out to them and Quinn peered at it closely. "I can't tell what it is either," they said with a shrug. They turned back towards Madame Celeste. "Let's do the divination. I'm ready."

The spellcaster's amber eyes narrowed at the jar in concern. She picked up a lavender-colored candle from the table and placed it in the center of a mat decorated with interlocking geometric patterns. "I will need a lens," she said. "One of my crystals is acceptable, but I suspect something with a personal tie will be more effective. Your glasses, please."

"My glasses?"

"Yes. Powerful symbolism around vision."

Quinn hesitantly handed the glasses over. Celeste's blurry outline examined them and nodded.

She snapped her fingers, shedding sparks that lit the wick of the candle and fed it into a healthy flame. Quinn squinted as Celeste laid their glasses down facing the tent wall. The candle light shone through the lenses, casting trembling shadows against the canvas of the tent.

"Residents of the unseen realms," Celeste said authoritatively. "I approach you with a question."

She waited. After a moment the candle flame leapt upward.

"Thank you. You who have seen everything, tell me. Who killed the werewolf Fenris?"

Another pause. Slowly, within the twin circles of the glasses frames, the shadows began twisting restlessly against each other. They crashed against each other and reformed, trying to form a coherent picture. Quinn leaned in, trying to make out any detail they could with most of their sight gone. Finally the shadows converged, the edges flickering and reshaping themselves, forming–

The tent buckled over their heads, canvas snapping taut. Ash and Quinn looked up in surprise to see Ciara leaping across the tops of the tents. Close behind her was a humanoid figure dressed in leather, its face hidden by a featureless mask of beaten metal. It swung at the vampire with a curved dagger as she ducked and weaved away.

"Hi kids!" Ciara shouted when she saw them. "Tell Jasper not to wait for me to start dinner." She dropped to the ground, turned, and took off in the direction she came. The masked figure landed smoothly after her and sprinted through the crowd. The lavender candle toppled over and the flame went out, and the still-forming mass of shadow projected against the canvas dissolved.

82

Quinn groaned in disappointment. Celeste handed them back their glasses and the candle. "Here. Take these and try another time. It doesn't take a psychic to see that your friend is in danger."

"Thanks." Quinn looked at Ash. "Who… what… was that?"

Ash groaned. "A beast hunter! If there's one out here, there's gotta be more."

"Like cockroaches," Quinn added absentmindedly.

Ash looked at them in horror. "Stop telling me bug facts! Please!"

"Sorry." The two began running after the hunter.

Ahead of them Ciara darted between the rows of tents, swerving around groups of passersby. Without the flaming color of her hair Quinn would have lost track of her right away. Reaching the stone circle, she bolted into the woods and was about to disappear when more leather-wearing masked figures stepped out to meet her. She stopped just before colliding with the tallest one and tried to turn around again, but the first beast hunter was right at her back. They dragged their dagger against the edge of their mask, producing a metallic shriek that made Ciara wince and stumble as the other figures closed in on her. The vampire's face remained still but the rapid flickering of her eyes between each hunter gave away her panic. She tried a teasing smile. "Evening, friends. Been a while, hasn't it?"

Ignoring her comment, the beast hunter unsheathed a curved blade at his side and swung it over his head. In one smooth movement she slid a knife out of her sleeve and blocked, spinning out of his grasp.

The other hunters continued closing in as the two slashed at each other. Ciara landed a hard blow on his head and he fell, quickly replaced by three more. She tried to retreat, ducking and swatting away their weapons, but they had her surrounded. As she grew tired she grew desperate and her relaxed human facade began to slip. She started lunging at her attackers with her teeth and swiping with clawed hands. When her knife was knocked to the ground she didn't even glance at it before slicing open the closest neck with her nails.

"We have to do something," Quinn stammered. "Let's find Jasper."

Ash nodded slowly, unable to take his eyes off the fight. One of the hunters drove a large blade through Ciara's shoulder, pinning her to the ground, and she hissed in pain. Ash screamed and ran towards the group with Quinn following close behind.

"Leave her alone!" Ash cried.

The beast hunters threw him a disinterested glance and turned away again.

"Go away, boy," the tallest one said. "This isn't your business. Who's harvesting the bones?"

Ciara raised her eyebrows. "Bad news about that. I'm sort of using my bones. You can have them when I'm done, though."

"It's my turn," said another one of the hunters, a short broad-shouldered figure. "I say we cut her apart. It's quickest."

Another beast hunter, thin with frizzy hair poking out around the mask, said, "Pin her to a tree and wait for morning. When the flesh burns away, the bones are all clean and ready to use."

The short one paused. Quinn got the feeling they were glowering. "That's no fun."

"But it's so much neater," the frizzy-haired one said. "Don't you remember how hard these outfits are to clean? I'm not paying the dry-cleaning bill this time."

"Vampire blood is especially hard to get out of fabric," Ciara agreed.

The tallest hunter growled, gripping the hilt of his dagger. "If you idiots can't agree I'll do it myself. And I don't like to wait."

"Don't touch her!" Ash cried, his voice shaking. "I'll– I'll set you all on fire."

The beast hunter regarded him for a moment. He barked out a short laugh and raised his blade again.

Quinn squeezed their eyes shut, not wanting to see what came next. A rustling in the branches above them followed by a loud thud made them blink back open in surprise.

Tosk had just landed in the ground in front of Ciara. He straightened up and held up his paws towards the lead hunter in a gesture of peace. "Hold on," he said.

The leader let out a frustrated sigh. "What in the nine realms do you want, Tosk?"

Tosk looked over his shoulder, flashing Ciara a reassuring smile. She watched him curiously.

"She and her friend are doing me a big favor. They're letting me stay with them while I look for a new home. Please let her go."

The beast hunter folded his arms and tilted his head. He didn't put away his dagger yet. "Do you have what you promised us?"

Tosk tugged nervously at the tufts of fur on his ears. "Kind of. It's complicated."

"Do you have it or not?"

The squirrel hissed in a nervous breath. "Can we talk in private? I *almost* have it, I swear."

Without a word, the hunter turned on his heel and walked into the woods, leaving Tosk to scramble after him. They stopped a short distance away and Quinn strained to hear what they were saying.

"He's dead," they heard Tosk say. Their voices dropped below their hearing level for a minute, then he said, "I might have something even better. I just need time…" Their voices dropped again and a few more minutes passed.

Eventually, the lead hunter strode back to the group with Tosk close behind. He silently knelt down, yanked the long blade out of Ciara's shoulder and tossed it to its owner, and disappeared into the woods. He gestured for the others to follow him with one hand, not looking to see if they were obeying.

When they were gone, Tosk helped Ciara sit up. Ash and Quinn raced over and knelt next to her.

"Are you alright?" Ash asked. He nervously examined the wound on her shoulder.

"I'll be fine. We heal fast," Ciara told him, letting him pull her to her feet.

"What was that all about?" Quinn asked Tosk.

He fidgeted for a second. "Uh… it's a private matter. I promised not to tell anyone."

Before they could ask another question they heard Jasper shout their names. They looked up to see him running over.

"What happened?" he cried.

"Beast hunters," Ciara said with a shrug. The movement

reminded her of her injury and she winced. "Tosk here saved my skin… and the rest of my components."

Jasper let out a sympathetic whistle as he looked at her shoulder. "Let's head home. I'll make you a healing balm." He checked his watch. "It's almost 1:30, anyway. We need to be in our rooms by 2."

"What happens at 2?" Quinn asked. They couldn't believe it was past 1:00 in the morning. It didn't feel like they had been out that long and they certainly didn't feel tired enough.

"Immune flush," he said simply. "You'd rather not know the details, trust me."

He started walking into the woods and Ciara and Ash followed him. Before joining them, Quinn turned back towards Tosk. They wanted to ask him a few more questions. Something didn't feel right about his conversation with the beast hunters.

They looked around, their stomach sinking.

Tosk was gone.

- 6 -

The next morning Quinn sat at the chipped stone counter in the lounge, hesitantly poking at their breakfast. Eating eggs felt a little different when the chicken who laid them dropped them off herself and shook your hand. Meat was firmly off the menu in a place where one guest was often another's prey, and carnivorous visitors were directed down the road to a diner that prepared every species of meat they could get their hands on, including human. But after meeting creatures here of every shape and phylum, Quinn found it hard to believe the fiddlehead ferns on their plate didn't have some kind of consciousness too. They decided they'd rather not know.

They were the last to finish eating, stretching out the time until they had to help Jasper with a repair in the kitchen. Ash doodled on a napkin to their left while Jasper and Ciara cleaned up. Near them sat the mug Ciara had been drinking from, ringed at the bottom with dried blood from the repurposed half-gallon milk bottle she had bought last night. The smell was richly savory and metallic.

They looked up as Delta walked in with Brooke on her hip. She sat at the counter, setting her daughter down in the seat next to her, and asked for a cup of herbal tea. Brooke slowly blinked her eyes open and studied the people around her. Her attention settled on Jasper and she took a few unsteady breaths, trying to force a sound out through weakened lungs. "Has-per," she finally managed.

Delta beamed at her. "Look how well she's doing! That's right, minnow. *Jasper.* She'll be well enough to swim soon."

Jasper turned around with a surprised smile. "She remembers me?"

"Of course she does!" Delta cried. "Everyone in our shoal knows you and Lev. We didn't forget what you did for us."

Jasper shrugged, looking a little uncomfortable. "It was nothing."

"We'd all be shredded if you hadn't pulled that bulldozer wreck out of the river."

"Lev's the one who found it," he said quietly. Ciara abandoned a glob of dough she had been kneading to make Delta's tea and Jasper picked it up, churning it in his hands to avoid eye contact.

"Well, you can't avoid our gratitude forever," Delta said. "You know people are starting to call this Jasper's place now."

Jasper's brow creased and he shook his head, still not looking up. "Don't. This is Lev's place. That's how it's supposed to be."

He drew the dough long and thin. Right before it snapped in two he pressed it back into a ball.

Ciara slid Delta the mug of tea, and she shrugged and blew steam off the surface. Scents of rose and apple mint drifted through the air. Brooke waved her hand in the steam and giggled as it dispersed. Delta smiled and blew the steam towards her daughter's face, getting another delighted laugh in return. Brooke delightedly swung her arms back and forth, tipped herself off-balance, and almost landed face-first on the counter before her mother pulled her upright. "Clumsy," she cooed. "Careful, minnow."

She straightened up and tried to look Jasper in the eye. His focus remained locked on the dough. "I'm not saying we should pretend he never existed. I just think you undersell yourself. There are creatures here who owe a lot to you."

Jasper silently continued to twist at the dough.

Quinn shifted nervously in the tense silence, staring down at their plate. The others didn't say anything either.

Brooke took a deep breath, blew a raspberry, and smacked her open palm into the cup of tea. Hot water flew in all directions and the mug spun across the counter. Jasper caught it before it could fall to the floor.

"Hey, hey," he said, cutting off Delta's rush of apologies. "It's all good. There are clean towels in the laundry room. I'll be right back."

He walked out into the lobby. Quinn hopped out of their chair and offered it to Delta, who gratefully placed a wailing Brooke onto the cool surface.

90

Searching for a new seat, Quinn's mood brightened when they saw Tosk sitting opposite Bertram the wood frog. They dropped into the seat next to him and smiled in fascination.

"You're amazing!" Quinn told him. "I've never seen a frog like you before. I have so many questions! Can you see in the dark? Do you absorb water through your skin? Do you push your eyes down to swallow your food?"

A cloudy film blinked over one eye, then the other, as the frog took them in. *The nictitating membrane*, Quinn thought with a thrill of delight. "Ah– well… yes, yes, and yes," Bertram answered. Confused, he said to Tosk, "I thought you were doing the interview."

"I am," Tosk said quickly. "If you don't mind."

"Sorry," Quinn said, reddening.

Tosk's hand was shiny with graphite from taking notes, and after several minutes of fidgeting so was the entire left side of his face. "Anyway, Bertram– you're not the first person to tell me this. A lot of his employees report severe injuries. Neighbors living near construction sites, too."

Jasper came in from the lobby, looking a little lost. A machine behind the counter that looked like a brass hairball gurgled in distress. He clucked his tongue sympathetically and began dismantling its coils as hot steam poured out. It must be the job he asked them to help with, Quinn figured. They ducked to avoid his gaze and hoped he would forget.

"I believe it," the frog said. "There isn't enough safety equipment to go around, so we either take turns or go without it. When machinery breaks down, it just gets left behind. Four years ago a bulldozer fell into the river and they told us it would be too expensive to move it.”

The brass machine squealed as Jasper wrenched it apart.

“And last month, we were supposed to do a controlled detonation there,” the frog continued. “Mr. Fenris came to the site himself to supervise. But no one was sent out to clear the area beforehand. Plenty of forest and river residents were around, and they had no idea what was happening.”

Tosk wrote furiously. “That’s horrible. Would you say it was due to negligence, or was it an intentional act?”

“Well…” the frog thought for a moment. “I’m not sure. If it was pure negligence, it was quite extreme. I’m not sure how he could have overlooked it.”

“What other parts of his construction sites were unsafe?” Tosk pressed.

The frog’s throat swelled as he grunted. “There are no guardrails or harnesses. Last year I fell off a sheer rock face and split my head open.”

“Whoa. For real?” Jasper spun around, looking the frog up and down intensely. Quinn frowned. Something was different about his movements. They were quicker and more impulsive than usual.

“Take a look and see.” The frog bowed his head to show off a long scar running down his skull.

Tosk scribbled the story down so eagerly he tore the paper. “We could really have something here. What did Fenris do in response? Did he provide compensation or medical care? Did you sign anything?”

“Let me see.” Jasper leapt onto the counter, and now Quinn knew something was wrong. They noticed the blue tongue and tiny sharp teeth too late.

Meena turned to look at them when she heard their gasp and ruffled their hair with Jasper's fingers, smiled at them with his eyes. "Ha! I got you!" she crowed triumphantly.

Quinn's mind swam. Meanwhile Meena shifted into her own humanoid form and inspected the frog's scar. "Wow, Bertram, I didn't know you got this at work. If Fenris wasn't dead you should have sued him."

Jasper- the real one- came in at that moment with a stack of fresh towels. "Don't worry about the smell, Frederick is-" he began, then he noticed the scrapped brass machine. "Hey! What's that about?"

"Meena did it," Quinn said quickly.

Meena glowered and jumped down from the counter. "Thanks for ratting me out, new guy."

Jasper sighed and combed over the dismantled pieces with his fingers.

"We had to take it apart anyway, right?" Quinn asked, joining him at the counter.

"It was working fine!" he said. "We were gonna fix the faucet!"

"Oh."

Jasper pulled a small sketchpad from his pocket and flicked through the pages until he found one titled *Elixir Distiller*. A detailed sketch of the machine was surrounded by notes in Jasper's crowded handwriting. At least half of what was written had been scribbled out and corrected in red ink, then scribbled out again and corrected in blue ink, then again in the original black ink. Jasper wiped off each of the pieces with a sigh and began undoing

Meena's damage, and Quinn did their best to follow along.

"I don't think I signed anything," Bertram said slowly. "Truth be told, it was a few weeks before I even remembered who I was. For several months my mind was foggy and I lost most of my co-ordination."

"What else?" Meena asked suspiciously. She was still examining his scar.

"Well, my head hurt of course, but it… I don't know, *tingled* for a long time."

"Like when your foot falls asleep? But cold?" Meena asked. Bertram nodded. She grunted thoughtfully. "I thought so. Go on."

"Hey, who's doing the interview here?" Tosk protested. She waved her hand at him to shut up.

"I felt better after a few months," Bertram continued. "But some things never went back to normal. Colors looked a little different, for instance. I get random urges to do things I never used to enjoy. And I think I'm allergic to slugs now."

Quinn fumbled with a machine part and dropped it. "You think your food allergy came from a head injury?"

Bertram shrugged. "I wasn't allergic before. And now I am. Shame. I love slugs."

Quinn clicked the part into place with a frown. Meena nodded along as if what he was saying was totally normal, then she ordered them to wait and raced upstairs in the form of a bat.

"We never got to thank you for your help last night, Tosk," Jasper said a little too casually. The squirrel jerked his head up nervously. "I didn't know you're friends with the beast hunters."

"Not friends," Tosk said quickly. "Not friends. Acquaintances,

94

maybe. Neighbors."

"What did they want from you?" Jasper asked.

Tosk scratched restlessly at his ear, smudging it gray. "They just wanted a specific map of the forest and I told them I could get it for them. And I didn't have it yet, because I'm meeting with the owner today." He smiled again, watching their faces carefully to see if they believed him.

"Why did you say you might have something better?" Quinn pressed.

"I just– I haven't met with the map guy yet," Tosk stammered. "He has a lot of things they might be interested in."

Meena flew back into the lounge, panting and lugging a large medical textbook. She dropped it on the table and it fell open to a richly illustrated diagram of the lupine circulatory system. Wedged between the pages was a bundle of notes. Shifting into her humanoid form, Meena pulled the notes out and shuffled through them. "Here it is. Lack of coordination. Mental fog." She flipped to another one. "Loss of sensation. Lack of coordination. Altered sense of taste." Another. "Mental fog. Paresthesia around the site of the injury."

Quinn curiously joined her at the table and peered at the textbook. Its spine was worn soft from years of use and its pages bristled with sticky notes. Flipping through the pages they saw the insides of bony gremlins, gooey invertebrates, sharp-toothed cave dwellers, and a variety of things Quinn couldn't begin to describe. They sighed, mentally listing off the crimes they were willing to commit to own one of these books.

Tosk leaned in to examine Meena's notes. "It looks like you've treated several of Fenris's employees. Have you heard about any deaths at his site?"

She shook her head. "I doubt anyone would tell me, though."

"I never saw anyone die at his sites, either," Bertram added. "Lots and lots of injuries. But never any deaths."

Tosk fidgeted, spreading graphite across both paws. "That's a shame. Err– I mean, not a shame that no one died. I mean it's a shame we haven't heard about it. There's no way, with all those injuries, that there wasn't at least one."

"Do you think Fenris was covering them up?" Bertram asked.

"Well– I can't prove anything yet," Tosk retreated, "but he and his family have a lot of influence around here. They're powerful people. They could do it if they wanted. In fact… there's something I *know* they covered up, but it's meaningless without more evidence."

"You have dirt on the Fenris family?" Meena said incredulously. "No way. They're squeaky clean and they like to stay that way. Just a bunch of stuffy developers."

"Not all of them," Tosk said. "Not everyone in Peter Fenris's family shares his name." He pulled a piece of paper from his breast pocket and smoothed it out on the table. "This is his nephew's arrest record. Toby Burke. He worked at the local hospital."

"Who?" Meena asked. "Never heard of him."

"Exactly," Tosk said.

"His nephew?" Quinn repeated. "The one he was visiting?"

"He gets out today," Tosk said. "Fenris must have come here to pick him up."

"What was he in for?"

Tosk looked up from the paper, his gaze bouncing restlessly between them all. "Desecration of a corpse."

There was a long, frigid silence. "Desecration of a corpse," Jasper repeated softly. "So you're saying…"

"I'm not *saying* anything about Fenris," Tosk retreated quickly. "Not on the record. I'm just passing on what I've heard. Which is that remains from his employer's morgue were found in his home. A *lot* of remains."

He pushed the paper forward for them to examine. At the bottom was a curt message which was not part of the official report. SUSPECT IS EMPLOYED AT OWASCO MEDICAL CENTER AS A PARAMEDIC. PRESENT ON 18 TRANSPORTS WHERE PATIENTS WERE REPORTED DEAD ON ARRIVAL. UNABLE TO ESTABLISH CONNECTION TO SUSPECT.

Everyone clustered around the table to read. Tosk watched their reactions with a mixture of satisfaction and dread. He tugged at the tufts of fur on his ears. "Don't tell anyone you heard it from me, okay? The Fenrises are not forgiving people."

"So," Meena mused, "The rich werewolf who's been huffing and puffing and blowing all our houses down has a body count. I knew there was something up with his employees."

"It sure looks like it," Tosk said. "But, again, I have no way to prove it…"

"You should be careful," Jasper said, returning to the counter with a shake of his head. "I don't like the look of that."

Everyone went silent as Ryan strode in, mumbling on the phone with someone he called "A-dog." He hung up, rubbing his face wearily, and set down a dappled ceramic mug. "How are my favorite tenants doing?" he said, trying to muster some energy.

Jasper shrugged. "Late night?"

"Not more than usual," Ryan answered, stifling a yawn as he sat down. "I've got a method worked out. See, what I do is I maximize my productivity by sleeping three hours a night. I've biohacked my system so that I can get all the rest I need in those three hours. It frees up five extra hours, and I keep my energy up throughout the day with caffeine. It's super efficient!" He slid the mug towards Jasper. "Can you fill me up?"

"You're just in time." Jasper patted the reassembled distilling machine. "The last thing we made with this was hemlock tea, but lucky for you we've done a full deep cleaning." Meena giggled.

"I have good news for you," Ryan said as they listened to boiling water rattle its way through the coils. "My dad says he's not selling anymore. Fenris stopped responding to him. I guess he lost interest."

Jasper froze, but he recovered quickly. "Oh," he said. "Glad to hear it."

Quinn looked up at the clattering noise of Dr. Lycosidae's many feet. She appeared in the doorway a moment later. Jasper excused himself and walked over to speak with her with Quinn trailing behind.

"I'm almost done," Dr. Lycosidae told them in a low voice. "Like you said, trauma to the face and body. Round marks from the lamp in that room."

Jasper nodded thoughtfully.

"Did you find anything on the body?" Quinn whispered. "From

the killer? Like DNA?"

"Or a fatal wound?" Jasper asked.

"Not yet," the doctor said. "I did find a small piercing wound on the chest. Could be an injection site, but there's no poison in his system, so I doubt it. The blows from that lamp were done using the left hand."

Quinn and Jasper grimaced. Behind them, Ryan gasped.

They whipped around to stare at him. He was looking down at his phone in dismay.

"What's wrong?" Jasper asked, trying to sound casual.

Ryan lifted his head. He looked heartbroken.

"StockShock. They're going out of business." He spread his arms in a silent request for a hug which they both ignored. Quinn heard Jasper let out the breath he had been holding. Dr. Lycosidae took the opportunity to duck back down to the basement.

"What?" Quinn asked.

"StockShock. The one-stop-shop for shocking stocks. They were totally disrupting the marketplace. They were too good for this awful world." Ryan sniffled. "It's okay, guys. We'll get through this. Don't worry."

Behind the counter Ryan's mug overflowed, and Jasper rushed to turn off the machine. Ryan took the coffee and sighed into the steam before taking a long swig. "At least I'm nearly done with this inspection," he said finally. "I've seen most of the floors. Only the basement and attic are left."

"The attic," Jasper said quickly. "Let's do the attic."

"Great," Ryan said, getting up. "I gotta get my notes. I'll meet you up there."

Quinn followed Jasper up to the third floor and down a side hallway, where a door led outside to a rickety spiral staircase. Quinn drew back as the staircase groaned under Jasper's weight.

"Uh, how old is that thing?" they asked.

He waved their concerns away with one hand. "It'll hold us. Come on."

They hesitantly stepped out and climbed the stairs, holding their breath. It led up to the roof, which was collecting leaves and bird nests at its edges. A collection of sun-paled patio furniture surrounded a couple of fire pits. Quinn gazed around at the tree canopy surrounding them in awe. Jasper crossed to the center and heaved open a trapdoor. They followed him down a ladder into the dark.

They choked on dust as they landed. There was a brief metallic scrambling noise, then a bare bulb sparked to life over their heads with a click. Jasper let go of the cord and looked around.

"Not bad," he said, knocking his hands together to shake off the dirt. "For a bunch of cursed junk anyway."

The space was filled with a random mix of old and broken objects. Plush toys with realistic eyes and decades-obsolete media players mingled with tattered, skeletal furniture. From the corner of Quinn's eye came twitches of movement, objects which stilled as soon as they looked at them directly. Some of the items gave off an aura which made them feel cold and anxious.

The space was low-ceilinged but somehow felt cavernous. Quinn realized with a start that it was the breeze creating that feeling. The pale beams seemed to contract and expand with it in the darkness. A firm, rhythmic breeze pushing back and forth, out and in...

Quinn's stomach flipped.

"Is it breathing?" they squeaked.

Jasper turned. "Hm? Oh. Yes."

"H-how? Why does it do that? Why can't we feel it anywhere else?"

"We could never figure that out," he said with a shrug. "Maybe if you stay with us long enough, you'll find the answer."

He slowly walked through the space, pausing by a large puddle of water. Above it a swollen spot in the ceiling had burst. "Well, cursed items are one thing, but Ryan can't see this," he said. He began to whistle, drawing the water up into a slender column and guiding it out from the hole in the ceiling.

"Whoa!" Quinn cried, running over. "What are you doing?"

"Another form of magic," he answered. "I'm using the frequencies of music to manipulate the water particles' movement."

"Teach me?"

"Sure." He gave them a similar explanation to their first try with the sigils and then stepped back to let them try. Quinn focused until they felt their face crease with the effort, trying their best to match Jasper's notes. It took several tries to get any movement from the puddle. They searched for that strange, budding feeling they had noticed last time. As soon as it appeared, they gave it a gentle tug.

With a loud crack and a groan, the floorboards buckled. Water began draining through the cracks.

The boards below Quinn's feet rippled, throwing them to the floor. The boards closed back in on their legs like angry teeth.

They looked over at Jasper, bewildered. "What was that? Did I get the notes wrong?"

He scratched his head and offered them a hand to pull them free. "It sounded alright to me. Usually wrong notes just abort the spell, or they make a big mess." When he saw their face drop, he added, "Now, wait. We don't know what this means yet."

Tears pricked at Quinn's eyes. "It can't mean anything good. I hurt the inn somehow. And now your repair is ruined!"

"Quinn. I don't care about–"

The inn grumbled, floorboards vibrating.

"And it's mad!" Quinn cried, panic rising. "Look!"

"Let's slow down," he said, reaching out to put a hand on their shoulder. "We can–"

"No!" Quinn twisted away from his touch. "I can't be here. I can't hurt anyone else." They bolted up the ladder and across the roof, leaving Jasper and his protests behind. They rushed down the spiral stairs and flung the door open in agitation.

Something heavy thudded against the door with a wet crack.

Quinn froze. They slowly drew back the door, a deep and cold pit forming in their stomach.

Ryan knelt on the ground and clutched his nose, which streamed blood. The red carpet eagerly absorbed each drop as it fell.

- 7 -

Quinn let out a strangled noise caught between a yelp and a groan. "Ryan! Are you okay?"

Ryan looked up. His nose was bent at an unnatural angle. "It's alright," he said kindly. Guilt scraped at Quinn's insides as they offered him a hand and he waved it away. "My mentor says we need to pick ourselves back up when we fall. So, really, you're giving me a learning opportunity!"

"I'm sorry," Quinn said lamely. They felt stupid. Nothing they could say would undo breaking his nose. As if the disaster with the ice wasn't enough, now they had injured someone.

"Don't worry about it," Ryan said, "It was an accident. Do you guys have a first aid kit?"

They led him down to the lobby in ashamed silence. The staff staircase rumbled discontentedly. Another reminder that Quinn didn't belong here.

"It's okay, really," Ryan said when he saw how upset they were. "I know you didn't mean to do it. It's like Delta said yesterday, when we were looking for her daughter. We have to take care of each other, or else… I didn't hear the end, because she went down to her room."

Quinn gasped, inhaling so much of his cloying body spray that they almost choked. "What? You talked to her on the third floor?"

Ryan stared back at them blankly. "Yes," he said. "Why?"

"Uh– no reason." They quickly looked away. "I just didn't know she went up there. That's all."

When they reached the lobby they called Meena, leaving Ryan with her and the first aid kit, and fled for the fourth floor.

They dug their hands through their hair as they climbed, wincing as their fingers snagged in the tangled spots. *Focus, Quinn.*

They felt horrible. Their parents were right. They were too impulsive and too emotional. Once again, they had acted without thinking, and now they had badly hurt someone.

Quinn groaned as they pushed open the door to the fourth floor. All they wanted to do was make a beeline for their bedroom, but they had forgotten what a cryptic mess the floor layouts were. They had even written down instructions yesterday for getting there, only to find that the number of turns wasn't right and they had miscounted the empty rooms they had to pass. If they didn't know better they would think the rooms were constantly changing places.

Quinn pushed their glasses onto their forehead and ground

104

their palms into their eyes. The color red gave them a headache in moderation, but here, covering every surface and surrounding them, it was way too much. They dimly remembered Jasper complaining about the same thing but saying he didn't want to change it because it was Lev's choice. They took a deep breath and struggled to regain their train of thought. Identical red doors and jaundiced wall lamps became blurred by hot tears.

"Quinn?"

They felt a touch on their shoulder and almost jumped out of their skin. Ash was behind them. They sighed in relief and grabbed his hand, as though if they let go he would disintegrate and leave them alone again.

"Are you okay?" he asked gently.

"Yeah, fine," they said shakily. "I'm looking for my room. I can't find it."

He nodded. "Oh yeah. That happens. Sometimes when I'm really tired, I just crash in a random empty room. Last week I did that and I found my lost hat!"

Together they wandered the halls until they ran into Quinn's room. They breathed a sigh of relief as they stepped inside. For the most part it still looked like every other room in the inn, except for their backpack lying open in the corner and a couple of zoology books sitting on top of the crumpled green quilt on the bed. With time they figured it would begin to look more like their own space. They hoped so.

Quinn scooped up the photos from Fenris's room which had been scattered across the desk. They groaned as they flipped through the photos. They didn't know what to think anymore.

"Could any of them really do this?" they asked in a small voice. They didn't need to explain what they meant.

"I… I don't know," Ash said. "I don't want to think of any of them as killers. Each of them has been coming to the inn for years. They're old friends." He wrapped his arms around himself and shivered.

Quinn nodded mutely. Their eyes fell on Madame Celeste's violet candle and they gasped. "Hey!" they cried. They seized the candle and turned to Ash in excitement. "Why don't we use this? We can finish the divination spell from last night!"

Ash's face brightened. "Yeah! Let's try it."

No matter how elusive their bedrooms were, the common room always seemed to be only a few steps away. Quinn followed Ash inside, mentally elbowing their worries and suspicions out of the way. Ash ignored the sofa and armchairs in favor of kneeling on the carpet as he redrew the geometric shapes from Madame Celeste's mat onto a page from their notebook.

"You remember all those shapes?" Quinn asked, impressed.

"They're the same ones in Jasper's tattoos," he answered. "The plants and animals and things are drawn over them, but I see them glow when he uses magic. Here you go." He placed the finished drawing on the coffee table.

Quinn stood the candle on the sheet of paper. Realizing they had no matches or lighter, they glanced around the room, but Ash leaned forward and blew gently. A bright orange flame sprang up on the wick.

Quinn's hands trembled as they took off their glasses. They didn't know why they felt so nervous all of a sudden. The late-morning sun drowned out the light of the candle and so they blindly stumbled to close the curtains. When they turned around, the shadows were already tumbling in agitation like boiling water.

They sat next to Ash, not daring to breathe. The projection through one of the lenses began to settle. An empty hallway of the inn appeared in silhouette. The shadows in the other lens continued to churn.

After a long moment the second lens cleared up. It was a guest room. Empty, just like the hallway. Quinn and Ash shared a confused glance.

The room didn't stay empty for long. Fenris's silhouette stomped angrily into view and pivoted to shout at someone. Quinn strained to hear what he was saying, but the projection made no sound. The other person lingered just outside the frame as Fenris growled.

The silent argument continued for a long minute. Fenris grew more furious, gesturing violently with his arms. A twitch of motion in the other glasses lens brought Quinn's attention to the empty hallway. The door to the staircase opened slowly as the person behind it looked cautiously around. Quinn leaned in, trying to make out any details on the figure. It looked vaguely humanoid.

Quinn froze as they heard voices drifting up from a lower floor. They struggled to make out the words muffled by layers of keratin and carpet.

The voice was Dr. Lycosidae's. She sounded upset. "I don't *care* what you need it for…" her voice dropped and became indistinct. They couldn't hear the other voice from this distance.

"No. And that's final." Her volume rose, irritation mixing with fear. She said something else indistinctly, then cried, "What are you–"

She screamed, loud enough for the whole inn to hear. Quinn and Ash bolted to their feet and out of the room.

Crashes and bangs were audible in the hallway. The sounds seemed to be coming from the staff staircase, which had its door hanging wide open. The two raced down the stairs as Dr. Lycosidae shouted for help.

"We're coming!" Quinn shouted. "What's happening?"

She kept screaming. They could hear Jasper and Ciara run across the lobby and throw their door open. Jasper called the spider's name in panic.

Abruptly the screams ended in a gurgle. The crashing slowed to a stop. Quinn nearly fell down the last flight of stairs with Ash close behind them.

They arrived just after Jasper and Ciara to a sea of violence. Everything in the basement that wasn't nailed to the ground had been toppled or thrown across the space. Broken glass and dented metal scraps lay among Jasper's unfinished projects. And in the center of it all lay Dr. Lycosidae. She lay rigid on her back, legs curled inward in the universal pose of every dead spider. A pool of rich blue hemolymph spread slowly around her.

The most confusing part was Fenris's body- or, more accurately, the lack of it. The trail of blood as it fell and the splatter where it had landed were there, undeniably real, but the body itself was nowhere to be seen.

The group stood frozen in shock for a short while. Ciara was the first to move. She crept across the room, as if she were afraid to wake the doctor, and leaned in to assess. "Dead," she confirmed quietly.

"I don't understand," Quinn said. "We just heard her screaming. Someone must have attacked her– but how did they get out before we got here?"

"Carrying a body too, probably." Ash pointed towards the blood streak marking the position where Fenris's corpse had lay.

"It couldn't be–" Ciara scratched her head. "No. Fenris was dead. *Is* dead."

"He is dead," Jasper assured her. "We made sure."

But the dreadful truth hung in the air between them. Someone, somehow, must have done this.

Quinn cringed at the thought of getting closer to the corpse, but they took a deep breath and steeled themself. A wealth of information could be on that body. Information that might help them find the killer. They had to do it.

Blinking back tears, Quinn approached the body and looked it over. The doctor's exoskeleton was punctured all over. The cuts were all different sizes, some crooked and some straight, some deeper than others. Quinn wasn't sure if it meant anger or incompetence. They took a deep, shaky breath. Then they did the only other thing they could think to do. They drew out their notebook.

Several stab wounds, uneven
Injection wound in pedicel
Front legs scratched up– self defense?

The bright blue liquid leaking from the body onto the floor looked so unreal that they had to remind themself they were looking at the spider equivalent of blood.

Ciara silently stepped up next to them, head bent but eyes dry. This was not the first friend she had buried.

"Find anything?" she asked quietly.

Quinn mutely showed her their notes.

She nodded. "Pedicel– is that what connects the head part and the back part?"

"The cephalothorax and abdomen," Quinn murmured.

"Right," she said, thumping their back. "Aren't we lucky to have you? You're a walking encyclopedia."

Quinn shrugged and didn't look at her.

One of Jasper's inventions lay near the body in a puddle of hemolymph. It was the little recording radio which he tinkered with the morning of Fenris's death. It looked like it had been knocked to the ground. Maybe it had recorded something. They turned the knob and it crackled loudly to life.

There was a loud *whump* on the recording followed by the clatter of several clawed feet. Dr. Lycosidae must have knocked the radio off the shelf and accidentally turned it on.

The group stilled to listen as the familiar voice echoed against the walls. "I *said* we can talk about it later," the doctor cried. "I've got my hands full as it is. And for me that's saying something. Ha!"

Quinn shivered, turning down the volume. Dr. Lycosidae's voice sounded cold and distant as it rang through the room that held her body.

Another voice murmured indistinctly for a few moments. The basement groaned on the recording, shuddering at the unfamiliar presences.

"I don't *care* what you need it for," the doctor replied. "This is an active investigation. I'm not handing the body off to anyone outside his family."

Another pause and another murmur. Quinn frowned in frustration. If this stupid radio had just been able to pick up a little more sound…

"No. And that's final," the doctor said. "Why don't you go upstairs? You're impeding a– hey… what are you–"

A loud scream followed by a long chain of crashes and thuds confirmed what they already knew. At some point there was a loud crack, a shrill cry of pain, and a stumble. "Stay back," Dr. Lycosidae panted. "I don't like to hurt people. But I'll do worse if you don't–"

She was cut off again as there was another long scuffle. This time the doctor was the one to cry out in pain, once and then again and again.

Quinn underlined the *self defense* phrase in their notes. *Killer injured- how?*

The crashing noises quieted. Finally there was only the metal rasp of something circular spinning to a stop on the floor, leaving the scene silent.

In the absence of the doctor's voice the room seemed emptier and colder than before.

Ash sniffed back tears. "I'll pick some flowers for her," he said quietly. "Some really pretty ones. She deserves them."

"And I'll search the woods," Ciara said. She restlessly clenched and undid her fists, nails pressing dark crescents into her palms. "They can't have gone far."

Quinn nodded mutely and began following them towards the

stairs. They froze in surprise at the sound of the front door slamming. A couple of voices were arguing loudly above them.

"Well if you weren't creeping around in the river, it wouldn't have happened!" one of the voices shouted. It was Hector.

"Creeping around?! What is wrong with you?" Delta screamed. "You could have taken my jaw off!"

The three rushed up to the lobby, where the front desk clerk was already digging through the drawers for the first aid kit. Vivid blue blood spilled down Delta's face and body as she clutched Brooke tightly to her side. Beside her Hector sullenly clenched a fishing pole in his fist.

"Are you okay?" Ash gasped.

"I'm–" Delta tensed. "I'm fine." She swatted his hands away.

"You should lie down," he fretted. "That rip in your cheek looks really bad."

"I'm *fine*," Delta growled. She turned back to Hector and pointed at the large hook on his pole. "What were you trying to catch anyway? A whale shark?"

"It's none of your business!" Hector stammered. "What were *you* doing out there?"

She froze for a moment. Quickly recovering, she rolled her eyes. "Do you mean in a river? Where I *live*?"

"Hey, wait," Quinn said, watching the bright blue blood drip to the floor.

"It's not as bad as it looks," Hector told them. "We just had a minor collision."

"How do *you* know how bad it is?" Delta hissed at him. "This was your fault!"

112

"*My* fault? I was just sitting there!" he cried.

The clerk approached nervously with a stick-on bandage that was about the right size to treat a papercut. Delta looked at him incredulously for a moment before turning back to Hector. The clerk slumped self-consciously and slithered away.

"Do you know what I think?" Delta cried. "You were hoping I'd get hurt. You were waiting for me, or some other poor forest dweller just passing through, to swim by and skewer themselves on that horrible hook!"

"Don't be stupid. I wasn't waiting for you," Hector said bitterly. "And don't act so righteous about the poor little forest creatures. There's nothing innocent in these woods."

"What's going on up there?" Jasper called from below. He appeared in the doorway a moment later, streaked in blue hemolymph from moving the doctor's body. He and Delta stared at each other in surprise. The blue liquid covering them both was almost identical.

"What happened to you?" Jasper asked.

"What happened to *me?*" Delta repeated. "What happened to *you?* Why are you covered in–" She froze. "No. Please, no, tell me there hasn't been–"

"Stop fighting, you two," Jasper said firmly. "Show some respect. This is a crime scene."

Ciara and Ash slinked out the front door, eyes to the ground. Jasper turned and walked back down to the basement. With some hesitation Quinn followed him. The confused shouts and protests of Delta and Hector faded out of earshot as they descended.

There wasn't much to do now but to clean up the room. Jasper

unfolded a fresh sheet and placed the body on top. As they prepared to wrap it up Quinn found their gaze wandering to the stab
wounds again and again. They looked away each time, feeling in-
vasive and ghoulishly curious, but each time their gaze was drawn
back. It was like they were tracing a pattern, but there wasn't anything there. Right?

They frowned, mentally going over what they knew. The stab
wounds were all over the body, but they weren't all the same depth.
The spot behind the eyes, in particular, had suffered a lot of damage. The heart and lungs were strangely untouched. Then there was
the puncture wound in the pedicel.

Suddenly it clicked. Quinn gasped.

Jasper startled beside them. "What?"

"Hey," Quinn said. "Where in her body is Dr. Lycosidae's
heart?"

He frowned. "There?" He pointed to the thorax, the section
below the head where a typical mammal's heart would be.

Quinn hopped excitedly. "No. It's in there." They pointed to
the abdomen. "That's where her lungs are too. Something the killer
obviously doesn't know. Fenris just had one puncture wound, a
small one. Whoever gave it to him knew exactly where to aim. But
this was totally different. They must have stabbed her all over looking for the right spot."

"Which means Fenris's puncture wasn't just intentional," Jasper
added with grim realization. "It was key."

Quinn's mind raced as they pulled out their notebook. They
hesitated for a moment, unsure what to write. Then they scribbled.
Killer unfamiliar with spider biology. Then, after glancing at the body

again: *Looking for something.*

- 8 -

All the screaming had drawn guests out of their rooms and a small crowd was now gathering in the lobby. They gathered in tight clumps and whispered to each other. Occasionally someone broke off from their group to ask Delta a question, and she waved them away without answer, lying across a sofa with Brooke at her feet and Jasper kneeling by her head with a cotton pad and a bottle of isopropyl.

"I bet the starling did it," someone whispered as Quinn passed by.

"It had to be that creepy human in the red hat," another said. "Always sneaking around the woods at night like he's up to something."

"Why does it need to be a murder? They told us the room was trashed. Maybe this place got an ulcer and started trying to throw

116

up."

Quinn would have loved to believe that. It was so much more comforting than the truth. No one could think the doctor had died in an accident if they had seen the body. Or the empty spot where Fenris had lay. Most of the guests had no idea he had died, and no one who knew was in any mood to tell them. Besides, the doctor's death was much easier to report. She didn't have layers of blood and controversy surrounding her the way Fenris did. The longer they could postpone the news of his death getting out, the better.

"It's a nasty wound, but it'll heal alright," Jasper said to Delta as they neared the sofa. "I'll have Meena wrap it up. You came straight here as soon as it happened?"

Delta sighed. "Yes. And I know what you're asking. I was out in the creek during this death and so was Hector. We're each other's horrible, horrible alibis."

She glared daggers at Hector, who was perched awkwardly on the edge of the other sofa. He was flushed as red as his hat. He ground his teeth anxiously, frozen in place by guilt. Meena and Tosk stood nearby and ran through the morning's events with each other, both swearing they had stayed in the lounge from the last moment the doctor was seen until her body was found. None of them was the person Quinn was looking for, so they wove between the sofas and headed towards the fireplace.

Sure enough, Ash was sitting curled up on the carpet with his back against the hot stone. He looked up at them and then back down at his knees.

Quinn took his lack of protest as an invitation and sat quietly next to him. They coughed awkwardly. "So, uh… how are you…

doing?" Their real question, the one they weren't asking, hung heavily in the air between them.

"Good," Ash said in a small voice. "I'm fine."

"No you're not," Quinn said before they could think about it. "We just found a body."

He shrank in on himself. Quinn winced.

"Sorry," they said quickly, "sorry." They tried again. "Do you… need anything?"

He sighed. "I don't know."

Quinn nodded and began to stand up. Usually when they were upset, the last thing they wanted was someone watching them. But they froze when he added, "… just… stay here, please."

Quinn looked at him in surprise. He didn't move.

"Yeah. Of course." They sank back down, grasping for something else to say and coming up empty. The two of them sat side by side for several minutes and said nothing.

Quinn's mind began to wander. The killer had wanted to take the body away. Why? Was Tosk desperate to keep up his end of the deal with the beast hunters? Did Delta want to dispose of the body before Dr. Lycosidae found claw marks? Did Meena, with her well-used anatomy textbook, think the corpse could be a valuable specimen? Was Hector indulging his grudge against werewolves after the death of his brother?

Their phone hummed frantically into their hip. Quinn pulled it out and answered.

"Hi honey," their mom said. "How was your second day?"

"It was… okay." They hoped their voice didn't sound too strained.

"Good. Did you spend time with your new friend?"

"Yeah. He's here, actually."

"Can we talk to him?"

"Uh– yeah."

They passed the phone to Ash. He introduced himself, then listened for a couple seconds. "Well, we're all really sad right now. A spider just died." A brief pause. "What? No! It was terrible! She's an old friend–"

Quinn grabbed the phone back. "Uh, they're, uh, calling us for lunch. Gotta go." They quickly hung up and stuffed the phone into their pocket..

"Your mom is nice," Ash said after a pause.

Quinn grunted. "Yeah. Nice. That's probably the best thing you could say about her."

"What do you mean?"

They sighed. "Once you've been around her a while, you see she's *just* nice. She doesn't really *care*. Or if she does, she's afraid to act on it. She just wants me to meet her expectations. That's all."

He nodded thoughtfully. "I guess that makes sense. I used to know people who were really nice to me, but when I hurt, they didn't want to help me. Nice isn't enough."

"Yeah."

"Why did she ask me about camp?" he asked.

Quinn's stomach flipped. "Oh– uh– I think she's confused. She thinks we're going camping this weekend. I told her we're not, but she probably forgot." The lie sat heavily in their chest. They tried their best to ignore the feeling.

Ciara and Jasper walked over to sit near them, discussing

quietly. "The same cologne, of course. But I smelled something else," she said. "Someone who'd been down there. A human."

Jasper stared back at her, unfazed. "A human? You mean like me, Quinn and a third of our guests?"

Her shoulders sunk a little. "Ah."

Jasper shrugged and knelt to slide awkwardly across the carpet towards Quinn and Ash.

"How are you two doing?" he asked softly.

Quinn shrugged.

"I'm fine," Ash murmured.

Jasper grimaced. "Yeah, I can't blame either of you." He ran his hand over his hair. "I mean, we've had plenty of troublemakers here. But a murderer…"

The two shivered. Jasper sighed and drew something out of his pocket. "I want you both to take these. Just in case something happens."

In his palm were a couple of joined pairs of plastic bricks. Quinn looked at them and then back up at Jasper in confusion. "Why? That's not enough to build anything."

"No, no. Look." Jasper broke one of the pairs apart and gently tossed the bottom brick to one side. He showed them the studs on top and then pressed one. In a blink he was gone, then he reappeared right where he had thrown the brick. He grabbed it and clicked the two back together before handing them to Ash.

He and Quinn let out an impressed *ooo*. "I need to know you have a little protection in case something happens," Jasper said. "A quick escape. Give it a try."

Ash took apart the pair of bricks and threw one away, then

120

pressed the button on the other. He quickly teleported to the spot where the brick had fallen. He gasped in delight and tried the device a few more times, sending himself farther and farther away.

When he was out of earshot Jasper leaned in. "Do your parents know about any of this?"

"Nope," Quinn said simply. Their parents would take them away if they knew. They couldn't let that happen.

"I didn't think so," he said, "since they haven't knocked down our front door yet and dragged you away." He paused. "I don't blame them. This is a pretty scary place for a kid right now."

"We're not kids," Quinn protested.

"Yeah, yeah. If they knew, they would want you home with them."

Quinn shook their head, struggling for words. "No. I can't leave. Not when you guys are in danger."

Jasper considered them for a long moment. Then he blinked slowly, recognizing the urgency in their tone, their desperation to belong. Even with a murderer on the loose, this was where Quinn felt safe. And he knew exactly what that felt like. He nodded almost imperceptibly and pressed the other pair of bricks into their hand, giving it a brief squeeze.

~ ~ ~

The next morning Quinn woke up to the rattle of heavy rain pouring against their window. The dull, wet weather drew everyone inside and they could hear the rooms buzzing with activity as they passed by. The lounge was almost full. The scents of coffee, tea, and other unfamiliar elixirs curled in the air and friendly conversation thrummed in Quinn's ears like cicada song. The pastry case on the counter was full of apple-sized rolls made of the dough Jasper was kneading the day before. Ash had pinched their tops into two peaks and stuck dried cranberries in for eyes before putting them in the oven, and now a miniature flock of horned monsters sat under the dome of the case. Quinn grabbed one and slipped between the tables of chattering guests to sit at a booth opposite Ash. A crochet hook dipped and twisted between his fingers as he wove a ball of red yarn into a flat disc.

"What's that gonna be?" Quinn asked.

He looked up at them. "A crab. I still need a name for her."

They thought for a moment. "Clawdia? Shellby? Crabigail?"

Ash smiled down at the disc. "Crabigail."

Quinn smiled too. The moment felt strangely normal. It was a comforting island in the middle of all the danger and sorrow. They relaxed just a little.

Ciara was pipetting tomato soup into thimble-sized bowls for a couple of mice when the front door slammed open. She froze and looked up, and her expression darkened. The guests nearby leaned and craned their necks to try to see what she was seeing from her spot behind the counter.

A tall, muscular man stomped inside and shook the rain off himself in a single careless movement. He had the same steely eyes as Fenris, but he was younger and attempting to remain clean-shaven against the persistent bristle of his thick hair. He glanced around the lobby with such an angry huff that Quinn almost expected to see steam rise from his nostrils.

"Where are the owners?" he asked the front desk clerk, a praying mantis about the size of a shoebox. The clerk lifted a mint-green leg and pointed it towards the lounge.

The man turned and strode towards the lounge, and his eyes narrowed in disgust. "I smell a vampire," he spat when he reached the doorway.

Ciara rolled her eyes and grumbled, "What a coincidence. I smell an ill-mannered boor." She extended her hand and forced a smile. "You're looking for the owners?"

He scowled and shook her hand, flinching at its icy touch.

"Jasper's upstairs," she continued when he didn't say anything. "So you're stuck with me. How can I help you?"

The man squared his shoulders. "I heard a rumor," he said slowly. "that my brother stayed here."

"That certainly would make sense, us being a hotel," Ciara said.

"It might," the man said, "except that I lost touch with him the day he checked in."

Ciara had clearly figured out what he meant by now, but she smiled innocently and said, "that's a shame. And who's your brother?"

The man darted his glare around the room before fixing it back on her. "Peter Fenris," he said with all the weight that the name carried.

The lounge erupted in concerned whispers. Most of the guests had no idea Fenris had died here, but the mention of the man destroying their home was enough. Delta and Tosk, tucked into separate booths against the wall, exchanged a terrified glance.

Fenris's brother raised his voice over the buzz. "I get it, Pete's not a popular man. I don't want to get mixed up in his personal drama. I just need him back home."

Ciara shrugged. "Terribly sorry, Mr. Fenris, but your brother's checkout time was yesterday afternoon. No one here has seen him since then."

All of it was technically true. The man dropped into a seat at the counter, fuming, and the mice turned over their tiny chairs as they rushed away from him. The pastry case rattled. "Let me talk to the other owner. I don't trust anything that comes out of a vampire's mouth." He sneered at Ciara. "And it's Burke, not Fenris. That stuck-up idiot is my stepbrother."

Quinn froze at hearing the name Burke. He must be related to Alex Burke, the nephew who was just released from prison. They peered at him curiously. The restless grinding of his teeth seemed to carry a current of worry underneath the anger.

They stayed in their seat as Jasper came in and talked to Burke. Jasper led the werewolf to the corner to prevent the others from hearing them, but it was clear from Burke's body language that he hadn't calmed down. Jasper didn't let it throw him off even as Burke loomed at least a foot over his head. His eyes danced back and forth, following the agitated swing of Burke's arms. Eventually he laid a soothing hand on Burke's shoulder, and the werewolf slowly stilled and quieted down. He didn't seem to notice the faint blue glow poking through the fibers of Jasper's sleeves. Burke let out a heavy sigh that rustled the pothos leaves on the ceiling and nodded, and he followed Jasper back to the counter.

"If Pete made someone mad enough to get rid of him, that's his fault," Burke growled as he came into earshot. "But he made it my business when he got me in on his stupid real estate racket. The whole thing's way more trouble than it's worth. He had to get me involved when he knew I was vulnerable, and now he's leaving me holding the bag! Just makes me want to–"

He seized an empty chair at his side. Before he could do whatever he was planning to do with it, Jasper quickly placed his hand back on his shoulder. "Hey, now," he said. "You have a right to be angry. But you will not put our guests in danger. Do you still want to see his room?"

Burke nodded, looking dazed. He glanced down in confusion at the chair as if he'd forgotten why he grabbed it. When he let go Quinn saw the deep marks his fingernails had made in the wood.

"I'm sure you'll land on your feet, anyways," Ciara said. "Yours is a big family, isn't it? They'd support you."

Burke's glare burned into her back as they started for the stairs. "Not anymore," he grumbled.

Minutes dragged by. Quinn fidgeted with a splintered spot on the table made by the impact of something pointed. When they couldn't sit still anymore they looked up at Ash. He took a moment to notice and return their gaze.

"What?" he said.

"What do you think he has to do with all this?" Quinn asked, leaning forward.

He blinked at them. "Nothing. He's looking for his stepbrother."

"But his name is Burke. Remember what I told you yesterday? About the nephew?"

"Quinn, I don't want to think about this stuff," Ash said. "Two people are already dead. We're making it worse if we accuse people of things we don't know about."

The table rocked as Tosk leapt onto it. "Are you two talking about the werewolf?"

Ash shook his head vigorously. "Yeah," Quinn said eagerly.

Tosk wrung his clawed hands. "That's Robert Burke. He's listed as a partner in Fenris's company, but Alex Burke's name isn't anywhere. The only information I could get on him was the arrest record, plus the note about his dead-on-arrival patients. Everything else must have been scrubbed."

Ash stood up, wobbling a little. He looked pale. "I don't want to hear about this. I'm going to my room."

Tosk slid into the seat Ash had just vacated and curled his tail around himself. "They never figured out what he was doing with the bodies," he murmured conspiratorially. "But his freezer was full of pieces from the hospital's cadavers. All sorts."

Quinn frowned. "Creepy. And they don't know why he was doing it?"

"He refused to say anything. He pled no contest and went straight to prison." Tosk tugged nervously at his ears. "The timing of all this is really bothering me. I think–"

He was cut off with a frightened yelp as Burke burst into the room. Ciara and Jasper trailed behind him like children being taken to detention. They traded frustrated scowls as Burke strode to the center of the room and raised something over his head.

"What I want to know," he growled, "is who left this in my brother's room."

There was complete silence as the guests in the lounge looked

126

at each other. Most shrugged and grumbled, and a few laughed quietly. Quinn squinted and saw that the thing in his hand was an old, thoroughly chewed pen. They turned to Tosk in disbelief, only to see that he was staring at the pen in wide-eyed terror.

"Are you serious?" one of the guests asked Burke.

"Yes," he cried. He was beginning to turn defensive as the laughter got louder.

"What's the issue, exactly?" Ciara asked. "You don't think your brother used a pen to go over those heaps of documents he brought?"

"Everyone watch out!" someone mocked him. "It's a big bad pen!"

Burke squeezed the pen in his fist and fumed. The plastic casing snapped and ink bled over his fingers. He glared around the room and his eyes lighted on Tosk.

"What about you, squirrel?" he asked, slamming one hand down on the table and shoving the broken pen into Tosk's face with the other. "You recognize this?"

Tosk swallowed. Failing to control the tremble in his voice, he said, "no… I don't know what you're talking about."

The laughter and chatter died down at his reaction. "These teeth marks are tiny," Burke continued. "Made by a twitchy little prey animal. It's yours, isn't it?"

Tosk pressed his lips shut, not trusting himself to speak, and shook his head rapidly.

"Why were you in his room?" the werewolf bellowed. The guests in the nearby tables winced.

"Hey, wait," Quinn said. "You don't know he was in there.

127

Fenris could have borrowed the pen. Or picked it up by accident. They were in the lounge together before he…" They thought quickly. "… checked out."

Burke snorted. "In case you don't know, kid, us werewolves can smell fear. And this little fella is coated in it." He leaned closer to Tosk, who whimpered. "If you didn't do anything wrong, why are you so scared, squirrel?"

His voice kept trembling, but Tosk managed to say, "I don't know. It might have something to do with the angry two-ton werewolf leering over me."

Burke let out a strangled cry and swiped at him. Tosk ducked as fur sprouted from Burke's skin and his bones shifted and snapped. His claws became lodged in the table and he growled through broad, sharp teeth. He thrashed and twisted, trying to free himself from the table, and Quinn and Tosk scrambled away. The werewolf opened his jaws wide and attempted to say something but he could only bark and bite at the air. Giving up on freeing his paw, he jumped at Tosk, dragging the table after him.

In two leaps Ciara crossed the room. She clamped an arm around Burke's chest and lifted him off his feet. Given their height difference, she almost had to bend backwards to do it. "That's enough now," she grunted, dragging him away.

Burke responded by sinking his teeth into her arm. She winced but held on as he attempted to squirm out of her grip. The table came loose and went rolling across the floor.

She pulled him towards the door and he bucked, trying to shake her off. Instead he knocked over the pastry case with a loud smash. He tried again, sending them both to the floor amid the rolls and shards of glass, and she gave up her composure and threw an elbow into his jaw. He swiped at her with his claws and she buried her fists in his ribs. The guests in the lounge watched them struggle in stunned silence for a few moments. Then they recovered, and laughter and amused shouts rang through the room. A couple of them made bets on who would win.

Ciara and Burke tumbled across the floor, trading blows and sending chairs skidding in all directions. Eventually she yanked him into the lobby and out the front door. Jasper gratefully shut it behind them. Quinn could hear the scuffle continue outside as he returned.

"Are you gonna stop them?" Quinn asked him in disbelief.

He laughed. "I learned years ago to just let her tire herself out. If she gets rid of Burke, even better."

He had barely stepped away from the door when Hector threw it open and trudged past him into the lounge. Rain soaked the top half of his body and mud caked the bottom half.

"Course it had to rain today," he grumbled as he slid into a chair at the counter. "Those mud patches out there are like sinkholes," he told Jasper. "You ought to do something about that."

"We can't guarantee your safety if you go off the path," Jasper said with a shrug. "If the forest wants to swallow you, it's gonna do it."

"Can you get me something warm?" Hector asked. "Coffee? I don't care."

A thick sort of green slime spilled down the stairs in the corner. It oozed into the lounge and drew itself high as it solidified, and Meena took shape, stretching her arms above her head. She dropped lazily into the chair beside Hector. "Gorgeous weather, huh?" she said.

Hector jumped and knocked over the coffee Jasper was trying to hand him. "You'd better stop that!" he cried, regaining his breath.

"Someone's jumpy," Meena said. "What happened to you?"

"Nothing," Hector growled. "Went for a walk and got lost."

"Looks like you were pretty lost."

"It's none of your business, okay?" he cried.

Rain continued to drum at the walls. It was soon joined by chatter and laughter as guests resumed their interrupted conversations. Quinn found a broom and swept up the broken glass. Peace was just beginning to return when Ciara dashed inside, banging the front door open. She glanced around at the guests with frantic eyes. She had been splashed with mud by the impact of something large, and the mud dripped softly to the floor in the silence.

"You," she said, grabbing Jasper by his elbow, "and you," grabbing Quinn by theirs, "come outside. Now."

Quinn wanted to protest, maybe ask for time to grab an umbrella, but before they knew it they were outside and the rain was gluing their hair and clothes to their skin. They shivered violently as Ciara led them down the hill.

The path they were following curved sharply around a large sycamore, and Quinn saw a big hunched shape come into view. They squinted through the rain. Burke, still in his wolf form, was curled in the mud and whining through gritted teeth.

"We tossed each other around for a bit," Ciara said, pointing towards him, "and then he had to go on his way, so we said

130

goodbye. I was halfway up the hill when he started screaming his head off. Look."

Jasper hissed in a nervous breath. A large metal trap with wicked teeth bit into Burke's torso. "What's that thing doing here?" he cried.

He knelt next to the werewolf and ran his fingers along the trap. "It could kill someone," he continued. "Are you okay, man?"

Burke growled and rolled his eyes. *Do I look like I'm okay?* his eyes asked.

Jasper sighed and closed his eyes in concentration. He placed both hands on the trap and his tattoos glowed, and the metal jaws slowly shrieked open. Burke rolled away and panted in relief.

"Okay. You'll be okay," Jasper said to him. "We have a doctor staying with us. You can—"

Before he could finish, Burke dragged himself to his feet, shook the rain and blood off his fur, and trotted away. He tossed a con-temptuous glare over his shoulder at them as he disappeared.

Jasper sighed. He tried to pick the trap up, but it had been chained to a nearby tree. He cast a spell around it instead to stop anything from touching it. The rain rolled over the enchanted spot in an odd dome. "I'll take another crack at that when it's dry." He stood up and winced as a large raindrop hit him right in the eye. "Let's get inside."

"I don't understand," Quinn said as they struggled back up the hill. The path was half-liquid by now and their feet sank and slid through the mud. "Why is there a trap out here? I thought lots of creatures live in this forest."

"That's right," Jasper said. "It's either irresponsible or very, very cruel." He sighed. "But what's worse is… I recognize that trap."

Quinn and Ciara both turned to stare at him in surprise. He nodded. "It's the same model as the one I tried to scrap for parts in my workspace."

They were all silent for a moment. Then Ciara laughed, trying to lighten the mood. "Taking up hunting now, are you?"

He snorted. "Yeah, right."

"So it might have been stolen from your workspace," Quinn realized. "In the basement."

They were quiet again. *The basement.* The basement which was supposed to be locked. The basement where a murder had just taken place. That basement.

"We should check if anything else is missing," Jasper said. The others nodded. When they came inside, they headed straight down.

A few minutes of rummaging through the shelves showed that nothing was missing, including the trap. The one down here had a set of impressive dents from Jasper's attempts to disassemble it. "So it came from somewhere else," Jasper said thoughtfully. He pulled his own trap down from the shelf to look closer.

He turned, bumping the radio off the shelf with his elbow. It landed on the playback button and wheezed to life.. Quinn covered their ears but couldn't escape the terrible noises.

"Could the guests hear that?" Quinn asked when it was over.

"No," Jasper said. "The doors down here are soundproof, and they're closed. I guess they were open when we heard the real thing happening."

They nodded, thinking. The events of last afternoon suddenly clicked into place in their mind.

132

"Awfully stupid move for someone so clever at killing," Ciara said.

"Or," Quinn said, "maybe it was a really smart move." The others looked at them in disbelief.

"Think about it," they said. "We came down as soon as we heard the screaming, but the killer was already gone, taking Fenris's body with them. How could anyone escape so fast? They didn't."

"What do you mean?" Ciara asked.

"What we heard couldn't have been the actual murder," Quinn continued excitedly. Of course. It was finally making sense. "It had to be the recording. The doctor was killed when the soundproof doors were shut, when the murderer had plenty of time to get out and move the body. They set up an alibi, then they came back and hit the button to play the recording when we could all hear it."

The others nodded thoughtfully as they put together what Quinn was saying. "So," Jasper said, "our timeframe was wrong. The killer didn't need to be nearby when we came down."

"Making everyone's alibis worthless," Ciara said.

Their shoulders sagged. She was right. They were back to knowing practically nothing about this death. If they were wrong about when it happened, Quinn realized, then it could have happened any time after she came up to talk to them. That was a wide window of opportunity.

Quinn shivered as they climbed back up to the lounge. All they wanted to do was peel off their wet clothes and change, but a sudden glimpse of Ryan made them freeze.

He was sitting at a table with three guests and a notepad, dabbing at his soaked shoulders and hair with a napkin. He waved cheerfully at them. "How are my favorite tenants doing?"

Jasper and Ciara waved but didn't stop walking. Jasper sighed and murmured, "This all really had to happen during an inspection?"

"I know," Ciara whispered. "Couldn't this horrifying murder have happened at a more convenient time for us?"

They left to change into dry clothes. Quinn almost followed them, but they couldn't resist listening to Ryan's conversation with the guests. Maybe one of them overheard something important.

Looking slightly deflated, Ryan turned back to the guests at his table. "What about visibility?" he continued. "Are the stairs too steep? Do the lamps in there give adequate lighting?" Quinn grabbed a rag and a spray bottle so they could look busy and inched closer.

The guest at his right, a large furry beast with papery wings folded neatly on her back, shrugged. "Dunno. I fly between floors anyway. I don't look around me much."

He nodded and wrote a few notes down. "Did you see anything broken or needing maintenance?"

The beast shook her head. "All seems fine. But it's too noisy. The third floor's supposed to be the nocturnal one, but someone was stomping around and screaming, woke me up. I thought I heard a woman crying too, but I'm not sure it was the same room."

Quinn's heart dropped. Panicking, they pretended to trip and fell against Ryan. The conversation cut off abruptly as he toppled.

"So sorry," Quinn laughed anxiously. "I'm clumsy today." They helped him scoop up the business cards which had fallen out of his pockets. There were so many, all with his name on them. *Agni's*

Kitchen, Eden Perfumes, Anubis Technologies, Bifrost Engineering, and countless others. He hurriedly sorted them into alphabetical order before tucking them away.

"Alright," Ryan said, checking his notes. "Where were we… right. Does the surrounding land seem well cared-for and accessible?"

Quinn let out a relieved breath and backed away.

The beast nodded. "Yeah. The trails are well-marked. I mean, if you follow them you get lost. But they're there."

"Off the trails it's even worse," the other guest at the table said. It had the body of a human and the head of a horse. "That creepy human has been wandering around out there every night. The one in the red hat. Have you seen him?" Quinn froze, pretending to scrub the adjacent table. "Last time I saw him, he grabbed at his knives and glared at me like he was planning to skin me."

"I haven't seen him," the beast said. "I see that squirrel all the time, though. The reporter? He's always running around in the woods and over the walls of this place. I even saw him go by my window last night. I wish I could still do that. Stupid arthritis."

"Hmm." Ryan jotted down a note. "Okay, final question. How safe do you feel here?"

Behind them, Quinn heard Delta choke. They glanced at her, then followed her gaze to the lounge door. She was staring open mouthed at someone who had just walked in.

When Quinn saw who it was they couldn't believe it either. If Delta wasn't about to faint, they would have thought they were hallucinating.

It was Peter Fenris.

- 9 -

Fenris banged his head on the doorframe as he walked in. He didn't stop or even seem to notice the large pink blotch growing on his forehead. Most of the guests glanced at him and continued to chat, unaware of the horrifying miracle stumbling past them.

Quinn couldn't move. Panic hit them in a wave and they struggled to breathe. They wanted to scream, or bombard Fenris with questions, or run away and hide, or anything except keep standing there. But with Ryan watching them, all they could do was stay still.

Fenris paused by the counter, grinding his jaw with the effort of thinking. They had to do something *now*. Impulsively, Quinn ran over, pulled out a chair, and offered it to Fenris. He dropped into it with a curt nod. They tried a few times to speak to him, each attempt ending in a nonsensical stammer. Finally, they said, "H–hi, Mr... uh, Fenris. Can I get you anything?"

He peered at them. After a long moment his eyes lit up with recognition. "Yes... Lennie. A mug of chaga tea, please."

Quinn paused. The offer had spilled out of their mouth automatically, but now they realized they had no idea how to make whatever Fenris had just asked for. They forced a smile onto their face, nodded, and walked nervously behind the counter.

Fenris's eyelids drooped and he slouched over. He startled, gasping, and pulled himself upright. "Are you okay?" Quinn asked him. A hundred other questions threatened to rush out behind that one. They bit their tongue to keep quiet.

Fenris nodded, scratching absently at the center of his chest. "Fine. I've felt better. Too many long nights looking over these infuriating contracts."

He noticed them staring, and Quinn turned away to study his reflection in the shiny refrigerator door. Fenris was here. He was *here*, and he was *alive*. They felt even more destabilized than when they had stared down at his motionless corpse. In a daze, Quinn drifted to the counter and studied the knot of brass coils that Jasper had reassembled the day before. They hesitantly poked it with one finger. Their skin burned immediately. They jerked back with a hiss, then crossed their arms and sighed, wondering how they were ever going to get chaga tea out of this mess. The thought had barely crossed their mind before the machine started rattling to life. Quinn snatched a mug from under the counter and slid it under the spout as a murky brown liquid began to pour out of it. When the mug was full the machine stopped with a polite splutter.

Curiously breathing in the bitter earthy scent, Quinn handed the mug to Fenris. He took it with a shaky hand.

Think, Quinn, think. One way or another, Fenris was here, and he didn't seem aware that anything was wrong. Now was the time to get information from him. Quinn smiled at him again, careful not to move too fast or too close. "Long nights, huh? Must be pretty bad if you're just getting back now. Where were you?"

He blinked slowly and frowned. "I was… ah…" He trailed off and pinched his brow, disturbed at his inability to remember. He pulled a small day planner from his pocket and consulted it. He tapped the page from two days ago, the day he died, in satisfaction. "Right. I met with Mr. Hare to discuss the sale of this land." He nodded towards Ryan and said to him, "Your father."

So he still thought it was the day he died. Fascinating. And a little disappointing, but Quinn didn't give up. He had to know something.

"Does that hurt?" they asked when they saw him rub absently at the middle of his chest. It was the second time they saw him touching that spot.

Fenris glanced down at his hand. He didn't seem aware of what he had been doing. "Err– yes." He unbuttoned the top of his shirt. The skin there was red and raw. Quinn couldn't tell if it was from him irritating the spot or from an injury. "Sort of an unpleasant tingle." His eyes drifted up to the menu and fixed on one of the items, a tea made from poison sumac berries. He scowled at it, trying to unearth a memory. "Perhaps your bartender gave me the wrong order this morning."

He shrugged and raised the mug unevenly to his lips. He took a sip, paused, and then began coughing and gagging violently.

Quinn watched him with panic rising in their chest. Was this their fault? Did they just poison him? They had no idea how they had made that tea, after all.

He recovered with a gasp, taking the napkin Quinn offered him and mopping his chin with it. "I'm not sure what happened," he said finally. "My throat– it wouldn't–" He made a grasping motion with his fist.

"Swallow?" Quinn hesitantly finished. Fenris cleared his throat and nodded, embarrassed.

At that moment Ciara appeared in the stairwell. She spotted Fenris and jumped back as if someone had thrown a lit match at her feet. Quinn leaned forward to block her from Fenris's view. "Maybe you need some rest," they suggested. "Want me to take you to your room?"

Fenris nodded. "Thank you. I'm always getting lost in those awful corridors."

He wobbled to his feet and followed them out to the lobby. Quinn wasn't sure they would be any better than him at navigating the hallways, but they weren't going to pass up the opportunity to observe him further. Something was clearly wrong with him physically, and he was acting a little different too. He was more polite, less sure of himself. He remembered who he was but nothing from the past few days. What did it mean? Quinn chewed their lip as they punched the elevator button.

As they stepped into the car, Hector came through the front door. His eyes blazed with agitation and he was soaked with rain. When his eyes fell on Fenris and Quinn, he gaped at them in shock.

He shouted for them to wait and began running towards them as the doors slid shut.

"What was that about?" Fenris asked with a frown.

Quinn shrugged, forcing a nervous laugh back down their throat. "I don't know."

When they arrived at the third floor, Fenris's room was right around the corner. Quinn could have sworn it was at least halfway down the hall, but they were grateful enough not to question it. They showed him what they hoped was a confident smile as he unlocked the door and turned to go. They didn't move away, though. They lingered, hoping they would see or hear him do something important.

A moment passed, then another. Quinn frowned, disappointed. Fenris didn't make any noise as he stepped into his room. That was it, then. They began moving away.

Fenris grunted. They turned eagerly.

"Where is the sheet?" Fenris asked.

Quinn peered into the room. The top sheet, the one Jasper and Ciara had used to wrap up his body, hadn't been replaced yet. "Oh– I– I don't know," they stammered. "I'll get you a new one."

He nodded and turned away. "Maybe ask someone to clean that up as well." He pointed at the curtains, which were streaked with dirt on one side.

Quinn's heart went cold. They hadn't noticed *that* when they found Fenris's body. The brown stains were on the part of the curtains that hung just below the window. Their mind began to race. Maybe someone came in through the window or left that way. Maybe whoever opened the window was wearing dirty shoes.

Maybe it wasn't dirt at all.

Quinn nodded nervously. "Of course." Fenris thanked them and shut the door. They shifted their weight back and forth, sinking unevenly into the carpet as they considered what to do next. Scouring their brain for ideas, they came up empty and turned back the way they came with a shrug.

After replacing the sheet with a fresh one from the laundry room, Quinn walked outside and down the hill towards where Burke had gotten caught in the trap. They paused there at the sound of something leaping through the trees overhead.

They looked up to see Ciara. She was wrapped up in long sleeves and gloves, her head swathed in a deep hood. She dropped to the ground in front of them.

"Well, the inn's haunted I suppose," she sighed. "Fenris stumbled past me as I was leaving, staring right through me. Not such a big change for him at least."

"He's not a ghost," Quinn told her. "He's really back."

"What?"

"I don't know what he is, but he drank a whole mug of tea. Seems pretty alive to me."

Ciara shook her head. "Let's hope he doesn't ask for a refund."

"What are you doing out here?" Quinn asked. "Doesn't the sun hurt?"

She shrugged. "Not as much as being murdered. I'm out looking for that churl."

"Have you found anything yet?"

"Not yet," she said with a disappointed sigh. "Almost had a run-in with the beast hunters. I hid just in time, but I'm lucky they weren't looking for me. They were complaining to each other about Tosk being late."

Quinn shivered. "That's not good. What do they want from him?"

"That's what I'm concerned about," Ciara said. "They're direct rivals with Fenris in trying to control these woods. Motive galore. Shame I can't ask them about their deal with Tosk without getting a knife in the gut for an answer."

Quinn smiled, excited. "Maybe I could–"

"No. Your uncle would kill me." She sighed. "Anyways. Look what Ryan had this morning. A box of unclaimed items he had people curse for him." She dug in her pocket and produced a fistful of little fuzzy worms with long snouts and googly eyes. "Mostly dolls and jewelry, plus these. Delightful, yeah?"

She picked up a worm between two fingers. It immediately squirmed to life, bit her on the thumb, and then went slack again.

Quinn stared blankly at the worms. "Do they do anything else?"

"Nah. Just bite. I think I'll build them a tiny house and give them all names. This one's Ebenezer."

Quinn picked up another worm. The resulting bite left a tiny ellipsis of red fang marks in their skin. "They're kind of cute, I guess."

"Adorable." She stroked one on its lifeless head. "It feels good to carry something dangerous again. Jasper thinks carrying around my sword near the inn is 'inappropriate,' if you could believe that."

"No way," Quinn said unconvincingly. "Hey. Did Ryan say if he had any suspicious orders? A cursed object could be a pretty easy murder weapon to hide."

142

"He didn't say. I'll ask him." Ciara tucked the worms back into her pocket. "Well, I should be off. Don't get killed out here. And if you do, tell us." She scrambled up a tree and was gone.

Quinn glanced around the site of Burke's trap again. The mud was churned up where he had thrashed in pain. They found nothing else there besides dead leaves and soggy pine needles. Disappointed, they headed towards the creek and sat under a big tamarack, pulling out their notebook.

They flipped through their pages of notes in an attempt to calm their mind. Everything was happening so fast, and none of it made any sense. Fenris couldn't have raised himself from the dead (*right?*) so somebody must be responsible for his return. Who? How? Why?

The idea of a cursed object felt promising. The puncture wounds on Fenris and Dr. Lycosidae were totally unfamiliar, bigger than a flu shot but much smaller than any stab wound they could imagine. And the victims' bigger injuries made them seem redundant. If the device that made those wounds wasn't a typical weapon, that might allow the killer to carry it easily while concealing its purpose. But what *was* that purpose, exactly?

They stared into space, chewing on their pencil. A stir of motion behind them made them twist around. Delta was approaching the creek with Brooke on her back. Quinn stood up, creating a shuffle of dead leaves which made her jump in alarm.

She relaxed when she recognized them. "Quinn! What is Fenris doing here? What's going on?"

Quinn winced. They weren't sure how much to tell her. "I have no idea," they said truthfully. "I don't think he remembers anything after he died."

"Did he say anything important?"

They shook their head. They decided not to mention the stains on the curtain or the tingling pain in the werewolf's chest.

Delta sighed. "I don't know what to think anymore. I've never been so afraid. I'm taking Brooke back to our den for a little while."

Quinn perked up as distracting questions flooded their mind. "Ooh! How do you go between the water and land? Are you oviparous or viviparous? Do you live in schools or herds?"

She glanced around and then smiled conspiratorially at Quinn. "Do you want to see our home yourself? It's nothing special, but-

"Yes!" Quinn said eagerly before she could finish. "Yesyesyes! Show me!"

Quinn followed her to the shore where she dove into the water. They shed their shoes and notebook and then paused, unsure what to do next. On an anxious impulse they broke apart Jasper's teleporting bricks and left the bottom one in their shoe. Just in case.

Delta resurfaced and held out her hand. Quinn took it. It was cool and wet, the fingers thinly webbed, but her grip was firm. The rocks on the creek bed were slick with some type of fuzzy algae, making it impossible to do anything more graceful than slide unevenly into the water, and so that's what they did.

The question of breathing occurred to them just as the water closed over their head. Delta raised her hands to her mouth and blew an air bubble between her fingers, then passed it to Quinn. They held the bubble to their lips and breathed it in. Their chest relaxed and the itch in their lungs disappeared.

Delta grabbed their hand again and took off downstream. They weaved through cool currents and patches of muted sunlight as the creek deepened into a small river. Long fingers of aquatic weeds brushed against Quinn's face and blue crayfish scuttled along the rocks below. Brown speckled fish gaped at them in surprise as they passed.

Something huge and angular loomed out of the murk up ahead. A construction machine of some sort, bristling with zebra mussels, its identity eroded by years of running water. Delta swerved easily around it but a jagged corner scraped Quinn's cheek as they followed. Blood warmed the water by their face.

After several bends in the river, Delta pulled them to the right into a still pocket of water. Dug into the banks on all sides were large holes, with slabs of driftwood and scrap metal serving as doors. As they approached another riverbeast poked his head out of a door and peeked at them curiously. His eyes fixed on Quinn and he considered them for a moment. Then he lunged towards them, teeth snapping.

Quinn shrieked as Delta yanked them out of the creature's way. They rushed through a door and upwards until they surfaced in an underground chamber. Quinn gasped and choked in the humid air. "What— what was that?" they wheezed.

"Sorry about that. My neighbor." Delta's voice came from beside them in the dark. The water threw up pale patches of light as it lapped against the walls, too weak to see by. Delta climbed out of the water and shuffled around for a moment before appearing in a burst of orange light. She held a stub of an old candle and a match. She pulled Quinn out and then laid Brooke down on a woven pad nearby. "He just wanted to eat you."

"*Just* wanted to eat me? What?" Quinn yelped.

Delta blinked in surprise and then grimaced. "Oh… this is awkward. Nobody told you?" Quinn shook their head. "Riverbeasts are carnivores," she continued. "We mainly eat humans."

Quinn's jaw hung open. They considered fleeing back out into the river. It wasn't far. Were they fast enough?

"But you're safe with me. Don't worry." As if that settled it, Delta turned away and swept the candle through the air to illuminate the space. "Welcome to our home!"

She smiled eagerly, waiting for their reaction. At one end of the chamber lay a cutting board with a pile of cleaned bones and a shell-handled knife on top. At the other end was the woven pad where Delta and her daughter slept. Cushions and a low table stood in the middle. Pressed water lilies and purple lupines were stuck to the walls alongside colorful shells and rocks.

"It's really nice," Quinn said. They meant it.

Delta beamed. She sat beside Brooke and gently stroked her hair. Quinn sat too and looked down at the little girl. Nothing seemed clearly wrong with her; the green tint of her skin was deeper and livelier, her stitches were healing- Quinn frowned. Her stitches? They hadn't noticed those earlier.

Brooke crawled away and toyed with the loose shells and driftwood on the floor. She pulled a small metal object from under the blanket and waved it around. Quinn squinted at the thing. A hollow needle and suctioning plunger connected to a clear bulb. The whole thing was about the size of a small orange.

Delta gasped and tore the device out of Brooke's hand. She returned it to a hole under the blanket and covered it up with mud.

"What is that?" Quinn asked.

Delta flushed deep green as she answered. "That's– not mine. My neighbor's. It's for shelling crayfish." She fiddled awkwardly with the blanket. "I should really get it back to him. It was helpful at first. Making use of all those little crayfish coming into our den. But they just kept coming, and soon I started to rely on my neighbor. I owe him so much that I can't ignore the crayfish anymore. And now I think I'm overwhelmed with crayfish, and I wish I never even *met* my neighbor, and I–"

Brooke squealed and snapped a stray shell in half. Delta abruptly went silent.

"Are we still talking about crayfish?" Quinn asked quietly.

She pinched her lips together and said nothing.

"What's… really happening with your neighbor?" they carefully prodded. When she still didn't answer, they said, "You feel trapped, right? You're scared of him? What's going on?"

Delta glanced around as if her neighbor could be listening right now. "I… I shouldn't say. I can't."

Surprised, Quinn watched Delta pick up Brooke and hold her close. Their eyes traced the long lines of stitches studding the girl's arms and neck.

"It's something about Brooke," Quinn guessed. "What happened?"

"She… was in an accident," Delta said evasively.

"What kind of-" As they formed the question the cut on their cheek reopened. They lifted a hand to touch it. They remembered hearing Bertram describe Fenris's hazardous worksites. Hadn't he said something about an incident by the river?

"It was Fenris's fault, wasn't it?" they said quietly.

She didn't answer.

"They didn't clear the area before a detonation," Quinn continued. "And she was hurt."

Delta sighed, then she nodded. She didn't meet Quinn's eyes.

"But I don't get it. Why did you bring her to the inn to recover? Couldn't she rest here?"

Delta frowned, considering how to respond. Eventually she said quietly, "After the accident, I took her to a human doctor. Our community doesn't trust humans and we hate relying on them for anything." She began talking faster, avoiding their eyes. "But our healers couldn't help her. I had no choice, really, I-"

"I believe you," Quinn said gently. "It's okay." Delta was shaking, her eyes gleaming with worried tears. Quinn was at a loss for how to comfort her. They leaned over and awkwardly patted her hand. The two stayed that way for what felt like a long time.

Eventually Brooke began to squirm. Delta smiled hesitantly, shifting the girl on her lap and sweeping the hair out of her face. "Could you take a look at her? Tell me if you find anything unusual?"

Quinn hesitated. They knew they were completely the wrong person to ask for help. They were young, new here, and not especially smart. But Delta was frightened for her daughter's life. She was probably desperate enough to trust any kind face.

"I can't promise I can help," they finally said. "I'll take a look at her, though."

Delta smiled and thanked them repeatedly as they leaned over the little girl. They checked her pulse (rapid) and her temperature (cold). Both were perfectly normal according to her mother. Those long seams of stitches made Quinn nervous when they imagined what injuries could have caused them, but the skin underneath was reforming smoothly, free of infection. Her breathing was easy and unbroken.

Quinn frowned in confusion. "This is weird. What are her symptoms again?"

"She's been sleeping a lot," Delta said, "just like when she first got sick. I made her a poultice with some valerian root, so I knew she'd be drowsy, but this is extreme. And she throws up anything I feed her."

"What have you fed her?"

"I've tried everything from our usual diet. Carp, walleye, perch…" she laughed awkwardly, "…human…"

"And she used to have no trouble with those?"

"They were her favorites. Er, not human," she added quickly.

Quinn chewed their lip, thinking. They weren't sure what it could mean. Apart from her lack of appetite, Brooke seemed okay. But her condition would quickly get worse if she didn't eat.

Their focus was interrupted by a muted thumping on the door which they had come in through. "Um," they said. "That door is strong, right?"

"More or less," Delta said. "Why?"

"I think your neighbor might have come back," Quinn said quietly.

In the ensuing silence the thumping got a little louder. Then it got faster– no– it multiplied. There was a second riverbeast behind that door.

Delta's eyes went wide. "They wouldn't– no–"

The thumping became louder and more insistent. She stumbled to her feet and pulled Quinn up with her.

"My neighbors wouldn't hurt you," she said, attempting a reassuring smile. "But, all the same… let's move away from the door."

They backed away from the den's opening. Brooke bleated in surprise as she was hoisted away.

The pounding got louder. Panic began to rise in Quinn's chest. They gasped, remembering the plastic brick in their pocket. Locking elbows with a confused Delta, they yanked the brick out, wiped off a few soggy rags of stray notebook pages, and desperately pressed the button.

For a moment nothing happened. Then all at once the plastic shattered and fell through their fingers. "No, no, no," they groaned. Even the earth was rejecting them now.

They desperately searched for other options. The door splintered. Delta stepped in front of Quinn protectively. "Is there another way out?" they asked.

She looked around at the mud walls and ceiling. "Not unless we make one."

They didn't get a chance to ask what she meant. Yanking Quinn after her, she dove into the wall.

Mud consumed them. Their skin screamed at the wet, shifting texture which pressed on them from every angle. Their lungs burned. They blindly held onto Delta for dear life.

The travel to the surface felt endless. Finally the mud released them with a damp squelch. Quinn gratefully pulled in deep lungfuls of air. The three dragged themselves onto solid ground and

150

collapsed, chests heaving.

Brooke was the first to roll upright. She waved her arms aimlessly and froze when her fingers brushed the leaves of a fluffy green weed. Brooke gazed at the plant eagerly and crawled towards it before seizing a few tufts of it in her fists.

"What is that stuff?" Quinn asked, still lying on the ground.

"I don't know," Delta said. "Don't touch that, minnow."

Brooke inspected the plant curiously. She looked up at her mother, then back at the plant, then in one movement uprooted a stalk and stuffed it in her mouth. Quinn gasped. It was the first time they had seen Brooke's teeth. They were big and at least as sharp as Delta's set. Brooke didn't even use them as she swallowed the plant in one gulp, then tore up a few more stalks and swallowed those too.

Delta watched her daughter in shock for a moment. Then she laughed in delight and relief. "She's eating! She's finally eating!" She tried a little of the plant to make sure it was safe before filling her pockets with it to save for later.

The three of them dove back into the water and swam upstream the way they came. Even against the current, Delta was so strong that the weight of Brooke and Quinn didn't slow her down. Sunlight parted the clouds and tinted the water gold. They passed the construction machine and followed the bends in the river. As the water shallowed below them, Quinn felt a sliver of curved metal brush through their hair.

They twisted to look. It was a fishing hook. A big one. It bobbed innocently in the stream as Quinn stared at it in horror.

Delta pulled them up onto the bank, disturbing a crowd of

water-skating bugs which fled in all directions. Quinn barely noticed the sweet taste of fresh air. Their eyes immediately landed on
the fishing pole. It was stuck into the rocks, its owner nowhere in
sight. A tackle box lay beside it. Quinn turned over the box. Just
as they expected, Hector's name was on the bottom.

Delta gasped. She pulled Quinn away from the pole and shoved
them behind her. She groaned when she saw Hector's name.

"That idiot never learns, does he? These humans are going to
kill us all…" She glanced at Quinn. "Er, I meant…"

"I know what you meant," Quinn said hurriedly. "We need to
get this thing out of the water." They ducked around her, grabbed
the fishing pole, and unearthed the end. The hook swung viciously
over their head. Delta yelped and grabbed the line to stop it, and
two of them slowly laid the pole down.

She took a large rock from the creek bed and brought it down
on the hook until it was dull and bent. "That should slow him
down, at least," she sighed.

There was a soft rush of wind over their heads. "Vandalism,
huh?" Meena's voice came from the waterlogged bat circling above
them. "Can I join?"

Delta stepped back. "Go ahead. It belongs to Hector."

Meena swooped down and snapped the fishing line between her
teeth, flinging the pole into a bed of cattails with a toss of her head.
"Good. That man's a creep."

Quinn pocketed the hook, knowing they couldn't leave it out
here to hurt someone else.

"He's been acting like a menace since he arrived," Delta complained. "What does he want with a hotel full of magical creatures

anyway?"

Quinn knelt down to put their shoes back on. They were soggy, but drier than the rest of their body and much more comfortable as a result.

"I think he's on some kind of revenge mission," Meena said conspiratorially. She glided lazily through the air as she spoke. "Do you hear the way he talks about werewolves? I tried to get him to spill by pretending I was Fenris on his first day here. He said something about a brother."

"A brother?" Delta repeated.

"It's revenge, I'm telling you. I'm not surprised. Fenris has more enemies than hairs, after all, and that's saying something for a werewolf." Meena dipped to avoid a branch and sprinkled Quinn's head with the rainwater her wings had been collecting. "I heard right before he died, he was in a big fight with someone about his nephew. I still want to know what happened. But I guess I'm too late to ask."

Quinn glanced around at the creek bed. "Hey."

"Oh, didn't you know?" Delta asked. She smiled, savoring the feeling of knowing something that Meena didn't. "He's back."

"Who?"

"Fenris."

"*What?!*"

"Hey," Quinn said again, louder. They frantically lifted rocks and fallen leaves and looked underneath. Panic rose in their chest.

"What do you mean he's *back*? You can't just go *back*. Is he a ghoul? A vampire?" Meena paused and considered it. "Can a werewolf be a vampire? No way. The teen girls would have discovered them by now."

"Where's my notebook?" Quinn shouted. They didn't mean to yell, but they couldn't think about anything right then except the empty stretch of rocks which their eyes raked over repetitively.

Meena dipped low and briefly examined the rocks. "Must be around here somewhere. Is this where you took it out?"

Quinn nodded and Delta did too. "I saw them," she said. "It was right here."

For the next several minutes Meena helped Quinn search the bank while Delta looked under the water. Brooke sat off to the side and helpfully clacked a couple of rocks together. The clouds, which had looked like they were clearing up, now gathered and darkened overhead, and the rain grew heavier.

Finally Delta stood up and sighed. "We've looked everywhere. I think it's gone."

"We should get inside anyway," Meena said, shaking the water off her body. "Sorry, new guy."

"No..." Quinn murmured. "No, I can't..." Their energy had slowly drained along with their hope as they searched. The area wasn't very big. None of them had seen the notebook, and if it had fallen in the creek then it could be miles away by now. There was no use in looking any more. Still, they couldn't force themself to move. They couldn't abandon their notebook.

Delta lay a hand on their shoulder. "We can look again tomorrow. There's no use staying out here now."

Quinn didn't look at her but kept staring blankly at the rocks. "What am I supposed to do without it?" The reassuring weight of that notebook in their pocket was their anchor. It held their

154

thoughts without judgment, kept their memories straight, and patiently listened to them without end. They felt blind without it.

"Come on, don't make me drag you back," Meena teased. "It won't be fun. I'll turn into something really horrifying. Like a gargoyle. Or a moose."

She gently tugged at their sleeve with her teeth until they stood up. Quinn groaned and allowed themself to be led away. They didn't know what else they could do. At least if they were going to be depressed they could do it in dry clothes.

Quinn looked back at the creek bed one more time as they all walked back towards the inn. Besides their despair they could feel something deeply wrong snagging in their mind. But without the clarity of paper and pencil it was all too tangled up to understand.

- 10 -

Quinn's room appeared blissfully close by when they stepped out of the elevator. They shrugged, lacking the energy to be surprised, and fumbled for their key.

They noticed the smell when they began peeling their clothes off. A foul blend of sweat, damp cotton, and whatever was in that creek. Quinn gagged and tossed the clothes in the sink to fester while they showered off.

They were just scooping the clothes out again when they heard the harsh squeal of complaining metal wheels in the hall outside. Quinn opened their door to see Ash struggling with a battered laundry cart. He looked up and gave them an exhausted wave.

"Oh! Are you doing–" Ash tried to shush them but he was too late. The word "laundry" slipped out before he could stop them, and the cart lurched to a sharp stop. Ash groaned.

"Yeah. Well, I'm trying to."

"What's wrong?"

"It hates water," he sighed. "I tried telling it we're not going to the laundry room, but it didn't believe me. Now it's never gonna move." The cart spun its wheels in an indignant shriek.

Quinn grimaced. "Sorry. But hey, can I add mine?" They darted back into their room and came back with the soaked clothes, dumping them on top. Ash wrinkled his nose. "I know, I know. Here, I'll help you push."

Even the combined weight of the two teens wasn't enough to budge the cart. Quinn considered it for a moment, then they gripped one end and gestured for Ash to grab the other. "Let's just carry it."

The cart's wheels screamed and its canvas walls thrashed in protest, but it couldn't stop them as they hoisted it into the air and down the hall. They waited for the elevator doors to close before setting it down. The car stopped and slid open on the third floor, and Quinn warily gripped its rim to stop it from ramming into whoever was on the other side. It was Fenris, clutching a sheaf of papers and blinking in surprise at the growling cart.

"Hello, children," he said with a stiff nod. "Are you going to the lau-"

"Yep!" Quinn cut him off as the cart shook in fury.

Fenris stepped back. "Perhaps you could wash my curtains while you're there," he said nervously. "Why don't you go and I'll bring them to you. You seem to be... capably handling that little... situation." He turned and quickly strode away as if the cart was about to bite him. Maybe it was. At this point Quinn couldn't be surprised.

The elevator stopped again on the second floor to let Bertram in. His golden eyes widened when he saw the cart. "Are you two–"

"Uh-huh," Ash said quickly.

"May I add a few of my things?" The frog hurried away without waiting for a reply. Quinn and Ash looked at each other and shrugged. Ash held the doors open while Quinn restrained the cart. Bertram returned quickly, and together they continued down.

On the first floor Ash led them past the front desk and around the corner. He unlocked a plain door near the back entrance and pushed it open with a puff of soap-scented air. The laundry room was cramped but neat, with an empty washing machine and a dryer churning around an old quilt. As they set the cart down on the floor, it trembled and tried to roll away, and Quinn quickly grabbed it.

"Hey," someone said behind them. Quinn turned to see Tosk clutching a bundle of clothes in his arms. "Do you mind if I add these?"

"Why is everyone so eager to do laundry?" Quinn grumbled as Ash helped them haul the cart into the room.

"The closest laundromat is in town," Ash said with a shrug. "It's a human town."

"Oh. And they can't be seen by humans?"

He shook his head. "The place only takes quarters. No one has change anymore."

They stuffed the contents of the cart into the machine, and

158

Bertram and Tosk gratefully shoved their items in. As soon as the cart was empty it shot away and disappeared. Quinn apathetically watched it go before turning back to the machine and pulling open the soap dispenser. They lurched back with a yelp.

At first they thought a toad had been trapped in the dispenser and crushed. They leaned closer, desperately calculating how they might do CPR on a toad, and realized they weren't looking at a toad at all.

Squatting in the soap dispenser was a very small, very bumpy yellow imp. It shielded its eyes from the sudden light and frowned at them. "Who are you?" it asked.

"I'm Quinn," said Quinn. "I'm new here."

"Can't help you," the imp said with a shrug. It began to pull the dispenser shut.

"Wait!" Ash cried. "They're in the system! They're an employee."

The imp paused. "You think that stomach talks to me?" it snarled. "I've got my own system."

"So add me," Quinn said. When the imp didn't move they added, "please."

The imp let out a long sigh. Grumbling to itself, it disappeared into the depths of the machine and appeared a minute later clutching a scrap of blue cloth.

"Is that from my hoodie?" Quinn protested.

"You're in my system now. Congratulations," the imp said. It sniffed the fabric thoughtfully. "Phew! I'll have no problem remembering that."

"I don't usually smell that way," Quinn said defensively.

Behind them Fenris stepped into the room. His dirt-streaked curtains were rolled up in his arms.

"Who are you?" the imp asked suspiciously.

"No one," Quinn said quickly. They took the curtains from him and stuffed them into the machine. "It's just me and Ash. Our laundry. Can we start now?"

Tosk and Bertram, who had been chatting outside, went quiet as Fenris joined them. Quinn gritted their teeth as they heard Tosk let out a string of surprised exclamations.

"Sure. Just as soon as we settle the payment, naturally," the imp said.

"I've got it," Ash said. He pulled a sleeve of crackers from his pocket.

The imp shook its knobby head vigorously. "Jasper gave me crackers last time. I'm tired of crackers."

"Then what do you want?" Ash asked helplessly.

The imp screwed up its eyes in thought, dramatically tapping a bleach-stained finger against its chin. "Wait. I gotta check the pantry." It ducked back into its chamber.

Out in the hall Fenris said, "I can't sleep either lately, not for the life of me. Not with these chest pains."

"Chest pains?" Bertram said. "It's my head for me. The humidity, I think."

"Why does he want his curtains washed?" Ash whispered. "He just got back to his room. How are they already dirty?"

"He noticed them as soon as he came in," Quinn told him. "The room hasn't been touched since his death. They must have gotten dirty around that time."

Ash nodded thoughtfully.

"I don't like this," Quinn continued. "It was confusing enough when he was dead. Now I don't know what to think. And I'm scared he's gonna say the wrong thing to–"

"Hey! I heard someone's doing laundry!"

Quinn flinched at the sound of Ryan's singsong voice. Tosk and Bertram took the opportunity to quietly return to the lounge as the man leaned against the doorway and grinned.

"Can I toss a few things in there?" Ryan asked. He carried several identical copies of the black t-shirt and jeans which he was currently wearing. When he noticed the strange looks he was getting he added, "It's a productivity hack. Wearing the same thing everyday boosts my efficiency by 50%. It's what Bill Jobs does. You guys should try it."

Quinn didn't have the energy for more than a weak smile as they opened the machine to let him stuff his clothes in. If the other appliances were as demanding as the washing machine, they thought, they would soon have no choice but to try his one-outfit idea.

The imp's door began to open, and they ushered Ryan out with polite urgency. To their dismay, Fenris broke off his conversation with Bertram to get the human's attention.

"I need to speak with your father," Fenris said to Ryan as he left the laundry room. "He appears very upset about something. I have dozens of missed calls from him. Is everything alright?"

Ryan looked at him in surprise. "Oh– well– no. He's fine. He just assumed you weren't interested in the purchase anymore."

Quinn strained to hear them as the two drifted away from the door. Did this mean Fenris was still going to buy the inn's land? This was the last thing they needed right now. They couldn't even write it down without their notebook. What if they lost track of some important detail? What else might they miss? They felt the dull buzz of anxiety in their chest.

"Cheese."

"Huh?" Startled, Quinn spun around.

"I want cheese," the laundry imp repeated. "Not just any cheese. Salamander cheese."

"Where would we find that?" they cried.

"Dunno. You figure it out. You want laundry, you gotta pay the price." It extended its tiny hand and closed its fingers in a fist a couple of times.

Quinn covered their eyes and groaned.

"Well, he hadn't heard from you at all in the last few days..." Ryan was saying.

"The last few days?" Fenris said, puzzled. "But I saw him yesterday."

Quinn swung their head up and shared an alarmed look with Ash. Without thinking they ran out into the hall. Ash trailed hesitantly behind. Fenris and Ryan looked at them, startled by the interruption.

Quinn frantically searched for something to say. "Hi. Um... any chance you two know where we could get... salamander cheese?"

Fenris frowned. "Salamander *what?*"

"Cheese," Ash said. "It's for Frederick."

Quinn's mind was too busy to process the fact that the laundry imp was named Frederick. "Yeah," they agreed. "No one's stuff is

162

getting clean unless we can get that cheese."

Delta was walking quickly out of the lounge, and at the mention of the cheese she froze. Brooke peeked over her shoulder at them. "Oh– I know where you can get that."

"Really?" Quinn asked hopefully.

Delta wrinkled the spot where her nose might have been if she were a mammal. "My cousin raises salamanders. His den smells awful, but he loves the little guys. I'm sure he can spare some cheese."

"Could you talk to him?" Quinn said. "The imp won't clean our clothes until we pay it."

Delta shrugged. "Okay. It's almost time for us to go out again anyway, isn't it minnow?" She ruffled her daughter's hair and turned away. "Stay here," she called over her shoulder. "I'll be right back."

"The papers are in my room," Fenris told Ryan. "Let's sort this confusion out tonight." He started for the stairs. Ryan drifted towards the lounge to wait for him and Quinn and Ash followed.

Ryan sat down at the counter where a half-empty mug of coffee sat by a pad of paper. He raised the mug to his lips to drain it in one swig with his left hand while scribbling notes with his right, then he slid the mug across the counter towards Ciara.

"Could you fill me up?" he asked her. "I'll need my boost to stay focused in this meeting."

Ciara took the mug. "I don't suppose we could bribe you with coffee not to sell?"

Ryan chuckled, but the laughter died on his lips when he looked up at her and Jasper's faces. They gazed steadily at him, their lips pressed tight together, as he squirmed in his seat.

"I'm sorry, guys," Ryan sighed. "It's not my decision to make. It's definitely not what I would do. Things will be a lot different without this place…"

"That's right," Jasper said. "The inn's an important part of the community. It brings in visitors and locals. Not to mention revenue. Did your dad think about that?"

"Fenris is promising the same thing, actually," Ryan told him. "Revenue. He wants to put up lots of businesses here instead of just the one." He paused and jotted down a short note on his pad. "This is what he's offering for the land," he said, confidentially sliding the paper across the counter.

Jasper blinked at the paper and looked back at him. "What is that?"

"It's his offer," Ryan said. "Read it."

"We're right here," Jasper said. "Just tell us."

"It's—" Ryan stammered. "It's what you're supposed to do when you— can you just take a look?"

Jasper rolled his eyes and picked up the paper. "I can't read this at all, man. Your handwriting is terrible."

Ciara squinted at it. "What is this, elvish? *Nac them tu pr—*"

"Okay, okay!" Ryan huffed, snatching the paper back from them. He beckoned for them to lean in close, even though the lounge was almost empty. Besides the three of them and Quinn and Ash, there was only Bertram, reading in a corner booth and clearly not paying any attention to their conversation. But Ryan still lowered his voice to whisper Fenris's price into their ears.

Quinn couldn't hear what he said, and they weren't sure they would know what the number meant anyway. But the way Jasper's face darkened and Ciara narrowed her eyes told them everything they needed to know.

"And you don't think that's suspicious?" Jasper said. "Why is he offering so much money for this land when he could just go somewhere else?"

"He's got money to throw around, I guess," Ryan said with a shrug. "It's a pretty attractive offer, you have to admit."

"But your dad never wanted to sell before, right?" Ash said. "He never told us so."

"Well… The thing is, he's getting old. He has to retire eventually, and…" He faltered, and a vein of insecurity ran through his voice. "…he's not planning for me to replace him. So he's liquidating."

"Then liquidate it to someone else," Ash pressed. "You can't sell. We live here. Lots of creatures rely on this place."

Quinn looked over at him in surprise. They had never heard him use that tone before- more stubborn, more self-assured than usual. They couldn't blame him. This was a tame response for someone in danger of losing the only real home he had ever known.

Ciara's voice turned smooth and sympathetic. "He doesn't trust you to replace him? That doesn't seem fair. You've worked for him for years, haven't you?"

Ryan scratched his ear self-consciously. "Well… yeah, I have."

"Tirelessly. You deserve a say in the big decisions by now."

"Maybe I do." Ryan sat up straighter.

"And aren't you the one who's been here, inspecting this place with your own eyes? You said this isn't the decision you would make. Why should he get the final say?"

Ryan frowned slightly, thinking. He gazed down into the fresh mug of coffee as Ciara slid it towards him.

The thump of sturdy footsteps down the stairs announced Fenris's presence. He lost his balance mid-step and braced his hand against the counter as he sat.

"Alright." He cleared his throat, rifling through the sheaf of papers in his hand and selecting one, "Let's get started."

Ryan looked up from his coffee, snapping out of his distracted daze. He smiled at Fenris and scooted his chair towards him. Jasper and Ciara traded a disappointed glance.

Beside them Ash buried his face in his hands and Quinn's heart softened. They reached over and gave his shoulder a stiff pat. He leaned into the touch, seeming to understand what they were going for.

Physical touch seemed important to him. They remembered sitting next to him yesterday, after he found Dr. Lycosidae's body, and feeling helpless to comfort him. Maybe they should try a hug next time. Not that they wanted a "next time" to happen, they thought with a shudder. They needed to focus. It was so easy to get overwhelmed right now.

They stepped aside as Hector came in through the stairwell. When Fenris noticed him he looked away with a nervous cough, but Hector had seen the werewolf and he paused, his eyes like ice. The energy in the room noticeably shifted. Nobody made a sound.

Fenris hunched over his papers and tried to ignore the human as he walked closer. Hector stopped behind his chair and cleared

166

his throat.

"If you'll excuse me," Fenris said quickly. "I'm in a meeting."

"You seem eager to buy," Hector said, ignoring him, "for someone with no money."

Fenris shifted uncomfortably in his seat. "I have non-liquid assets," he muttered. "It's not the same as having money for a settlement."

"*Don't* lie to me." Hector slammed his hand on the counter and leaned in. If the lounge was silent before, now it felt like a January midnight.

"It doesn't matter anyway," Fenris said, holding his gaze. "Toby hasn't been affiliated with our family for years."

"Yeah? Who is he affiliated with, then? Who's answering for him?" Hector snorted. "I know *he's* not paying up."

"I know you're upset, sir." Fenris put a slight, patronizing emphasis on the word *sir*. "But I don't control the verdict. Maybe it's time you move on."

"Move on?" Hector squinted at him in disbelief. He elbowed Ryan out of the way to take up Fenris's whole field of vision. "*Move on?* And how do you expect me to do that?"

Fenris let out a long sigh. Finally he dipped into his breast pocket and dropped a few hundred dollar bills in front of Hector. "Here. Are you happy?"

Hector's complexion was already red, but at this he practically turned mauve. "Is this some kind of *joke?*" he roared. He snatched up the bills and held them up in front of him. "*This* is what my brother's life is worth to you?"

Quinn glanced at Ciara, wondering if she was going to grab

Hector the way she did to Burke this morning. She just watched
him with her lips pursed. Ash and Jasper were still too, watching
the fight with disturbed interest. They may not have especially liked
Hector but they seemed content to watch Fenris get a good scold-
ing. Quinn had to agree- besides, if the men kept arguing maybe
they could figure out what was going on between the two of them.
They just wished they could write all this down.

Hector scowled at Fenris and took a slow step forward to loom
over him. Fenris looked the human up and down, considering him,
then he stood up himself. Fenris stood at least a head taller than
Hector. "I hope," he said evenly, "you're not inviting yourself into
a fistfight with a werewolf. You may not like how it turns out for
you."

Hector's face soured, wrinkling up like a withered apple. He
turned and stormed out of the lounge, pausing for a moment in
the doorway. "You–" he stammered. "You all think you can do
whatever you want. Just because you can scare the rest of us. You
won't scare me off. You'll see." He crossed the lobby and flung
open the door, almost slamming it right into Delta's face as she
came in. He stomped out and she ducked to avoid him.

Delta glanced in confusion between each face in the lounge and
eventually shrugged and sat down. None of them said a word. The
horrible tension in the room began to flow out in Hector's wake.

Clutched in Delta's right hand was a small wheel of red wax
which Quinn recognized from the little cheeses at the grocery
store. The wheel had been emptied, refilled, and resealed with a
tarry brown substance. "Here you go," Delta said. She gagged
slightly as she handed the wheel to Quinn and they soon

understood why. The little wheel of cheese stunk of curdled pepper and ammonia.

"Thanks," they said softly. They fought the urge to put it in their pocket, not wanting the smell to spread to their clothes, and settled for closing their fist around it as they walked to the laundry room.

"Oh, it's you again," Frederick said when they knocked on the door of its dispenser. It squinted up at Quinn and Ash and sniffed the air, and a delighted grin split its face. "You have my payment!" it cried. "About time." It reached out its tiny hands and did the same grabby motion with its fists from earlier.

"Wait." Ash reached out in front of Quinn, stopping them from handing over the cheese. "What do we say?"

The imp rolled its red-streaked eyes. "Now."

Ash shook his head. "Not quite."

"Or else," it tried.

"It's always the same thing, Frederick," Ash hinted helpfully.

The laundry imp let out a long, dramatic groan. "*Please*," it said finally. Ash smiled, plucked the cheese out of Quinn's hand, and placed it into the dispenser. The red wheel was almost half the creature's size.

Frederick rubbed its hands together in pleased anticipation. It slammed the dispenser shut and the sounds of several levers being pulled issued from the machine. In another moment water and soap swirled over the clothes inside.

They watched the rhythmic movement of the machine for a few moments. Then Quinn sighed. "This is still better than quarters."

That night, Quinn twisted restlessly back and forth between the sweat-dampened sheets. The day's events cycled rapidly through their mind over and over. They shut their eyes, trying to focus on the sounds of soft cricket song and creaking keratin as guests walked around downstairs. Hector's furious face as he stood over Fenris filled their head. They rolled over and counted the geometric feathers crisscrossing the wallpaper in front of them. Memories seeped in anyway. Burke threatening Tosk. Delta crouching over her daughter in concern. The worried expressions of their friends faced with losing their home. After almost an hour of this, Quinn groaned and sat up. They climbed out of bed and opened the window. A chill breeze slid inside. Some mid-sized animal scrambled across the wall of the inn, or maybe it was one of the trees, and the last fireflies of the year drifted lazily through the moist air.

It had been hard to sleep every night since they found Fenris's body. Mingling with the usual suspicion and anxiety were newer, gentler feelings. Logically, Quinn knew someone in this inn had to be a murderer. But the more time they spent with the guests, the more they started to like, or at least sympathize with, them. Meena's playfulness, Tosk's anxious fidgeting, Delta's protectiveness, and even Hector's grief over his brother changed them from strangers to complicated individuals, and that made it harder to stay neutral.

Quinn sighed, turning away from the window. The fishing hook which they had taken out of their pocket earlier gleamed on their desk. They picked it up, examining its harshly bent shape. Hector had surprised them today. He seemed to hate Fenris from the start, and his constant fishing and trap-setting showed a disregard for most other creatures as well. But his confrontation with Fenris shook Quinn's whole understanding of him. What had Hector said on that first day? *"A werewolf killed my brother, I'm sure of it."* Quinn sighed, shaking their head. They had been quick to imagine a violent mauling in the woods. The truth seemed a lot more insidious.

They slipped the hook into their pocket and walked out into the hall. It didn't seem like they were going to sleep tonight anyway, and they were too restless to lay down. They wandered the halls for a few minutes before finding their way to the common room. Shelves of books lined the wall behind the sofa, dozens of books varying in size and style and age. Quinn dropped to their knees on the sofa and swept their eyes over the titles. *Exorcisms For Dummies. Gnomish Architecture of the 13th Century. Care and Keeping of Squonks.*

The door whined on its hinges as Ash walked in. Quinn sank down to sit cross-legged, and he rubbed his eyes and sighed. "You can't sleep either, huh?"

"Yeah," Quinn said. They picked at the fibers of the sofa's armrest. "I can't stop thinking about… uh, everything I guess."

"Today was crazy," he agreed. "I think I have something that can cheer you up, though," he added. "I was gonna tell you tomorrow."

They looked up. "Yeah?"

"I got another purple candle from Jasper," he said. "We can try the divination spell again!"

Quinn gasped. An excited smile spread across their face as the gloom in their mind lifted. "Really? That's awesome! Let's do it now!"

They both rushed to their rooms to grab the pieces of the spell and assemble it. The world went blurry as Quinn handed Ash their glasses to place in front of the candle. Finally they both sat restlessly on the carpet, waiting for the whirling shadows on the wall to take shape.

The empty hallway appeared in one lens, then Fenris's room in the other, just like last time. Fenris entered the frame and began to shout at someone, just like last time. Quinn frowned in concentration as if they could force his unseen companion to step into view. Was someone actually in there with him, or was he on the phone?

Again Fenris grew angrier. Again the door at the end of the empty hallway opened slowly. When the figure inside saw they were alone, they walked out into view towards the door, gaining detail. A human. A man. The baseball cap and the way he swung his arms as he walked were unmistakable.

Quinn hissed in a tense breath through their teeth. "Hector," they said at the same time as Ash.

Quinn's mind reeled. "I can't believe… no. I knew it." They stood up shakily. "He left all those traps around. He hates magical creatures. He has some kind of history with Fenris."

"Wait," Ash said. "We don't know if he did anything yet."

Hector's hands were dug firmly into his pockets as he walked to one of the doors and stopped. He tilted his head to the side, as if he was thinking intently or listening to something. After a few moments he snapped out of his daze and knocked.

Inside his room Fenris stopped shouting and turned.

The sound of tires crunching on gravel outside made Quinn and

Ash jump. A car door slammed and they could hear Hector– the real one– grumbling to himself as he walked towards the inn. Quinn peeked out the window. He was holding the bloodied bear trap which had injured Burke, and the look on his face said he wanted someone to blame.

"Let's go. Before he hurts someone else." They grabbed Ash's arm and pulled him out into the hall. He scrambled to snuff out the candle flame between his fingers as he stumbled after them.

The two raced down to the lobby. In the lounge they could hear Hector's voice raised in anger. "What do you mean, no one's touched it?" he shouted. "I've got eyes. I know when someone is messing with me."

"Will you please relax, man?" Jasper's voice was heavy with exhaustion. He and Meena were drooping over steaming mugs at the counter opposite Ciara. Brooke sat in Delta's lap nearby, poking at Bertram's spotted arms as he turned the yellowed pages of a book. An enormous moth and a child-sized possum chatted softly in the corner over their lunch. "No one's messing with your nasty traps."

"Why were you out there anyway?" Quinn asked when Hector stomped out into the lobby. "It's the middle of the night."

Hector scowled at them. "What do you care?"

Quinn looked back at Ash. He nodded. They took a deep breath and asked in a quiet, determined voice, "What were you doing at Fenris's room right before he died?"

The man's eyes bulged. "I–" he spluttered. "I didn't go near him. You're lying!"

"We saw you in our divination spell," Quinn pressed. "You went to see Fenris. Why?"

Hector took a furious step towards Quinn. They held their ground, doing their best to ignore the uneasy feeling that they were making a big mistake. "You had better watch your mouth," he spat. "Going around spreading lies will get you in a lot of trouble."

Quinn swallowed nervously, but the next question was already on their lips when Ash gently tugged them back by the elbow. "He says he didn't do it, Quinn. Maybe he was at Fenris's room for some other reason."

"I *said* I wasn't there!" Hector insisted. His eyes blazed for a moment, but he seemed to change his mind and he turned away. "I'm going to my room. If you nag me about this again, I'll report you both and get you fired."

Quinn grimaced. After all the chaos and murder, it was just their luck that a customer complaint would send them home. They sighed and punched the elevator button. Hector stepped in after them for what was sure to be an awkward ride.

As the elevator ground its way up, Quinn slid their hands mindlessly into their pockets. They pricked their finger on the fishing hook inside and flinched. All of this was so confusing, they thought as they took it out and rolled it between their fingers. These contradictions and loose ends were overwhelming.

"Where did you get that?" Hector asked sharply.

Quinn looked up. He was glaring at the hook in their hand. "I—" Quinn stammered. "I found it. By the creek. It was gonna hurt someone."

"That's mine," Hector growled. "You ruined my fishing gear for no good reason."

The elevator lurched to a stop at the second floor. Hector

174

jammed his left arm into the doorway to stop it from closing and threw out his right hand, palm open. "Here. Just give it back so we can all go to bed."

"I don't think I should do that," Quinn said quietly.

"Yeah," Ash added, "it hurt Delta's face really bad."

Hector sprung forward, trying to snatch the hook away. Quinn ducked around him and out of the elevator. Ash followed close behind.

Hector let out an angry chuckle between gritted teeth. "You think I'm some kind of killer? Come on." He walked towards them with slow, even steps. "I was just fishing. How do you think that beast gets her food? It was an honest accident."

He jumped for the hook again. Quinn twisted out of his reach, behind Ash, and Hector shoved the boy out of his way. Ash yelped and nearly fell to the ground. Over Hector's shoulder he and Quinn looked at each other and made a quick, wordless decision: RUN.

Quinn turned and bolted. Ash ran after them, grabbing the bear trap out of Hector's hand as he passed him. "You shouldn't have this either!" Ash called as they fled. "It almost killed a werewolf!"

But that was the point, wasn't it? As they rounded a corner Quinn cursed themself for ignoring the obvious signs that this man was violent. Could they have saved Dr. Lycosidae's life if they had seen it earlier? Could they have prevented Burke and Delta's injuries?

Something still felt wrong about this whole thing, a vague nagging sense they had no time to think about. They pushed it aside as they swerved to avoid the opening door to the stairwell. Meena stared in confusion as Quinn and Ash ran by.

"What are you kids doing here?" she called after them. "It's almost 2."

She turned at the sound of more footsteps and saw Hector chasing after them. Without another word, Meena started running too.

They ducked around another corner, trying to lose Hector in the maze of hallways, but he only drew nearer. Meena transformed into a mountain lion and caught up easily. "Hello! Did you hear me? It's 1:58. You have two minutes."

Ash stumbled and went pale. Quinn frowned uncomprehendingly. "Until what?"

Meena and Ash spoke at the same time. Her voice was loud and urgent while his was hushed and fearful. "The immune flush." When Quinn didn't answer, Meena continued, "Didn't Jasper tell you?"

Quinn vaguely remembered him saying something as they returned from the night market. So many things had happened that night, they had hardly paid attention. "Um... I think?"

Meena shook her head. "We have no time." She stopped at the nearest door, shifting into her humanoid form, and tried the knob, finding it locked. Stretching her fingers into long, thin shapes, she stuck them into the knob and made a few sharp movements. The door opened.

"Hey, wait–" Quinn began, but Meena was already pulling them and Ash inside. She shut the door just as Hector caught up with them.

Hector bellowed in anger and pounded on the door. Nearly

blind with panic, Quinn shoved the lock into place and threw all their weight against the door. The keratin was cool against their back as they caught their breath.

"You can unlock doors?" Quinn demanded when they could speak again.

Meena rolled her eyes. "Relax. I never do it without a good reason." She glanced around the dark room, letting her eyes adjust. "And look, I rescued us. Good thing this room was empty, right?"

In response, the bedside lamp clicked on. Pale yellow light spilled onto the bristling face of a very alarmed tarsier.

A relieved giggle escaped Ash. "Sorry, friend. We'll be out soon. We just–"

Thunk. The door shuddered as a hunting knife pierced through right next to Quinn's shoulder. Quinn shrieked and jumped back. The knife disappeared and landed again in a new spot. Hector stabbed the door again, and a long crack opened down its length.

"What–" Quinn gasped. "What do we do?"

Meena scowled and stepped between the two teens and the door. "I don't know," she said quietly. "You two stay behind me."

Another stab. The crack lengthened. Quinn's throat closed in fear. They watched the knife go into the keratin again and again. The door was shaking and splintering, it was going to collapse, it was going to–

A loud rumble drowned out every other sound. Meena's shoulders sagged in relief when the stabbing stopped. Quinn tried to shout, to ask what was going on, but their voice was swallowed by the noise like rocks tumbling over a tin roof. Outside Hector screamed, and then…

Nothing.

Nobody moved. Quinn's eyes darted between Meena and Ash. Their faces revealed nothing. Slowly the rumbling got quieter until it faded away.

"What just happened?" Quinn demanded.

Meena didn't answer as she approached the door. Quinn and Ash crowded together behind her.

She took a deep breath and opened the door.

A rattle and a snap. A full set of human bones tumbled over each other as the door pushed them back.

- 11 -

"There was an… accident. Nothing serious," Jasper lied, pacing as he spoke into the phone. He paused and rushed to the sink to catch the stack of dishes Ash had precariously balanced on the edge. His nerves made him clumsier than ever today. He was off balance. They all were.

Quinn stared ahead, trying not to listen. They listened anyway.

"No, no. Everything's fine, Mr. Hare." He listened for a moment. "Okay. You too." He hung up.

Ash stumbled and paled at the dry clack that followed. It wasn't the first time he had tripped over the bag of bones— in fact, he was the reason they had already moved it several times this morning. Jasper gently dismissed Ash's apology as he picked up Ciara's worn garment bag to find a new spot.

Quinn shivered into the steam of their lavender tea. They hadn't slept at all. Every time they tried, visions sprang up of their friends, their classmates, even their parents collapsing into piles of bones. There were so many bones in a human. Quinn's hours of admiring illustrations and museum specimens never prepared them for that. Little finely shaped ones, big sturdy ones that toppled over like they were made of wood. Sprung loose from their bindings of skin and muscle, an elegant organic symphony dissolving into a jumbled pile of death–

Jasper sat beside them, interrupting their thoughts. "How are you holding up?"

Quinn sighed. "Bad."

He put a hand on their back. "Take it easy on yourself. I know it's hard."

They shuddered. "But it shouldn't be. I can't stop messing up. And every time I do, I cause more hurt. Maybe… this was all a mistake."

"What do you mean?" he asked.

"Maybe I'm doing more harm here than good. I'm bad for this place."

He paused. "Do you… want to leave?"

They winced. "I… don't know. No. But I should. I think."

Jasper silently took that in. He didn't look at them. "I can call your parents," he said eventually. "See if they can pick you up to-morrow."

"I'll do that," they said hurriedly. They were going to tell him eventually that their parents didn't know they were here. Honestly.

180

But this wasn't the right time.

"Okay." He tried a small smile. "I guess we have a day to try to convince you to stay," he teased. "Chores are canceled."

"Look on the bright side," Ciara added, striding into the lounge and shrugging off her muddy overcoat. "You may have gotten rid of a murderer. We should thank you."

Jasper swatted at her. "Hush." He paused, examining the smattering of small cuts on her face. "What happened to you?"

"Nothing," Ciara said unconvincingly. She sat and smoothed out her hair, which was matted with blood.

"Yeah, right," Jasper sighed. "Who tried to kill you this time?"

She lowered her eyes. "Who do you think? Our friends from the night market."

"Those beast hunters are becoming a real problem," Jasper said. "They think they can do whatever they want."

"One of them stole my stuffed octopus once," Ash complained. "I left it behind near the pond, and when I came back for it he held it ransom for 20 acorn caps. I think just to mess with me."

At a table behind them, Meena elbowed Tosk playfully. "Tell your buddies to lay off."

Tosk froze, eyes wide. "I can't tell them what to do! I– I mean– I mean they're not my buddies. We barely know each other."

"It hardly seems that way," Ciara huffed. "At least ask them to wait a second before they shoot. Imagine if they used a stake." She raised the hem of her shirt to show off a deep wound between two ribs. She plucked an obsidian arrowhead from the wound and tossed it aside.

Ash gasped and ran to grab the first aid kit. Jasper grabbed a few jars of herbs from the cabinets to wrap up with the wound. "I don't want you running around out there anymore," Jasper told her. "Look what happened. And for what? You still haven't found anything."

"Yet," Ciara added quickly. "I picked up a smell in that basement. Human- I couldn't tell anything more without a blood sample, but I would know it if I found it again."

She grasped at her temples in frustration. "I simply need to search harder. The person who left that smell moved down the hill towards the creek, then back into this inn, last night. They are *still here.*"

The others looked over at the bag of bones, then back at her.

"I know," she said. "Maybe it *was* him. And the killer is already taken care of. Spirits willing." She clapped Quinn on the shoulder and they shivered. "Good work, eh? Maybe." Jasper approached with a bandage and a poultice wrap, and she allowed him to plaster it to her side.

"Thanks," Quinn said drily. "How does Jasper put up with you?"

"Bribery," he sighed over her shoulder. "She smushes all the bloodcrawlers so I don't have to kill them. I've got no choice but to keep her."

Ciara looked up as the front door opened. "That'll be the ningens." She grimaced. "We forgot to freeze their furniture, didn't we?"

"I remembered," Jasper told her. He pointed his thumb at the large freezer in the corner, where a set of alphabet magnets spelled out profanities Quinn had never heard of. "Stuck everything in last night."

"And that's why *I* put up with *you*," Ciara said with an approving nod. "Symbiosis."

She pulled herself to her feet with a grunt and walked out to meet the guests. Quinn stared into their mug, shaking it gently and watching the ripples spread.

"Do you think she's right?" they asked quietly.

"About what?" Ash said.

"That Hector was the killer?" If it was true, they weren't sure how they felt. It was a relief to think the killer might be out of the picture. Hector had acted plainly suspicious and aggressive over the past few days, and Quinn couldn't deny that it was somehow comforting to think it was him. They were slowly beginning to like the other guests for the gentle and vulnerable sides they showed. Hector, on the other hand, was easy to mistrust.

Well, until last night he was. Confronting Fenris, crumpling the money in his hand, he looked almost… fragile. What if they were wrong about him? What if they had killed an innocent man?

"Well… he might have done it," Ash acknowledged. "We don't know. But no matter what, it was an accident."

"We told Hector about the immune flush when he checked in," Jasper pointed out. "He should have gone into his room instead of chasing a couple of kids." He started for the door. "Besides," he added before disappearing. "Ciara's wrong about almost every-thing."

He almost walked straight into Fenris on his way out. The were-wolf stumbled, pressing a hand to his chest, and dragged himself toward a seat at the counter. He was looking worse than the day before, wiping sweat off his pale brow with a trembling hand.

When he noticed Quinn he coughed awkwardly. "I think I may have something of yours," he said stiffly.

Quinn looked at him. "Really?"

He fumbled in his breast pocket. "Your name is on it."

He pulled out the item and set it on the counter. Quinn's jaw fell open. It was their notebook.

"Wha–" they stammered. "How– how did you get this?"

They picked up the notebook and flipped through the pages. All their notes were still there. The pages felt a little loosened, as if someone had searched through them in a rush.

"I met a stranger last night," Fenris said thoughtfully. "While I was walking in the woods. A figure in a cloak. They offered to take away my bad dreams in exchange for a valuable item. I think there's been some sort of mistake."

Quinn smiled in amazement as they shut the notebook. "Well, thanks for giving it back. They were right. This is really, really valuable."

The two of them stared at each other awkwardly, unsure what to say. Eventually Fenris cleared his throat and stuck out his hand. Quinn slowly took it and they stiffly shook hands.

Jasper eyed them in surprise as he returned. "No business deals without checking with me, Quinn."

Quinn smiled and settled back in their seat. They craned their neck to look out the door, hoping to catch a glimpse of a real ningen.

Jasper screamed.

Quinn whirled around, heartbeat skittering out of control.

184

Jasper wasn't supposed to make a sound like that. He was their adult. He was safety. The mindless sound he had just let out made their nerves go into overdrive.

They jumped out of their seat and ran to him. The freezer door stood open. Jasper stared inside, a hand covering his mouth.

"What? What's wrong?" they asked urgently. They peered in after him.

Bertram lay crumpled against the wall of the freezer, his coarse brown skin bristling with tiny ice crystals.

Quinn choked. They stood frozen in place while Ash and Ciara ran up behind them. Fenris frowned, leaning over to look inside. "What is going on?" he asked tremulously.

No one answered. The guests in the lounge stared down at their laps. Ash shrank back in fear. Jasper and Ciara passed a worried murmur back and forth. After a few moments of staring at the frog in shock, Quinn slowly stepped forward for a closer look.

The lenses of Bertram's eyes were fogged with frost. His hardened limbs lay at unnatural angles as though he was carried in here and dropped without a second thought. Quinn reached out and ran a finger along Bertram's brow. The tiny grains of ice scratched against their skin. Grief echoed through their body as they remembered seeing the frog for the first time. They had been so full of wonder and delight. Faced with a talking frog in a suit, anything seemed possible. So much had changed since that night.

Behind them Ash shook his head and murmured, "we need to move him. He can't stay here."

"Why not?" Ciara asked. "He's well-preserved here. He may need to stay for a while until the toad arrives."

Ash let out a soft choking sound.

"She's right, bud," Jasper said gently. "It will be easier on his husband to see him in good condition."

Ash took a shaky breath. "Just… let me gather his flowers? Then we can put him back in here. After we say goodbye."

Jasper and Ciara held a silent conversation in their eyes. Finally Jasper sighed and said, "Alright. Only a few minutes, though."

Quinn grabbed Bertram's shoulders and Ash took his feet. Carrying him out to the lobby was difficult in his twisted position. As they watched the ice on his skin twinkle, the only thing Quinn could think was *why?*

There was the usual *why,* of course, as in why someone would find it in their heart to murder another living being. But another *why* nagged at their mind as they carried Bertram away. Why him specifically? Who benefitted from his death? And why was this death so different from the others?

Fenris had his impact marks and Dr. Lycosidae lay in a pool of blue carnage. In contrast Bertram looked almost peaceful. And he was so well-hidden in the freezer. The other bodies had been left out in the open, as if the killer was proud of what they had done.

The memory of something they had written down suddenly rushed back. They checked the page on Dr. Lycosidae's body. There it was— *looking for something.*

Someone stole the notebook and read that page, and the next morning a new body appeared with a totally different cause of death. It fit together too well. This happened, Quinn realized with a lurch, *because of them.*

What else did the killer know?

Quinn choked on guilt as they set Bertram down on a sofa. Would the killer use their notes to hurt someone else? How would they do it? Which of their new friends had Quinn sentenced to death?

They lay down the body and Ash hurried outside. Quinn sat on the floor beside the sofa and looked into the frog's blank eyes. Jasper and Ciara followed them out at a distance, speaking softly but intensely to each other.

"Tomorrow's not soon enough. If something happens to them here, I…" Jasper's voice faltered. "I don't know what I'll do."

"It's not exactly wise to keep *anyone* here," Ciara told him. "I hate to say this, but… maybe it's time to close."

Quinn swallowed the sour taste rising in their throat and tried not to hear. They busied themself tracing their eyes over the brown patterns on Bertram's skin instead.

"No," Jasper said flatly.

"Didn't we say," Ciara tried again, "that we would reassess if things got worse? What would you call this?"

Quinn sighed through their nose and focused harder. Thin lines running down the head, spots rippling across the legs where one pant leg slid up, thick raccoon bands around the eyes… *Wait…*

Quinn knew this frog. Not this one, exactly, but dozens of his tiny non-magical cousins living in the pond behind their parents' home. Some of the first animals Quinn ever met. The realization made their heart ache.

"Our purpose," Jasper insisted, "the whole reason we're here is to be a safe place for those who can't go anywhere else. That was Lev's dream."

"Of course, but–"

"These creatures are relying on us. Now more than ever. And what will we do? Throw them out in the cold?"

Quinn whipped around to look at them. Jasper flushed, surprised, at their reaction.

"What did you say?" Quinn said in a rush. Something twitched in their mind, struggling to put itself together.

"I– it was a poor choice of words, I didn't mean–" Jasper stammered.

"The cold…" Quinn whispered. The thing knocking around in their brain half-formed was a memory. A memory of wood frogs. Small, muddy footprints from the door to the sofa. Their mom screaming at the frogs nestled in her throw pillows, ordering them to put the little slimeballs back outside, *now*, she didn't *care* if it was snowing. The next morning, tears dripping onto frozen lumps of frog as they padded a shoebox coffin with tissues. An hour later, a miracle.

Quinn shrieked in delight, startling both adults. "I got it!" they cried.

"What?" Jasper asked warily.

"He…" Quinn paused for dramatic effect. "…is a *wood frog!*"

Ciara squinted at them in confusion.

"And they *freeze,*" Quinn pressed. "In the winter. Let's thaw him out! He'll be fine!"

Jasper looked down at the body doubtfully. Quinn had to admit it looked pretty dead.

"Listen. In the cold his liver produces a ton of glucose, which keeps his blood from freezing! His heart and lungs stop and he goes into a torpor. And while ice forms in his body cavities, it's prevented from forming in his vital organs and puncturing them! All wood frogs do it. Plus the gray treefrog, spring peeper, and boreal chorus frog! Cool, right?"

Quinn paused for breath. They realized, self-consciously, how much they had just been talking and how fast. They lowered their eyes to the floor.

"Glucose, eh?" Ciara said. She crossed the room, swiped her finger across Bertram's forehead, and examined the frost she had picked up. "You're saying if we crack him open, his blood will taste sweet?"

Quinn paled and opened their mouth to object. Ciara gently punched their arm. "Joking. Are you sure this will work?"

Quinn nodded eagerly, then paused. "Well– kind of. I haven't tried this on the giant magic variety of the frog yet. But it will work. It's science."

Jasper frowned nervously. "I don't know, Quinn. If this doesn't work we could damage the body."

Quinn chewed their lip. He was right. If this idea failed they would feel awful. But if they had a chance to save Bertram, they had to take it.

"Please," Quinn said. "If it goes wrong, I'll take responsibility."

Jasper tilted his head, thinking. "Fine," he said finally. "Let's give it a try."

He rubbed his hands together as he approached Bertram's body. He knelt and slowly pressed his palm onto the center of the frog's chest. The room held its breath as Jasper's arms glowed and the body warmed.

Fear and hope fizzled together in Quinn's chest as they watched. They could see the frost on Bertram's clothes melt, collapsing into round drops of water and sinking into the fabric. The lenses of his eyes thawed and the white fog disappeared. A fine steam rose from the body.

Ash came back inside as the body finished thawing. He paused in surprise, his hands full of flowers, and joined the others watching in quiet wonder.

Finally Jasper pulled his hand away. The four leaned in expectantly. Bertram didn't move.

After a minute, Quinn sat back on their heels with a sigh. It hadn't worked. Of course it hadn't. Why did they think–

Bertram's limbs jerked. Ash shrieked, scattering the flowers.

The wood frog's eyes popped open and swiveled experimentally. He coughed and took a deep breath, then turned to look around himself.

"Ggh-" Bertram choked and cleared his throat, spat out a few ice crystals, and tried again. "Good morning!" he managed.

Quinn grinned in amazement. Ciara thumped their back in congratulations.

Jasper leaned in and patted the frog's shoulder. "Hey Bertram. You feeling alright?"

"Just fine," the frog said, looking puzzled. "A tad sluggish, maybe." He glanced around again. "Oh dear– I fell unconscious, didn't I? I'm terribly sorry. I was sure I would make it to my room…"

"You didn't reach your room?" Ciara asked. "You seemed alright last evening."

190

Bertram scratched his head curiously. "Well, I remember finishing my tea and growing unusually drowsy. I walked up the stairs, and then out into the hall, and… well…" He frowned. "That's all."

Quinn frowned at the uneasy feeling lurking in their belly. "You might have been drugged."

"When was this?" Jasper asked.

"The treewalkers came in around midnight," Ciara told him. "It took the better part of an hour to get them and all their luggage settled in. When I came back, Bertram was gone. It probably happened then."

"Who else was in the lounge?" Quinn asked.

Bertram thought for a moment. "Delta and her daughter were in the lounge with me. Fenris and your landlord's son were discussing something quietly. It looked serious, although I couldn't hear them. And…" He smiled. "Tosk was sitting very close by. It was clear he was trying to listen in on Fenris's conversation."

Jasper huffed out a short, bitter laugh. "That's not surprising. He might be disappointed to know Fenris is only planning to buy and destroy this place, though." He sighed. "You might be right, Quinn. We'll check the kitchen. Why don't you get some rest, Bertram, and we'll tell you what we find. We're glad you're alright."

They set Bertram up comfortably on the sofa to let the rest of the ice work out of his system. Then they entered the lounge to look for clues of what might have happened the night before. Ciara opened the dishwasher to pick through its suds-soaked contents, while the moss-hued imp who normally operated the device watched in confusion, its pointed tail coiled around its body.

"It all depends," she said, "on who could get close enough to drug him. Someone hanging around in the lounge, or someone following him waiting for an opportunity." She sighed, setting down a mug and turned towards Jasper. "Are you finding anything?"

He shook his head. He was studying a small, flat rock which he was moving around to different spots in the lounge. "I'm not seeing any unusual traces of magic. Just levitation, a couple of youth charms, and…" He poked a playful finger at her. "Necromancy."

"There I go again, mucking things up getting my necromancy all over," Ciara murmured. "Ash?"

Ash walked over and held his hands above the counter where Bertram had sat. Spots on the stone sparked and burned below his fingers. "There's little traces of perfume and hand lotion. Nothing else."

Quinn gasped and rushed to his side. "Woah! That is so cool."

Ash shrugged. "I guess. I didn't find anything though." He looked up. "Does this mean he wasn't drugged?"

"That, or it was *very* well hidden," Jasper said. "Same goes for a spell. But there must be something left behind. Even magic leaves a trace."

Quinn sighed in frustration. "Even if there were traces last night, they could be gone by now. What will we do then?"

The others were quiet. No one had an answer. They slowly returned to their searches.

"Try this. It was his." Ciara placed one of the mugs on the counter in front of Ash. He hummed softly, focusing intently on it. Quinn could feel the air heat up a little. There was a snap as the handle sparked, and smoke began to drift upward. Quinn's eyes darted between the other two for a clue of what they should be waiting for.

Then they smelled something. Pungent and foul, it was a little overwhelming. Ciara gagged and turned away. "Valerian," she managed. "That's plenty, Ash." He extinguished whatever substance was on the mug.

"That might be it," Jasper said. "Valerian produces drowsiness. But it's common in skin products and medicine, too. If it was used to drug him, he would need to swallow it. It might mean nothing."

"Is there anything in the cup part?" Quinn asked eagerly.

They held their breath as Ash attempted to burn the small puddle of tea at the bottom of the mug. Nothing happened. Their shoulders slumped in disappointment.

"It was a good idea," Ash said consolingly. He set the mug down and tried to smile at them. But Quinn could see the worry and defeat in his eyes.

"What does it matter?" Quinn said. "It was useless. That stuff's probably just moisturizer. It's not like Bertram was swallowing the–"

They froze. "Wait."

"What?" Ash asked. They barely heard him. Their mind was racing frantically.

"Are we sure this was his mug?" Quinn asked.

"He picked it out himself," Ciara said, tapping the curly red lettering on the side. "He thought a sugar mommy was a type of candy. I wasn't going to correct him."

"If that's right," Quinn said slowly, "then Bertram might as well have been swallowing it."

"What do you mean?" he asked.

"Frogs don't just ingest things through their mouths," Quinn said. Their eagerness was returning. "They do it through their skin too. When Bertram held this handle, it would have gone into his bloodstream."

"Whoa," Ash said, backing away from the mug warily.

"The killer drugged him," Quinn mused, "then dragged him into the freezer so he wouldn't have any wounds for us to analyze." They scratched their head. "What I don't get is how they knew about frog skin but not spider hearts."

"Huh?" Ash said.

"When I saw the way Dr. Lycosidae died, I assumed the killer was someone who didn't know a lot about anatomy. But they knew the best way to poison Bertram without attracting attention."

"It could have been a different killer," Ciara pointed out.

"Or someone who's more familiar with aquatic animals than bugs," Jasper said.

"The source of the valerian product would help us, too," Ciara said. "I'm already going into town this afternoon. I say we do a bit of snooping."

"Ooh! I want to snoop!" Quinn cried.

Bertram wandered in, rubbing ice crystals out of his eyes. "Would someone walk me to my room, please?" he asked politely.

"I've got you," Quinn said. Snooping could wait a little. They would make sure this living miracle made it to his room safely this time.

"Thank you, friend," he said, following them to the elevator.

They stepped inside. Quinn shivered as the numbers on the panel rose towards the third floor. They hadn't visited this floor much since finding Fenris's body. It was the nocturnal floor and so they hadn't met many of the guests here.

"So… it's pretty cool that you can freeze like that," Quinn began. "Did you always know you could do it?"

Bertram shook his head as they stepped out into the hall. "Not until I collapsed in the garden several winters ago. It gave my Teddy such a fright." He went thoughtfully silent. "He can be quite forgetful. Especially when he's upset. If he had arrived before you moved me out of the freezer, well… I'm not sure what would have happened."

Quinn's throat pinched and they swallowed. "Oh. Yeah. It's a good thing we warmed you up. I didn't know if it was gonna work. I mean…" They trailed off. The memory of the guests who had already died was painfully clear.

"It was your idea?" Bertram asked. Quinn nodded mutely. They reached his door and stopped.

He smiled and grasped their hand. His grip was cold and slippery. "Thank you."

Quinn flushed and returned the gesture. "Uh— it was nothing. I just wanted to help. That's all."

"Well, you may have saved my life. You took a chance to help me. I'll always be grateful to you." He smiled again and disappeared into his room.

Quinn took the stairs down two at a time, riding a warm wave of triumph. Bertram was safe. He would have a future full of little moments with his husband like the one he just described. Whether these moments were full of joy or sorrow, he would have them. And Quinn helped it happen. Their silly, obsessive hobby had saved a life.

The energy in the lounge was more relaxed when they returned. Having just a little information made them all feel more prepared to confront the danger looming over them.

"We should check the guests' rooms, too," Jasper was saying to Ciara. "I can do it while you go into town. Ash, will you give me a hand with that?"

He looked up at Quinn as they came in. "After that… I guess we should arrange getting you home, Quinn." There was regret in his voice, but he kept it controlled.

"Actually, I, uh…" Quinn paused, considering whether they really wanted to say the words that almost rushed out.

After what just happened, they didn't feel useless or dangerous anymore. They felt capable. And they felt grateful for the friends whose lives suddenly felt so fragile. They glanced back at Ash and Ciara. She raised an eyebrow at them. He smiled and waved.

They swallowed and turned back towards Jasper. "I think I changed my mind. I want to stay here."

He blinked in surprise. A wide grin spread across his face and he covered it with his fist. "Really? I mean– yeah. Good. Whatever."

Quinn smiled, relieved. "So are chores still canceled?"

"Definitely not." He tossed a sponge at them. "Start with the puddle of frog water in the lobby."

They groaned playfully and walked out.

- 12 -

Something small and pointed bounced off Quinn's head. They caught it and glanced up into the boughs of the trees, where Ciara was leaping along above them. "Hey," they said. "You dropped another tooth."

Ciara jumped to the ground and took the tooth from them, tucked it back into her shoulder bag, and gave them a quick nod of thanks before darting up the closest tree.

She was clumsier with her injured side, but she pretended not to notice the pain as she pushed herself forward. Quinn's requests for her to slow down for her own good had been pointless. They didn't feel like they had a right to order her around, but seeing the lack of care she acted with towards herself was a little alarming. They supposed everyone was more on edge after Bertram's near-miss. Still, it was clear that beneath her casual act was an increasing desperation for answers. They let their gaze drift back towards the ground and tried to think about something else.

"I still don't get why he needs so many," they said. They were walking down the narrow trail towards town, feet rustling rhythmically through damp sycamore leaves.

"Garnet is a very prolific potion master," she reminded them. "And creatures around here need their potions. He goes through vampire teeth like… ah, what do humans go through? Fingernails?"

Another tooth hit their shoulder. "You dropped another one," Quinn said. "I think it's all the jumping. Try walking regular."

"Walking regular is for mortals," she huffed. But she dropped to the ground to walk beside them. Quinn sighed in relief.

The two went quiet. The shuffle of their feet and the calls of distant birds were suddenly audible. Quinn grew nervous in the silence, but Ciara didn't seem to notice. They weren't sure if they were supposed to say anything or not.

There had been a definite shift in the air after they said they wanted to stay, like a breath they were holding since this morning had been released. Jasper tried to act unaffected, but his excitement was obvious, and Ash and Ciara seemed hesitantly glad too. They just hoped their decision wasn't burdening their friends. That feeling was a little too familiar.

"Is it ok that I'm staying?" they asked. "I mean, with the way you and Jasper were talking about shutting down?"

"Oh, I doubt we'll ever shut down with him in charge," Ciara said with a shrug. "Him and his morals and his emotions. He's

198

starting to infect me with them, I suppose."

"What a beautiful way to describe having friends."

"Oh hush."

Quinn smiled, letting out a relieved breath. "If you're such a loner, what are you doing here?"

"I made a promise." She shrugged. "This isn't a bad setup either. Probably my most permanent residence since I died. And one of the most comfortable– second, maybe, after that giant sea crab swallowed me." She grabbed a sapling and swung around it to follow a fork in the path. A couple more teeth fell from her bag. "We didn't plan any of this, of course. Jasper and I never wanted to see this place again after our friend, the previous owner, disappeared. But once Lev had the idea he fell in love with it, bless his heart… and then of course I had to go and steal a child… and, well, here we are."

"Steal a *what?*" Quinn yelped.

Ciara looked at them. "Oh. I figured Ash would have told you. It's his tale to tell, really." She tilted her head, debating whether to shut up.

"Tell me!" they said eagerly.

She smiled, unable to resist a good story. "Fine. We'd all been hearing stories of a researcher in the city doing cruel experiments on magical creatures. We had no idea who it was, until someone came to my bar in an awful mood and began cursing out every enemy she'd ever made. Being the troublemaker that I am, I thought I'd check out the address she gave me. The lab was already ransacked by the time I arrived. Whether it was hatred or greed, I don't know, but no one had looked closely enough to find the hidden door to the back room. That's where I found a whole lot of papers and empty cages, and a frightened little boy."

Quinn was silent with shock. They stared back at Ciara, wide-eyed.

"I suppose those papers could have explained to me what I was seeing. But I never got to read them, because at that moment I became aware of Ash's unique talent for starting fires." She laughed quietly. "He's come a long way controlling that. Singed off half my hair. I'm amazed we got out of there at all. I'm no great lover of children, but my first impulse was to pick him up and run, and so I did. I can still hear the panic in Jasper's voice when I got back!" She pinched her brows together in an imitation of her friend. *"Ciara! You stole a kid?!"* She laughed harder.

Quinn shook their head in amazement. "Whoa. I'm gonna need to have a talk with Ash later."

"You should." Ciara pointed down the hill, towards town. "Just as soon as we finish our business out there."

The path curved towards the creek, where Quinn could see the very top of the abandoned tractor poking out of the water. They frowned at it, wondering how Brooke was doing. After a long stretch the path curved away. The trees thinned before dropping off around the basin of a long, thin lake.

The squat town of Deep Hollow sat on the opposite shore. It wasn't a town so much as a huddle of snow-beaten houses clinging to the sheer slope of the earth. A few fossilized Victorian structures loomed over the rest, with peeling gold lettering marking them out as the town hall or the library. The two approached a narrow brick building with a green awning labeled PHARMACY.

200

Quinn paused in surprise on the porch when Ciara didn't follow them. Instead she veered off towards a large dead tree next to the building. She knelt and knocked on the dry wood.

A small door opened near the bottom and a knobbly tortoise poked his head out. "Ah! Ciara!" he said, adjusting his spectacles to peer at her.

"Good morrow, Garnet," Ciara said. "I have some teeth for you."

The tortoise produced a wicker basket and she poured a startling quantity of teeth into it. "Thank you kindly," Garnet said, passing her a dark glass bottle. "Here is your sunblock."

"Did you make anyone a potion containing valerian recently?" Quinn asked, eagerly bounding up to the tree.

Garnet blinked at them in surprise. Ciara quickly introduced them and Quinn shook the tortoise's scaly front foot.

"Hmm… let me see…" Garnet tapped one claw against his chin in thought. He disappeared into the tree trunk and appeared again with a well-worn ledger. "Oh yes. Quite a common request. I had three last week and another just this morning. An effective sleeping aid."

Quinn's shoulders sagged. "Oh."

They thanked Garnet and he withdrew into his trunk. The two of them turned to face the road.

"Where should we go next– *woah!*" Quinn jumped back with a cry as something large and furry hurtled by. They spun to see Tosk running past them. He leapt onto the roof of the taxidermist's and disappeared without glancing at them..

"Where do you think he came from?" Ciara asked excitedly.

The two glanced at each other and, without a word, took off in the direction Tosk had come.

They raced down the street, looking for a sign of the squirrel. Suddenly Ciara stopped dead, sniffing the air, and led them down a side road to a small half-shuttered building. A greyhound-sized black-footed ferret wearing a waistcoat stood in the doorway, chewing a licorice root.

"Hello Ermie," Ciara greeted him. "Was Tosk here? We just saw him go by."

"He just left," the ferret said. "Was saying he was late for something. In a big hurry."

"Can we talk to you about him?" Quinn asked. Ermie shrugged and waved them inside.

The room was cramped and dim. Any sunlight was blocked by stacks of newspapers ready to go out. Ermie wove deftly between the stacks and dropped himself into a scratched chair behind an old metal desk.

"Coffee? Tea?" he asked. They both shook their heads. He settled into his chair, scratching the black band between his eyes. "So what do you want to know?"

"Where was Tosk going?" Quinn asked. "Did he say?"

Ermie shook his head. "Tosk's pretty protective of his sources. He's always been that way. He's interviewing someone, that's all I know."

"Any clue what the interview was for?" Ciara asked.

Ermine's whiskers twitched as he thought. "There's a few things in that direction. The state park. Seneca Falls… closest town that way, my doctor lives there actually…" He yawned. "There's also… the taxidermist, the hair salon, the pharmacy…" Ermie frowned. "And there's the woods, but that area belongs to the hunters. He wouldn't go out there. Bunch of dangerous creeps."

Quinn and Ciara exchanged a glance. "Can you tell us more about them?" Quinn asked.

"Sure. Come upstairs, I got some beanbags up there." Ermie waved them towards the stairs.

Quinn started to follow him, but Ciara grabbed their elbow. "Psst. Stay here and look around. See if this lot's hiding anything."

Quinn blinked at her in surprise. "Huh? Me?"

"Who else?"

"But what if I get caught?"

"Lie. Say your contact lens fell out and you're looking for it."

"But I'm wearing glasses."

She waved her hands impatiently and disappeared up the stairs after the ferret. Quinn lingered at the bottom, dumbfounded.

What were they supposed to do now? They had seen people spy and sneak around in movies. They supposed it should look something like that. They took a tentative step towards Ermie's desk— and stepped right onto a loose floorboard which croaked loudly in protest. A crash sounded above them as Ciara knocked something over to mask the sound.

Quinn winced. They slowly scooted around the edge of the room towards the biggest stack of newspapers. Grabbing the one on top, they skimmed over the pages.

THE CAYUGA CHATTER was the name of the paper. Articles described upcoming bonfires, tips to care for one's paws during the icy season, and the latest arboreal fashions. Quinn spotted Tosk's name and paused.

Tosk's column had a noticeably darker tone than the others. *The Fenris pack's stranglehold on the central Finger Lakes continues. The apparent death of Peter Fenris caused a brief scramble for power within the pack, but his family headed by his stepbrother Robert Burke won out, wasting no time continuing evictions in Long Oak Forest. Peter's return appears to cement this new status quo. Anyone in need of emergency housing is encouraged to contact the author.*

Quinn shivered sympathetically at the news. It didn't tell them anything new about Tosk, though, so they put it aside. They inched over to the desk and began sorting through the drawers.

Ermie's desk was full of paper clips, crumpled sticky notes, and stained business cards. Quinn picked carefully around the thumbtacks until they found a sheet of paper. It was a doctor's note signed by Dr. Meena Lisham. Meena's neat, looping handwriting described Ermie's treatment for chapped whiskers in blue-purple ink the same shade as her feathers.

Nothing interesting here either. Quinn backed away and glanced around the room. Their eyes landed on another desk in the corner, covered in papers. They eased towards it.

The piles of notes and red-inked drafts were clearly Tosk's. His writing was messy to the point of panic and smudged from using his left hand. Quinn squinted, feeling a bit of visual whiplash at the difference between his writing and Meena's. The notes for his latest article were on top, and below it were outlines and interview transcripts describing recent evictions. The contents of the drawers were mainly the same… except–yes– there was a flimsy false bottom on one. Quinn lifted it eagerly.

204

Below lay a collection of notes and articles detailing Peter Fenris's recent actions. Every move the werewolf made was there, from the guest lists of relatives' birthday parties to his personal credit card statements. Some of these things looked nearly impossible to come by, especially by legal means. There was also a large book at the bottom– Meena's anatomy textbook, with all of its familiar sticky notes and illustrations. If the rest of the stuff in this drawer was any indication, Meena probably hadn't given it to him willingly.

Momentarily forgetting their mission, Quinn flipped through the book, admiring the richly detailed pages. A red sticky note caught their eye and led them to a page near the back. Silhouettes of a human, an insect, and a fish were marked with silver arrows flowing throughout their bodies. The page was titled LIFE ENERGY. They jolted in shock, toppling an open jar of ink with a clatter. Upstairs Ciara coughed loudly.

Before the jar could hit the ground Quinn grabbed it, spilling ink across their body. They would worry about that later. They wiped off their glasses to read the page's text:

Life energy is the oldest form of magic, animating every living being. While this force is poorly understood, it is thought to flow through the body in a manner similar to blood or hemolymph.

Investigation of life energy is HIGHLY UNETHICAL. This includes attempts to identify the location of energy channels, adjustment or modification of an individual's life force, and extraction and/or containment of energy. Opportunities for harm far outweigh any possible benefits.

If a patient is suspected to suffer from an ailment related to their life energy, provide appropriate medical care and do your best to minimize suffering. DO

NOT attempt to manipulate their life force.

In her familiar blue-purple ink, Meena had labeled the human and the insect diagram with a variety of names, each pointing to a specific spot on the model's body. *K Hyde. T Amaretto. J Doe.*

Footsteps approached the stairs. Quinn quickly shoved the book and papers back into their hiding spot and backed away.

Ermie arrived first, his nose twitching at the smell of ink. "Hey. Are you okay over there?"

"Uh… yeah." Quinn scrambled to look natural. They ended up leaning awkwardly to one side. "Sorry about the mess. I just, uh… lost my contact." They winced.

Ermie frowned. "But you're wearing glasses."

"Oh… uh…" Quinn smiled painfully, their mind racing. "Not, uh… not for these eyes. My other ones. In the back. All humans have them."

Ermie looked startled, then shrugged. "What do I know?"

"So," Ciara said eagerly as they walked away from the news office, "your stumbling panic means you've found something big. What is it?"

"Hey," Quinn said. But they told her what they had found.

Ciara pursed her lips. "That's no good. You can do some disturbed things meddling with life energy. Manipulate someone's magic, toy with life and death, or bring things to life which really shouldn't be alive."

Quinn shivered. "So you think Meena is doing something with them?"

"Possibly. Or she has a morbid sense of curiosity. I happen to know someone just like that. Walking right next to me, actually."

Quinn snorted. "Well, you're a bad influence for telling me to snoop around. What's next, car theft?"

"Much too advanced," Ciara said. "You'll get there one day. Car theft's not until after tax fraud and embezzlement."

They started up the hill towards the inn. A warm stir in Quinn's heart surprised them. They were actually excited to return. They could recall the place's jagged shingles and snarling overhangs with a new familiarity. It carried a hesitant promise of home.

Quinn smiled.

Inside, they put in their key to take the elevator to the fourth floor. To their surprise, their room appeared in front of them immediately without the usual hide-and-seek routine. They shrugged and ducked gratefully inside to change out of their ink-stained clothes.

Quinn balled up the stained items and brought them out to take them to the laundry room. In the hallway they turned a corner and nearly ran into Ash, who flinched away from them. "Hey," they said. "Are you okay?"

He shrugged and looked away. Then, like he was changing his mind, he looked back up at them with a frown. "Why did you have me lie to your parents?" he asked quietly.

- 13 -

Quinn's stomach plummeted. They actually stumbled a little.

"Oh– well, uh…" they stammered. Their mind raced, trying to shift focus from everything they had learned in town to what was happening now. How did he know about their lie?

"Jasper just called your parents," Ash continued. "They think you're at some kind of summer camp. I don't get it. Don't you trust us? We wouldn't tell anyone you're here."

Quinn cringed. "I didn't mean to involve you in this," they said. "But I didn't think I could stay any other way. You have no idea, that camp is horrible. It would be–" They stopped themself. That wasn't important.

They focused back on Ash. "Uh– it doesn't matter. I should

have been honest with you." They studied their feet. "I'm sorry."

There was a long pause. Quinn's face flushed as they waited for him to speak. The silence stretched on. Being yelled at would be better than this.

"When you were on the phone with them, and you passed it to me," he said eventually, "you were making me help you lie. Weren't you?"

Quinn's face burned. "I guess so."

"Why?"

"I– I didn't mean it that way," Quinn stammered. "I wasn't really thinking."

"Well, I wish you were." He fidgeted. "That– that really hurt me."

"The whole thing was a bad idea." Quinn shook their head. "My parents won't be mad at you, though. I think they like you."

Instead of reassuring him, Ash looked sick at the comment. He turned away towards the staff stairs, and they followed him. A murky feeling grew that they had said the wrong thing.

"What?" Quinn said. "They do like you. That part was real."

"Was it?" he cried, swiping at his eyes. "Does it matter? You don't need me to help you lie anymore. Are you done with me?"

Quinn jolted with a horrible realization. The memory of Ciara's story about how she met Ash came rushing back. "Oh no," they said faintly. Then, louder, "no, no, no! Ash! Wait!"

He was already running down the stairs. They struggled to keep up with him.

Of course this hurt him. They should have remembered. Ash had grown up surrounded by people who only cared about him as long as they could use him. Those people had probably lied to him constantly, possibly even convinced him to lie to visitors so that nobody would try to rescue him. Quinn had no idea what he had been through, and they were an idiot to assume his boundaries.

"Wait!" they cried. "Please! I didn't mean it!"

The staircase shuddered with the rapid movement. They both reached the first floor and burst out into the lobby. Quinn grabbed Ash's shoulder. He tried to twist away, but they held firm, at least for a moment.

"I'm sorry," they said. "Seriously. I never meant to use you. Never." They let him go.

He drew back a few steps, but then he paused, examining them. They could see confusion flickering in his eyes. Conflict between fear and hope, both directed at them.

"I'm completely serious," Quinn said. "Tell me how I can make it up to you and I'll do it. Anything."

He looked down at his feet, beginning to turn away, then looked back up at them with unusual intensity. "You want to make it up to me? Find whoever is killing us. Protect our home."

"I…" Quinn's voice cracked. They wanted to say *I can't,* but the words wouldn't come out. It was too much responsibility, they thought. Despite what they said to Jasper, they were just a kid. They couldn't hold the lives of everyone in the inn between the pages of their notebook. If they failed— *when* they failed— it would be catastrophic.

But Ash's gaze didn't waver. A little hope was the least they owed him. "I will," they heard themself saying. They didn't know how. They doubted they even *could.* But they would do everything

210

in their power to try.

Squeezing their ink-soaked clothes between their hands, they turned towards the laundry room. "Just as soon as I put this stuff in the wash," they added lamely.

They opened the door and immediately jerked back with a shout.

Frederick the imp sat on top of the washing machine with its head in its hands. On the floor lay Bertram. His throat had been slashed in one movement, narrow but deep and final. He was most certainly dead this time.

Ash, Jasper, and Ciara came running at their call and stopped cold behind them in the doorway.

Jasper groaned. Ash sniffled quietly. Ciara swore in a few different languages. The group clustered around the body and slowly turned Bertram over, finding no other wounds or impact marks.

Quinn groaned, grabbing their head in both hands. They stumbled past the body and out of the room. Bertram was dead. Their efforts to save him the first time had been pointless. Grief dug into them with cold, cruel fingers, dragging their heart towards the ground. They felt too heavy to move. And so, for several minutes, they didn't. Just the movement of their breath and the feeling of their face resting in their palms was almost too much.

And their grief didn't move either. It continued to weigh on them, and the longer it did, the heavier it got. The reality of these murders wouldn't disappear if they gave up. And their friends were relying on them. They made Ash a promise. He may have felt furious and hurt, but he must still trust them enough to ask that. The least they owed him was a little hope.

They straightened up, steeling their nerves. There was nothing else to do now, nowhere to hide. They had to find whoever did this.

They reentered the laundry room and looked over Bertram's body again, blinking back tears. "This, uh… is different from the earlier attacks," they said.

"Change of plans after the freezer didn't work," Ciara guessed. "Let's check him for an injection wound."

They did. The angry red dot on Bertram's chest matched the one Fenris had. On a closer look, something silver glinted out of the throat wound. Ciara carefully drew out a little sliver of metal. A piece of the murder weapon.

Jasper looked up at the imp. "Frederick, did you see what happened?"

Frederick shook its tiny head. "I was in the machine doing delicates. The frog came in to get his laundry and I went right back in after I gave it to him. Pretty soon I heard the door open again, and I thought he was leaving. But I heard him go, "Hello there! Are you–" The other guy cut him off there. Must've grabbed his throat from the sound he made. I heard a sort of fleshy noise, then he hit the ground, and there was a little shuffling around. By the time I opened my door they were gone."

"Do you smell anything?" Jasper asked Ciara.

"Cologne," she said with a grimace. "The same scent as in Fenris's room and the basement. But I didn't smell it in the freezer."

With new twin senses of dread and resolve, Quinn took several notes on the scene. They helped the others wrap the body in a freshly washed sheet and carry Bertram back to the freezer where they had found him that morning.

The group clustered in the lobby, trying to assemble a plan out of thin air. It felt impossible. It was hard to tell what, and who, could have done this. Frederick's description was barely helpful. If only he had *seen* what happened–

Quinn straightened up with a realization. "Hey. We should try Madame Celeste's spell again."

Ash nodded silently. He liked the idea even though he was still sore at them.

"What's this?" Jasper asked.

"We bought a scrying spell at the night market," Quinn said. "It hasn't helped us so far, though."

Jasper rubbed his chin. "I might be able to help with that. Let me see."

Quinn and Ash eagerly led the way up to the common room and assembled the spell. Jasper examined each piece and carved a few notches into the candle, erased and wrote over some symbols, and gave Quinn's glasses a thorough polish.

"You still need to teach me this," Quinn reminded him.

"If you find our killer, kid, I'll teach you whatever you want." He brushed some wax shavings off the table.

"This little modification won't blow us up, will it?" Ciara asked. "I quite like this blouse."

"Have some faith," Jasper said. "When's the last time I blew someone up?" He paused. "Actually, don't answer that." He dusted off his hands and stood up. "Try it now."

Ash lit the candle with a snap of his fingers. The room disappeared.

Quinn gasped. Around them the void shimmered and struggled to reassemble itself. Slowly, atom by atom, the world returned. They were not in the common room anymore but in the third-floor hallway. It was the same angle as Madame Celeste's projection, with the world still half-drowned in shadow but with more color and detail than their last attempts.

Quinn tried to turn, to take a step forward, but found that they couldn't move. They called out to their friends, panic starting to rise.

"I'm here!" Ash called. "I can't move, though. Where are you?"

"What have you done now, Jasper?" Ciara teased.

"We're still in the common room! All I did was modify the spell," Jasper cried. "I'm not Merlin."

"Someone's coming," Quinn hissed. The others fell quiet.

The lamps, now sunken cores of darkness housing dim points of light, outlined Hector's figure as he stepped into the hall. Quinn shifted their gaze to the dark panes of Fenris's door and strained to listen.

"Toby is barely more than a child," the werewolf was saying. "He doesn't understand the weight of his actions." His voice and that of the other person dropped below their hearing.

Hector trudged over the mottled carpet. He lifted a hand to knock, just as before.

"Absolutely not!" Fenris shouted. Hector froze.

Quinn listened closer. There was the murmur of the other person's voice, a soft shuffle, then a loud bang. Hector drew back.

Another bang. He looked anxiously down the hall, unsure what to do.

214

Another, and Hector turned, melted, and flowed down the hall as fast as he could.

Quinn blinked. *What–*

At the end of the hall, the mass reformed, opened the door, and ran down the stairs in the shape of a woman. *Meena.* Quinn groaned.

There was no time to process this, as more banging sounds were joined by Fenris's cries of pain and attempts to argue, then plead, with his attacker. Eventually a heavy, dreadful silence fell.

Quinn shuddered. They heard Ash's breath hitching as he tried not to cry.

"We… need to see into that room," Ciara said haltingly. "The attacker is still inside."

"I'm on it." Jasper audibly fumbled with the tools of the spell, hissing when he burned his finger on the candle. "It'd be a little easier if I could see what I was doing."

"Another stroke of engineering brilliance."

"What's that?" Ash cut in. They all paused to listen.

A footstep in the real hallway outside, steady, deliberate. Then another.

"Impossible," Ciara muttered. "How could–"

The doorknob turned. The spell's projection rippled with movement.

It was hard to tell what happened next. The thud of a small, hard body against keratin must have been Ciara throwing herself against the door, too late to stop the tumble of footsteps from the intruder. A cold, sharp-nailed hand grabbed Quinn's shoulder. They shrieked and twisted but couldn't get free until one of their friends punched blindly at the attacker. The blow must have landed somewhere soft based on the low grunt they choked out. Quinn scrambled away, kicking vaguely in their direction.

The projection shook violently. Someone's elbow connected with Quinn's head. Sounds of fighting surrounded them. They tried to crawl away, collided with a wall, and tried a new direction. The low central table dug into their shoulder. *The spell!* Quinn swept their arms across it, trying to dismantle it. Someone landed on top of them. They smelled their hair burning as the candle fell, then went out.

The world went black.

Downstairs, guests cried out in shock and confusion. Quinn felt someone run past them and grabbed blindly. Their fingers snared in soft, lightweight fabric. The figure tore out of their grasp and ran away, leaving them clutching a scrap which they shoved in their pocket before trying to follow. The doorframe intercepted with a painful *crack*.

After a lot of shouting and bumping into furniture, the four located each other.

"Could anyone tell who that was?" Ciara asked.

Ash's hair rustled softly as he shook his head, then seemed to remember they couldn't see him. "Nope."

"Someone who knows how to throw a punch," Jasper groaned.

"I ripped off a piece of their clothes when I tried to grab them," Quinn said. "It'll be more useful when we can see it, I guess."

"How did this happen?" Ciara asked.

"This scrying spell uses shadows," Jasper said. "Something must have gone wrong in the fight. It doesn't look like our visitor

216

did it on purpose, but it sure helped them out."

"That was scary," Quinn said. "The next murder could have been one of us."

"It's a good thing we were together," Jasper agreed. "As long as we're all safe, we–"

A scream on the floor below cut him off.

Ciara's rapid footsteps bolted out the door. Jasper grabbed her, Ash grabbed him, and Quinn grabbed Ash, and the four of them went stumbling and shouting into the hall.

"We can't separate!" Jasper scolded.

"Faster, then!" Ciara cried. She pulled them towards the staff staircase, where they slipped and tumbled over each other to the third floor.

The air here stank of sulfur. Two nearby voices were shuddering and whispering to each other.

"Everyone okay down here?" Jasper called, disentangling himself from the others.

"Someone tried to break into our room," said a voice high above Quinn's head. "They're gone now. I shot my quills at them."

"And I sprayed them," said another voice by their feet. "Picked the wrong couple to mess with."

"Which way did they go?" Ciara asked.

The two paused. "Uh– to the right, I think," said the tall voice.

"I thought they went left," said the small voice.

Around the corner, behind them, came another scream. The four ran towards it.

"What happened?" Ciara cried.

"There's a quill in my eye!" wailed a high, wavering voice.

"And one in my knee!" growled another voice behind the first. "Er… or there was. I'm bleeding everywhere! Where's the freak who did this? I'll show 'em…" The speaker pounded the wall in frustration.

"You!" a new voice shrieked. A grunt and a thump as one large body tackled another. "Taking advantage of the dark to break an innocent kid's nose? You should be ashamed of– aagh!"

"Hey," Quinn said anxiously, "Wait! Don't fight– There's someone–"

Another scream.

They didn't all stay together this time as they ran, with Ciara and Jasper in the lead and Quinn and Ash scrambling to follow their footfalls. But they arrived together to the snap of electricity and the smell of ozone.

Someone was using magic. A current of furious heat rushed past Quinn's ear. *Violent* magic.

They ran through the halls, too late each time as the intruder stoked up more terror and chaos. Magic crackled, puffed, and zinged through space. The air smelled of lilacs and fish and mint and citrus and decay. Guests screamed at each other, some in human speech and some in animal chatter and some in an ancient-tasting language which lingered just a little too long on the eardrum.

Quinn became dimly aware that Jasper and Ciara were no longer with them– and then brightly aware that they were falling down another set of stairs. Ash pulled them to their feet, saying something they couldn't understand, and they sneezed up a cluster of warm bubbles. The sensation made them laugh, and then someone punched them in the stomach, and they laughed harder. Ash tugged them in some direction or other, and like plunging into cold water their giddiness disappeared. They shook themself, brushed snow out of their hair, and gripped Ash's hand tighter.

They smacked into a wall– but that couldn't be right, they were tracing the wall with their free hand– and ran around it. A deafening sound, a great sycamore snapping like celery, and they ran into another wall. And they both knew what was happening.

"The house!" Ash gasped.

"It's… breaking." Quinn groaned. The floors groaned with them.

The inn was having some kind of reaction. To the intruder, or to all the magic, or to something else, they didn't know. But a fierce hot wind knocked them to the carpet, and Quinn knew they didn't have time to find out.

A crack opened up in the floor, tossing them to the side just as frantic hooves pounded over the spot where they had just been. Quinn reached out blindly and ended up with a fistful of Ash's hair. Hauling each other to their feet, the two kept running.

Noises of shouting and scuffling led them around a corner. A cry accompanied the wet slice of a stab, and a body slammed into a wall.

"Hey! We can't fight now!" Quinn cried. "We need to get out. The house is–"

"Help!" one of the figures screamed, "Help me!"

Quinn's blood ran cold. The other person paused, letting the first slump heavily to the floor. Running footsteps, then impact as they slammed into Quinn.

Quinn fought to catch their breath, waiting for the attack, but none came. The runner was aiming for the stairs behind them and hit them by mistake. The runner scrambled out of reach, dropping something with a small metallic *ding* in their wake.

"Are you okay?" Ash asked the voice who had screamed.

"I'm bleeding," they groaned. "That sicko stabbed me in the chest."

"We'll get you to a doctor," Quinn promised. "As soon as we can."

"Well, it's not too urgent. They cut into my heart, but I've got a couple spares."

The heavy *whump* of a door told them the other figure had escaped down the staff staircase.

"How–" Quinn murmured.

"No one should have access to that staircase but us," Ash finished their thought. "If someone's not in the system, the house should reject them."

And a second later, it did.

A tremor swept through the house, as if it were sick or very afraid. Then another. Then a long bout of shaking accompanied by a groaning– no, a tearing– no, a *retching* noise which drowned out every other sound. Quinn and Ash fell down, and without enough stability to climb to their feet, began to crawl. Each time a wave of shudders came along, something above their heads or to their side came loose. A chunk of keratin pinned Quinn down and they barely wriggled out in time for another to fall. They thought they heard Ash scream, the noise swallowed by the wooden roar of another quake.

No one was fighting anymore as guests searched for shelter and cast spells to keep the walls together in vain. Panicked legs tripped over Quinn's back and directionless tails swiped their face.

The carpet opened below their knee, quickly followed by the floorboards, and before they could react a huge gap yawned open. The floor on either side splintered and tilted violently. Quinn grasped desperately for Ash as they tumbled down the rapidly sloping carpet.

They fell into a corner and had to scramble right back out as the walls folded in on them. A doorknob dug painfully into Quinn's shoulder. They tried it and the door opened easily.

"A closet!" they cried as bottles and brooms slid out around them. "Ash! Get in here!"

The gap widened with a loud groan. Ash's fingers tore away from their arm as the floor buckled, sending him sliding backward. Quinn gripped the doorframe and screamed his name.

Ash flailed in the dark and caught their outstretched hand. They tried to pull him towards them, but the angle of the floor sharpened and made it harder to hold on.

Quinn grunted with effort as they tried to pull him up. "Come on!"

"Quinn," he said quietly. His feet slipped off the floor with a quiet shuffle.

"We can make it," they said desperately. They were beginning to lose their grip on the doorframe. "I can do this. You–"

"I'll be fine," he interrupted. "Just like always. But you need to take shelter." He raised his voice above the crackling of the ceiling. "Right now!"

"No!" Quinn cried. "I won't let you fall."

"It's okay." Ash's voice was oddly calm. "Then I will."

They heard him brace his feet against something. Then they were thrown backwards as he shoved them into the closet. The sound of him tumbling into the gap was quickly swallowed by the chaos.

Quinn grasped the door, choking in horror. He was gone. Everyone was gone. They were alone.

The walls continued to crumple with a thunderous shriek. Quinn slammed the door and retreated into the closet, which was splintering but held steadier than the hallways.

They didn't know how much time passed after that. They lay curled in the firmest corner of the closet, not daring to imagine what was happening to their friends, not daring to think about anything else. Without sight their mind was free to fill the space with looming disasters and unseen attackers.

Eventually their tear-stained face lifted at the sound of a mourning dove's gentle *coo*. If they could hear that, the walls must not be tearing apart anymore. They listened and realized it was true.

The quaking was over too. They slowly uncurled their body and stood up. They still couldn't see. Was this permanent?

They found the handle and pulled the door open. Quinn gasped as light flooded over them. The spell was broken. Their vision was back.

They leaned out, eagerly glancing around. Abruptly their stomach dropped. Their throat pinched.

Yes, they could see again. Every detail of the inn had returned before their eyes.

And it was in desolation.

- 14 -

The first thing they saw, of course, was the huge gash in the floor. Exposed boards poked up into the air on either side and torn shreds of carpet trembled in the breeze.

The breeze? Quinn looked up. The outer wall had peeled apart from the ceiling, allowing light and cold air to pour in. So the sun was still up.

Overwhelmed, they slowly sat on the edge of the hole and let their feet dangle into darkness. Their brain felt like a shaken can of soda. The inn was still standing, but it was transformed. Everything in sight was torn or shattered. Even if their friends were okay, even if the place could be fixed, it would never be the same.

They let that thought sink in for as long as they could stand it. Then they did the only other thing they could think to do.

They called their parents.

Quinn's mom picked up right away. They could hear her calling their dad over and fussing with the speakerphone.

"Um… hi," they said quietly. Their mind went blank. They had no idea why they were doing this.

"Is everything okay, honey?" their mom asked anxiously.

Quinn let out a shaky breath. "No. I… I messed up. I really messed up."

"It will be alright," their dad said definitively. "We're not happy that you lied to us. Something bad could have happened to you out there."

"I know," they whispered. They watched water bleed out of a burst pipe on the wall.

"But," Quinn's mom added quickly. "We're happy you're safe. We just want to know why this happened." Her voice got a little softer. "Why did it happen?"

They wished they had an answer. All of it– being sent away from home, the small disasters they had caused each day, and now this collapse– felt like reminders of their deep and persistent *wrong*ness. Their parents, this inn, magic itself all recoiled from them.

"Nothing," Quinn heard themself saying. "I just don't belong where you wanted me to go. Maybe I don't belong here either. Or anywhere."

"That's not true," their mom reminded them. "You'll always belong with us. What's happening over there?"

"They're mad at me. They should be, I guess. But now… now we're all in trouble. Everything is all wrong."

"Then you make it right," their dad said.

"How?"

"You'll know how. Quinn, you may be strange, but you have a good heart."

"... thank... you?"

"When you see what someone needs, you give it to them. Let them take their time to forgive you and don't push it. And when things are right again, you'll know."

Quinn frowned, turning that over in their mind. "Okay."

Someone cried out in pain down the hall. Quinn stumbled to their feet. "I think I should go. Like you said. I have to make things right."

"Alright, honey. Good luck."

"Call us again soon," their mom said.

"Thanks. Bye."

Quinn began walking. They felt a new energy but a strange new weight in their heart too. They passed by more and more destruction. Sobs trembled up from their abdomen and threatened to choke them. They wiped the tears away and kept walking.

Quinn followed a soft groaning sound down a side hallway to where a pair of antlers poked out below a slab of fallen keratin. They pushed against the slab until it rolled over. The big orange slug below rippled its body out of the way, gratefully bowing its antlered head towards them. They lifted a nearby door off the floor to free a family of stag beetles and pulled a troll out of a newly created pocket in the floor. The hall slowly came to life with cautious movements as they walked.

Turning a corner, Quinn jumped back to avoid stepping on someone who lay on the floor. They knelt to look. It was Fenris.

226

He was motionless, glassy eyes staring forward. He had no pulse and he wasn't breathing. Quinn's stomach dropped. They frantically checked him for stab wounds, or puncture wounds, or *anything*, all in vain. His body was untouched.

They sat back on their heels, confused. He was curled inwards in pain, one hand clutching at his chest. His heart had given out.

It made horrible sense, they supposed. Ever since Fenris returned he seemed unwell. This may not have been a straightforward murder. But whoever had caused this disaster had killed him nonetheless.

After covering Fenris with a torn rag of carpet, Quinn continued on. They hadn't been here long enough to know the inn's rhythms, but they thought they could feel the pain simmering through its structure. Tremors and groaning noises echoed up from below the earth. Exposed rafters hunched inward like self-protective shoulders around a broken heart. Quinn wished they could speak to the inn, apologize to it somehow. They paused to place a hand on the exposed keratin where some wallpaper had peeled away. They lingered there, uncertain, and finally gave the wall a little pat.

Hearing a familiar grunt, they ran down a side hallway to where the walls clamped together like stubborn jaws. Jasper was there, heaving the walls apart with his hands. He groaned, muscles straining and tattoos shining, and finally the walls split. Four ocelots spilled out of the newly freed door and gratefully nuzzled his ankles.

Quinn shouted happily and ran towards him, grabbing him in a hug which nearly knocked him over. The familiar smell of wood shavings on his shirt was strong and comforting. Surprised, he laughed and laid a heavy hand on their back.

"Man, am I glad to see you," he said. "Not in these circumstances, but… still. I bet you're regretting coming out here now."

"No," Quinn said honestly. "I regret lying to you, yeah. But this is where I want to be. Even now."

He smiled a little. And then a little more. Blinking away tears, he pulled them back into the hug. As he pulled away, he said, "We're not done talking about that. We'll make a long list of nasty chores for you to atone. I'm sure Ciara wants some help with that week-old sky buffalo carcass."

Quinn winced. "Where are the others, anyway?"

"I lost Ciara when a stray spell knocked us in different directions," he said. "She's probably running around somewhere feeling furious at herself for letting that creep get away. I can't say I feel any different. And last time I saw– uh, *heard*– Ash, he was with you." He cocked his head to the side, looking at them. "You don't know where he is?"

Quinn's stomach burned with guilt, remembering the way they had separated. "No," they admitted. "The floor cracked open and he fell. He, uh…" They swallowed. "He pushed me into a closet before he fell. He protected me."

Jasper sighed, smiling sadly. "That kid really needs to remember he's still a kid."

He ran a hand over his hair. "He must be around here somewhere. A lot of guests are trapped or missing too. We'll find him. If we just keep moving." He said the last sentence more to himself, an aching murmur.

228

Quinn nodded and walked beside him down the hall. They watched him out of the corner of their eye and saw his shoulders sagging, just a little. He held his head up with visible effort.

They stopped to pry open a door which had buckled inwards on itself. A grizzled old gnome was wedged under the fallen wardrobe inside. They helped him out and he shook both their hands before hobbling away.

They continued that way for a little while. Quinn didn't know if they were imagining it, but each time they moved on after helping someone, Jasper seemed to slow down a little more. Eventually they had to try not to outpace him.

"Are, uh…" Quinn asked awkwardly. "Are you okay?"

He grimaced. "Don't worry about me, Quinn."

"So you're not?" they pressed.

He paused, then shook his head. He gestured at the wreckage surrounding them. "I can't be okay. Not with this place gone." He started walking again.

Quinn hurried to catch up. "Wait! What do you mean?" The inn wasn't gone. They were standing right inside it.

"I knew I couldn't run this place on my own," he said, trying to muster a playful tone and failing. "I just thought I would have blown it up or something. You know?"

He stopped in front of the elevator. It gaped open, edges ragged, car nowhere in sight. Several guests who couldn't use the stairs clustered sorrowfully around it. Jasper poked his head in to look down the empty shaft and groaned.

Quinn fumbled for something comforting to say. "We… we can fix it," they said eventually. "Right?"

He leaned back against the wall. "I don't know," he said softly. "I don't know."

Alarm rose in Quinn's stomach. "Hey," they said uneasily, "let's keep moving."

He looked at them and didn't say anything. They took his hand and the two started walking again, even slower than before.

They reached an intersection between hallways, where a chandelier similar to the one in the lobby had once hung. It now lay shattered on the floor, shards of red and gold crystal flung outwards in a gruesome ring. Jasper froze in front of it and covered his face with his hands.

"What?" Quinn asked. "What's wrong?"

"This was his," Jasper said quietly. His voice was hoarse. "All of the decorations and little details. Lev chose them all."

"Oh gosh. Sorry."

He sank to his knees, then to the floor with a thud. Quinn stood behind him, feeling powerless to help.

"Um… hey," they said. "I think we should keep moving. It won't be so bad once we clean up."

Jasper stayed right where he was.

"You know," they said, talking faster, "we could get the guests to help, and…"

"What's the point?" Jasper murmured. "It's gone. All gone."

"Uh… I, uh…" Quinn stammered.

"Go find Ash," he said. "I can't help you. I can't help anyone." His face was still in his hands.

Quinn stood, staring at the back of his head, for a few long moments. Eventually they swallowed, nodded, and turned away.

They found the staff staircase and stumbled down. There wasn't as much damage in here. For the first time, the stairwell didn't rattle or retch as they passed through.

The lobby was empty. The chandelier had fallen here too, crushing the front desk, and the sofas were overturned. No one was in the lounge either, where the wall of bottles had toppled to spread a sea of broken glass over the floor. Quinn hesitated nervously for a moment before descending to the basement.

Jasper's workspace didn't look so different from its usual state of disorganization. The supply shelf lay on its side, a suspicious green liquid leaking out around it. They could deal with that later. Quinn took a deep breath and pushed through the moisture-swollen door at the back.

The inn's great stomach sat deceptively still, a rhythmic hum coming from deep underground. Quinn slowly approached, gazing up at it, and reached out to lay a hand against its side.

They immediately jolted back, blinking away tears. Raw pain and fear roared through the wooden organ, a wounded ferocity which only a wild animal could know. Quinn's arm tingled like it was full of angry bees.

They sighed. "I'm sorry," they whispered.

"Quinn?"

They startled and looked around. They couldn't see anyone. Was the house speaking to them?

"I'm back here. I'm stuck."

Quinn knew that voice. They cautiously squeezed around the side of the stomach. Ash was wedged high up against the wall there, below a jagged tear in the ceiling which had snagged a few shreds of his tee shirt. The side of his body pressed against the stomach was reddened from pressure and heat.

"Ash!" Quinn gasped. They wriggled closer to him. "Whoa. Are you hurt?"

He smiled weakly. "I'm fine." He tried to lift one arm to wave at them but found it pinned in place.

Quinn frowned. He certainly didn't seem fine. "Are you sure?"

"Yeah." He squirmed. "Of course. I'm hard to injure, remember?"

"I guess." Quinn didn't feel good about that answer, but they decided to drop it. "How do I get you out of there?"

"I don't know. The stomach was contracting when I fell. When it expanded again I got stuck."

Quinn glanced around, assessing their options. Apart from a few brushes, shovels, and a bucket with some cleaning supplies and antacids, the stomach was the only thing occupying the dim, cramped room. They braced their back against the wall and swung one foot, then the other, against the stomach. They had climbed countless trees before. This wasn't so different. One more ancient, living surface which they were just borrowing space on for a moment. They could do this.

They shimmied up to Ash's level and met his eyes. His glinted tangerine with hope and anxiety. Quinn hoped their own didn't betray how afraid they were.

They took a deep breath. "Okay. Don't worry," they told him. "I'll get you down."

They kicked at the stomach a few times, then threw their weight against it. The organ didn't move at all.

They began climbing down. Ash grabbed their hand frantically. "Don't go," he said.

"I'm not going anywhere," they promised. They gave his hand a squeeze before pulling away and descending.

They tried a few more things without success: tickling the stomach's side, wedging the shovel against it, pounding the base with frustrated fists. They leaned against the wall with a defeated sigh.

"Any other ideas?" they asked.

Ash didn't answer. They heard his breath start to tremble.

"Hey." They looked up at him. "We'll figure this out. I'm not leaving without you."

He squirmed. "I don't know. Maybe you should. You might get hurt if you stay."

"No," Quinn said flatly.

"I can get myself out," he said uncertainly.

"You don't need to," Quinn insisted. "Ash. Let me help you. Please."

"I'm okay. Really," he repeated. His voice was strained.

Quinn groaned internally. "Fine." They stared stubbornly up at him. "Get yourself out, then. I'll wait."

They watched him struggle for a few minutes to no result. Eventually he slowed, flushed and panting, and looked down at them with embarrassment.

"So?" Quinn asked.

"I… I might not be okay," Ash murmured.

"Yeah," Quinn said, softening a little. "It's alright, though. I'm here with you."

He nodded.

Quinn turned back to the stomach, thinking. The last time it had moved was during the fight, once their attacker had fled down the staff stairs. This reaction was the reason Jasper had needed to add Quinn into the "system" with a strand of their hair… for all the good that had done. The stairs still recoiled every time they were inside. Quinn perked up with a realization.

If they had set off the house's gag reflex before, they realized, they could do it again.

Ash's voice rose in protest as they heaved the stomach's hatch open. Intense heat immediately washed over them. Quinn grabbed the shovel from the corner, threw Ash what they hoped was a reassuring smile, and leaned into the stomach.

Quinn glanced around in the dim glow of distant blue fire. Ash's pleas not to go any further grew muffled. They shifted the shovel in their hand and experimentally clanged it against an inner wall.

Nothing happened. They frowned. Did they need to climb inside? Just entering the stairwell had set it off before. That nagging feeling from earlier came back, but they couldn't spare it any attention.

They hitched one knee up on the hatch to push more of their body inside. The sizzle of denim didn't come fast enough to warn them away, and hot pain soon shot through their knee. They jerked back and stumbled away from the stomach, dropping the shovel.

Ash sighed in relief when he saw them alive. "Don't do that again!"

"I'm being careful," they said defensively, if not truthfully. Their knee stung. "Relax. I'm helping you, aren't I?"

"It doesn't feel like it," he muttered.

234

"What does that mean?"

"You're gonna burn up in there. Watching you get hurt doesn't feel like help to me."

Quinn paused. "Fine. I won't go back in." They kicked at a shard of charred bone on the ground. "Why does it bother you so much?"

Ash squirmed. "It's scary to see you in danger. I'm still kind of mad at you, but… it doesn't matter, right? We're in this together. I can't help it." He sighed. "And maybe it's dumb, but I still want to be friends."

Quinn blinked back tears as something hopeful and vulnerable stirred in their heart. "That's not dumb. I… I still want to be friends too. I mean, I hope we're friends. Are we friends?"

That got a smile from him. "Yeah. I think so," he said.

They nodded. "Good."

They looked around in vain for more options. Ash squirmed uncomfortably against the stomach. This was getting urgent. If they couldn't free him, they didn't know who to call for help. Jasper was shut down with grief and Ciara was gone. It was up to them.

As they moved, they felt something poke up from their pocket to brush their belly. Quinn pulled it out. It was Brooke's moss-green hair ribbon, still in their pocket after all this time.

Quinn beamed at it in amazement. Then, without a moment's hesitation, they flung it into the stomach.

Blue fire roared up inside. The stomach groaned at the intruding sensation, its walls trembling and finally contracting once, twice, three times. Ash dislodged and fell to the floor. Quinn rushed to pull him out of the way before the giant organ expanded again. The two backed away and watched as the stomach heaved and thrashed in the cramped space.

Eventually its movements began to slow. The expansions and contractions began to resemble steady breathing, then ground to a stop. The stomach lay still as if nothing at all had happened.

Ash leaned heavily on Quinn's shoulders as they climbed up to the lobby. He was hurt worse than they had thought. His entire left side was bruised and one leg, though seemingly not broken, was weak and numb from the crushing. The fall had opened a small cut on his palm.

"Stay here," Quinn said as they helped him to a sofa. "I'll find you some help. Maybe Meena's still around."

If we can even trust her, their tired mind added. *If she's not the one who caused all this.*

With Ash safely settled, Quinn eyed the front door nervously. There was only one place where they hadn't been since the fight, one place where their remaining friend could be.

The woods.

A stiff breeze bit into Quinn's exposed knee as they stepped outside. Maple and sycamore leaves didn't crunch underfoot but lay limp and soggy with leftover rainwater. The angle of the sun was low and sharp.

Quinn wrapped their arms around their torso and shivered as they walked down the hill. Maybe this was silly. The woods were massive. They couldn't possibly find–

Something rushed by, missing them by a hair. Quinn's feet left the ground as they were pulled upwards by the collar.

236

Ciara's frantic green eyes bored into them, pupils drawn painfully tight. She looked Quinn over, sighed in dismay, and dropped them. The breath rushed out of them as they hit the ground.

"You ought to be careful," Ciara said, jumping from the tree branch above to land silently on her feet. "You're spilling rogue smells everywhere. I thought you might be our intruder."

Quinn looked up at her. She was shifting restlessly from foot to foot, clothes streaked with dirt, hair tangled with leaves and twigs. Her face and neck were an angry, peeling red.

"What happened to you?" Quinn asked, climbing to their feet. "You look awful."

Ciara tucked a few strands of hair into place and scowled. "I look perfect."

"The sun is chewing you up. How long have you been out here?"

She folded her arms, shifting her gaze into the distance. "It won't be up much longer," she murmured. "I need no light to find the bastard, anyway." She sniffed the air and grimaced when she didn't find anything.

"You're looking for the killer?" Quinn asked. She nodded. "It's been too long," they continued. "They're gone by now."

Ciara shook her head, turning away. "No. Not too late. Can't be too late." She froze, head cocking to the side at some sound Quinn couldn't hear, then took off in a blur of motion.

Quinn yelped and tried to run after her, but soon found themself lost among the trees. They gulped down a quick breath and tried not to panic. Where was the inn? It must be up the hill... but where was the hill? Their knee throbbed in protest at all the motion.

Ciara ran by again, colliding with them from behind. She grabbed their shoulders and righted them before they could fall. She was about to start running again when she saw their knee. "You should wrap that up," she said. "It smells delicious, a fact which is rather nauseating."

"Can you come inside?" Quinn asked. "Things are bad at the inn. Everyone is scared. Ash is hurt. Jasper is…" They didn't know how to end that sentence. "You should go talk to him."

"They've got reason enough to be scared, as I see it," Ciara said. "None of them would be in this situation if I had found that idiot by now."

"Don't–" Quinn began. She was already running.

Alone again, Quinn groaned and kicked a pebble off the trail. They trudged in a randomly chosen direction until their knee strung enough to make them stop.

"You're just making things worse," they complained to the empty air. "This isn't helping. You're just hiding away."

Only the cold breeze answered. Quinn sighed.

"And what would you expect?" Ciara's voice came from a tree to their left. She was perched on a branch, eyeing the ground like it was unsafe. "It's horrible enough in there. No one's asking a bloodsucker to come in and make things worse."

"What are you talking about?" Quinn asked, squinting up at her.

"Pursuing this villain is bringing out the predator in me," she spat. "Before you say, Ciara, you Byronic twat, stop brooding and come down from that tree, let me tell you I've been around long enough to know. I lose a little more control every time I chase a figure in the dark. Every time I get protective, and then angry, and then ravenous. Every time…" She frowned.

"Every time you get attached?" Quinn finished. They edged closer to the tree.

"Something like that." Ciara sat back against the tree in a show of feigned ease.

"Well… getting attached to people isn't so bad," Quinn said. "I mean, it was scary for me. I understand."

"That's where it all starts," Ciara mused. "Nothing to hurt until you attach. Nothing to disappoint or betray or destroy. I brought it on myself." She shrugged.

Quinn wasn't sure what to say. At least she was staying in place for now. "I don't think your friends see it that way. Ash likes you a lot. And Jasper could really use your help right now."

"They might think so," Ciara said quietly. "Right now they need to heal. Having a monster around will only make things worse."

Quinn stared up at her in shock for a moment. Then, unable to restrain **themself**, they burst out laughing.

Ciara peered at them curiously. "Alright, then mock my pain," she teased, but she seemed unsure how to react.

Quinn's laughter slowed enough for them to speak. "A monster? Seriously?" Then they laughed some more.

"Well… what would you call me?" Ciara asked defensively.

"Dude… we live in an inn full of all sorts of magical creatures. No one can be a monster here."

Ciara set her jaw, thinking. After a long moment she leapt smoothly down from the tree. "Let's go, then."

Quinn blinked at her in surprise. "Huh? Wha–"

"To the inn. That's what you wanted, yes? Can you walk on that knee?" Without waiting for an answer, she scooped Quinn up and tossed them over her shoulder. The movement was made awkward by Quinn being larger than she was, and their hair dragged on the ground as she ran.

"Why–" Quinn choked. "What is happening–"

"If you must know…" Ciara's voice didn't even tremble with the exertion. "You benefit from an uncanny appearance to someone I'm already attached to. Not just physically, but you got lucky by reciting his "no one can be a monster here" bit. Something he said to me long ago in a situation not so dissimilar from this one. As I said, I brought it on myself. I expect it will destroy me someday. But not today, I think."

Lev. Quinn knew enough to stay silent about that. Not that they could speak right now anyway.

Trees and matted leaves blurred by until Ciara stopped to deposit them at the back door of the inn. "Where is Jasper?" she asked as they entered.

"Somewhere on the second floor," Quinn wheezed. "He's shut down. He thinks everything is over."

"A common, if idiotic, fallacy for someone not half a century old," she said. "I'll knock him into shape. Ash, don't pick at that." She pulled a handkerchief from her pocket and quickly wrapped up Ash's cut hand. "I'll sew it up if we can't get a doctor. Suppose Meena's too clever not to run. Pity." She disappeared up the stairs.

Quinn dropped onto the sofa beside Ash with a sigh. They were exhausted and aching but their mind raced. Ciara was probably right– Meena was smart enough to flee, and they hadn't seen Delta or Tosk either. Fenris had looked like he was on his way out too. This disaster was the perfect opportunity to get out and cover your tracks.

But whose tracks needed covering? The answer to the whole thing felt so frustratingly close, yet almost impossible to reach. Quinn pulled out their notebook and flipped restlessly through the pages. Lines of gore and fear and confusion flew by without any apparent solution. There had to be some meaning to all this, some missing piece to join it all together. A werewolf, a spider, and a frog– did that count as three murders or five? – and a shady doctor, a paranoid journalist, and a protective mother. All seemed to have something to hide. But what–

Quinn froze. Their eyes locked on the page they had just skimmed, from the morning of Dr. Lycosidae's death. The crime which had put Fenris's nephew in prison. *Desecration of a corpse.*

Quinn covered their eyes and groaned. It was all falling horribly into place. Vivid, grisly, and too well-connected to be false.

Ash startled at the noise. He had been dozing off in exhaustion but now gazed at them curiously. "What's wrong?"

"I have it," Quinn said weakly. "Not all of it, not yet. But I know why these deaths have been happening. And more. Many more than we know."

He rubbed his eyes. "Huh?"

"Are you two alright?" Jasper stood in the doorway. His eyes were ringed with red but he was upright. Ciara was behind him. Quinn and Ash nodded. "Good. You should both rest. Quinn, I'll make you a salve for that knee." He ducked down to the basement and came back with some packets of herbs and a metal bowl, which he hung over the fire.

While he worked Quinn continued. "Fenris's nephew is at the center of all this. He was arguing with someone about Alex right before he died. And I saw him on the bus coming here. He was picking Alex up from prison."

Ciara perched on the armrest beside them. "Are you certain it was him? Why would the most powerful man in town be taking the bus?"

"Exactly because he's so powerful," Quinn said. "He didn't want anyone recognizing his car. He needed to keep his nephew's business a secret." They stood up and began pacing in excitement. Their knee twinged with each step. They didn't care. "And what business was that? Tosk told us. Desecration of corpses. He worked at the medical center where patients arrived mysteriously dead. Alex might have caused their deaths, or maybe he just allowed them to happen and didn't help. Then he took the bodies when no one was looking."

Their friends stared at them in shock and horror. "That… can't be right," Ash said shakily.

"It happened to Hector's brother," Quinn said. "He knows it. That's why he confronted Fenris."

"But why?" Jasper asked. "Why would anyone do this?"

Quinn swallowed. They weren't as sure about this part. "To harvest something valuable. To give it to others. You were wrong, Jasper. Zombies exist. At least, they do now."

Ciara laughed softly, folding her arms. "So I have undead company? I have to hear this."

"Bertram told us about an injury he had at Fenris's worksite and showed us his symptoms of lost coordination and sensation. Meena has been seeing patients with those symptoms for months." Quinn flipped to their notes from that day and showed them. "I think Bertram and all those other patients weren't just injured. I think they died."

"But that's almost impossible," Jasper said. "No one's ever successfully revived a dead body. At least, not without turning it into a vampire or some other creature."

"It's possible," Quinn said. "Bertram and the others had major changes in their behaviors and preferences, even allergies. Like they came from someone else. Like they're animated with someone else's life energy."

"You mean…" Ash's voice trembled. "Those deaths at the hospital…"

"Yes," Quinn said. "At least, until Alex was arrested. Then his partner– whoever helped him do this– had to find a new source. I bet his partner is the one doing the operations, since they continued while he was in prison."

"Hold on," Ciara said. "This entire process you're proposing relies on fresh life energy from victims. One life for another. What's the point of going to all that trouble?"

"It's not just for themselves. They're performing a service," Quinn said. "For the most vulnerable customers in the world. Customers who would give anything to have their loved one back, who will always keep the secret out of shame or fear. Partners, friends, parents…"

Jasper's quiet hiss of realization told them he was catching on. "Delta," he said softly. "Brooke was in that accident…"

Quinn nodded eagerly. "She's so sleepy and hardly speaks. She doesn't like the same food anymore. And Delta is terrified of her community seeing Brooke and knowing something is wrong."

A grave silence settled heavily over the group. Quinn cleared their throat. "Um— yeah. So that's what I think. Alex's partner killed Fenris, probably during a dispute over his role now that he's free. Then they killed Dr. Lycosidae and Bertram to silence them and to steal their life energy."

Another stunned pause. Eventually Ciara said. "That's all well and good. But who is it?"

Quinn looked at each of their friends. "Someone willing to kill to take advantage of grieving families. Someone who lied easily to our faces this whole time." They pulled out the scrap of fabric which they had torn from the attacker and held it up.

"It's—"

- 15 -

Ryan strode down the hill, dusting some more of that brown crud off his shirt. He didn't understand what had just happened in the inn, but he was delighted with the results. He couldn't have asked for a cleaner escape. Well, maybe he could, if he had succeeded at getting rid of the nosy kid. But he knew he had to look forward, not back. Keeping a positive mindset was crucial to the success of his energy supplement company.

Fenris would understand if he had the perspective. It was just business. Ryan didn't want to kill him right away. He wanted to give him a chance. But then he started talking about pulling A-dog– or as Fenris called him, Alex– out of the partnership. They couldn't lose such a valuable asset so soon. And so Fenris had to go, and Ryan had to improvise. Simple.

What he really did to the werewolf was a favor, anyway. Fenris should have seen that. As a businessman, he knew the value of image. Pulling A-dog out would have led to a scandal one way or another. With him out of the picture, and Alex quietly back where he belonged in acquisitions, the Fenris family could continue to enjoy a relatively clean image. It took ambition to see that, and foresight. Willingness to sacrifice short-term comfort for long-term goals. Like when that stupid spider broke his nose, and he covered it up by pretending Quinn hit him with the door. Success instinct. You either have it, Ryan supposed, or you don't.

He sighed, wishing he had taken his headphones with him. The walk to town was long and he could have spent the time finishing that audiobook on amateur phlebotomy. He couldn't go back, though. The kid was close to figuring him out, or maybe they already had. And now that he had A-dog back and Fenris gone, there was no point in keeping up the lie that his dad wanted to sell the place. He didn't want to step foot in there again anyway. It gave him the creeps.

Sounds of thrashing and panicked chittering drew Ryan's attention. He stopped and looked up. Tosk was tangled in a net trap high in the boughs of a tree. The trap was unfamiliar, nothing like the ones Ryan had stolen from Hector's room. Tosk saw him and called to him in relief. Ryan let out an annoyed sigh, slapped a smile on his face, and waved.

"Hi Tosk!" he shouted. "What are you doing up there?"

The squirrel laughed nervously. "Uh, funny story. There was just a little misunderstanding between me and one of my sources." Anxious for a diversion, he cleared his throat. "How's that nose feeling?"

Ryan winced. He hated being reminded of the damage that stupid spider had done to his face. She had been difficult to kill, but once Burke and his cronies started putting pressure on him to return their leader, he had no choice. "Better," he said. "Do you need a hand with that?"

"Yes please," Tosk said eagerly.

Ryan began to pick at the complex knot tethered to the trunk. He was careful to continue visibly using his right hand. It made him awfully clumsy, but he couldn't afford to be seen using the same hand which dealt the blows on Fenris's body. At least doing this was easier than writing that way- it made his handwriting unreadable.

This knot was clearly made by beast hunters. He wondered what Tosk had done to anger them. And whether it had anything to do with the disheveled state of Fenris's room when he had entered. Fenris was normally a neat and careful man, and Ryan had been surprised but not especially interested to see his papers all in a mess and the windows open. He was glad he hadn't touched anything. Maybe the whole thing would get pinned on Tosk if he was lucky.

The thought reminded him of why he left the inn and why he wasn't coming back. And he realized this didn't matter. He didn't need to be everyone's friend anymore.

Ryan stopped trying to untie the knot. Tosk shouted down to him in confusion as he backed away and began walking on. Eventually the squirrel's cries faded among the wind and birdsong.

On impulse Ryan tapped the two round-bellied syringes in his pocket. Safely capped, always, after an accident last month which left him dizzy and craving raw fish for a week. Waste not, want not. At least this whole inconvenience had provided him with some valuable supplies.

This was the part of production that tended to make people most uncomfortable. He usually left it out of his investor pitches. He rolled his eyes, remembering the way Delta had reacted when she learned where energy supplements came from. She just *had* to walk in right as he was covering his scent with an unsellable cologne, looking for her daughter. Maybe if she had kept a closer eye on the little brat, she wouldn't have died in the first place. Delta had cried, screamed at him, and even thrown up, all while he patiently explained to her that life energy is rare and needs to come from somewhere. She should have been grateful. No one else was doing this procedure. At least, not until he could figure out how to scale production. A reminder of how lucky she was to have her daughter back, and of how easy it might be to lose her again, sent her running.

He thought he would need to do more to keep her in line. But she was committed to the role, so committed that when he ordered her to tear open her face to cover his tracks, her performance made him want to shove his fingers down her gills. She could have used some of that conviction when she poisoned Bertram. Sure, it wasn't her idea, but she could at least show enough enthusiasm to get the job done. She wasn't a very good team player.

He would have preferred to let her take the fall for Bertram's death, but in the end he needed to step in and use the usual method. Ryan had one condition for his clients– *secrecy*– and if the frog was going to start talking to reporters and doctors, then he didn't have to keep up his end either. That's just business.

Finally he reached town. People smiled politely as they passed him on his way to the taxidermist's shop. He frowned back, uncomfortable with the attention. Now that he was done with this small town he'd try convincing his partners to go somewhere a little more anonymous. He could really clean up in Toronto.

He stepped onto the shop's porch and dug through his pocket for his keys. The glass eyes of the animals displayed out front bored into him. Ted's genuine passion for taxidermy helped their cover, but it also creeped him out. It didn't help that Ted kept rotating the display so he never got used to it. Today there was a wolf, an otter, a muskrat, some kind of huge black bird–

Before Ryan knew what was happening the bird was launching itself at him, star-speckled wings flung wide and talons aimed straight for his face. He screamed and stumbled back. The bird slashed at his face, slicing his cheeks and reopening the cut on his nose. He raised his arms to protect his eyes and his sleeves were quickly shredded. He found his key and desperately jammed it into the lock as the bird's beak ripped at his back.

The door mercifully opened. Ryan darted inside and swung the metal grate open again to slam into the bird. It fell with a squawk. The thing rolled, twisted, and climbed to its feet in the shape of a woman. Ryan's stomach twisted in disgust. He should have known.

Meena glared at him and reached for the lock, stretching and lengthening her fingers. He knew this trick. He snapped the door out and back in, crushing her fingers in one smooth movement. She roared in pain and threw herself uselessly against the gate.

Ryan regarded her warily from the other side. This was where he would say something about a little bird if he was any good with puns. "What are you doing here?" he said instead.

Meena smirked. "A little bird told me I could find you here." *That* was it.

She pulled a business card out and showed it to him. It was his card for Anubis Technologies, and the address was this shop. "Anubis? Are you some kind of idiot?"

He glowered at her. "It's called branding." He folded his arms. "So what do you want? Interested in some taxidermy?"

"I'm here about your other business, believe it or not."

"You can't prove anything."

"Oh, can't I?" She counted on her broken fingers. "Brooke recognized you when she came out of that vent. And I heard you were asking guests about the wall lamps in the stairwell, but there aren't any in the public stairs. Only the staff stairs. I should know, I've been in there without permission plenty of times. And you're the only murderer on earth who would use those flimsy pyramid scheme knives, even when they're breaking apart mid-job. What would you call all that?"

He smiled. "A few coincidences. And maybe a little paranoia." He tilted his head. "From a doctor who treated all the victims, in fact. And who can shapeshift."

"That won't work. No one suspects me." But she was shifting nervously on her feet, avoiding his gaze. Maybe if he played this right he could get her to leave.

He remembered something from Quinn's notebook. "They're suspicious of your methods. Isn't it true that you've been trying

250

out untested treatments on your patients?"

She stammered in shock. "I– how did… Well, what else could I do? Nobody has ever treated this condition before. I had to–"

She stopped and shook her head. "I don't need to defend myself to the body snatcher. Are you enjoying that ooze, you creep?"

"What are you talking about?" he asked.

"Mr. Amaretto's jar of ooze? Thick gray stuff? It was coming out of all his orifices and he collected some for me to test." She held up her hands. "I do *not* want to know why you wanted it."

Ryan wrinkled his nose. "That's disgusting. I didn't steal your ooze jar."

"Huh? Then who did?"

"I don't know," he growled. His patience was running out. "Meena. What do you want from me?"

She put her hands on her hips. "I want you to stop. Leave our town alone."

He clicked his tongue. "We're providing an invaluable service to grieving families, you know. Do you want to take that away from them?"

"I'll create another grieving family the minute you step outside. Try me."

Ryan sighed. "Fine," he drawled. "I'll go somewhere else."

"You won't go *anywhere*. I will find you if you do. You'll stop killing. Period."

He gritted his teeth. "Fine."

"Promise," she said. "Perform a binding."

He resisted the urge to reach out and strangle her. He knew how that would end. "I promise," he lied in a tightly controlled tone of voice, crossing his fingers in his pocket to negate the spell circle he was drawing in the air with his other hand. "Now, are we finished here?"

"I guess we are." She began turning away. "Remember. If you try this again I'll find you." She leapt into the air, transforming into her bird form, and flapped away. Good riddance.

Ryan double-checked the lock on the door before turning to walk through the empty shop. He wondered if Ted heard any of that. The man already got so paranoid, no matter how many times Ryan explained the business model to him.

It was Ted's skill with these animals which made him so valuable for the final phase of their process, the revival. From their perches around the shop, coyotes sneered at him, hawks hovered overhead, and rabbits cocked their ears in perpetual caution. The fading sunlight gleamed off dozens of glass eyes. The seams were well-hidden and the preservation was flawless, just like on all of Ted's work. Those who complained about sloppy wound repairs might change their tune if they knew what kind of state they arrived in. But customers always find something to complain about.

The door to the lab blended easily into the wood paneling on the back wall. Ryan unlocked and pried it open– and immediately staggered back at the smell.

The first thing he saw was the blood. Hardening in far-flung drops in each corner of the room, streaming off the edges of the operating table, filling cracks between tiles and carrying little scraps of viscera towards the central floor drain.

The second thing was Ted's mauled body. Most of it lay on the operating table, feet formerly facing the door if Ryan was judging

252

the position of those exposed ribs correctly. The same way their clients lay during operations.

The third thing he saw was the message scrawled in blood above the counter, punctuated by Ted's head. NO MORE BOTCH JOBS. YOU'RE NEXT, HARE. Ryan shuddered as he read his own surname. Concise, angry, and not very intelligent. Burke. He must be in charge of Fenris's pack now. Definitely time to get out of this town.

Ryan sighed as he surveyed the scene. Ted would be expensive to replace. Who else could do the operations? Maybe Meena would be easy to frame and blackmail. It couldn't be that hard to get ahold of starling feathers…

He began to pace in thought. His foot sank into a deep puddle of blood, knocking aside a stray toe, and he cursed. Ted was still causing him problems even after his death. These shoes were limited edition, and it wasn't like he could just bring them to a dry cleaner. They were–

Ryan froze. He remembered these weren't the only items he had gotten stained with blood. In the aftermath of his murders, it had been easy to shed his bloody clothes and change into something identical without suspicion. But he had left those clothes in his room back at the inn, soaking in the scents of each of his victims. The vampire would know what he had done as soon as she entered his room. Escaping from that place was pointless with a blood-tracking creature on his tail. He couldn't believe he had done something so thoughtless.

He groaned, running his hands through his hair and skimming through his options. No– there were no other options, not really.

To make a clean break, there was only one thing he could do.

He had to go back to that horrible inn.

~~~

Quinn's friends stared at them in mute amazement. Around them lay a flurry of newspaper scraps, photos, hand-scribbled notes, and business cards, plus a torn piece of a familiar black t-shirt. They stood up and caught their breath.

"Wow," Jasper said finally. "This… this is impressive. But it's a lot, Quinn. Are you sure?"

Quinn nodded. "Totally sure. There's no one else it could be." They handed him their notebook. "Take a look."

He opened it and began to flip through the pages. As he did, a tattoo on his finger brushed against a page and ignited a blue spark. Within the blink of an eye the notebook was engulfed in cobalt flame.

Jasper cried out as he dropped it. With a flick of his wrist he enclosed the book in a blue bubble which extinguished the flames.

"I thought you couldn't use magic," he said.

"I thought so too!" Quinn cried.

"Then why is there a hex on this thing?"

"A *what?*"

"Magical sabotage. Counteracts the effects of any spell you try to use it for. Some can even repel nearby magic." He groaned, putting a hand over his eyes. "Of course. When he arrived, Ryan said he works with curses."

"But he didn't touch–" Quinn gasped. "Wait. When we found
~~~

Fenris's body. I dropped my notebook and he gave it back to me." Their head spun. "So… wait. It wasn't me. Those times I ruined your spells. It wasn't me!" They hopped in excitement.

"It wouldn't matter if it was," Jasper said, but he smiled.

"So what do we do now?" Ash asked.

"Presumably, we thoroughly beat Ryan's sorry hide and then hand him over to whatever governing body rules him," Ciara said. "But we need him for that, don't we?"

"He's probably long gone by now," Jasper said. "But maybe he left something in his room that we could turn in. We should search the room."

Ciara frowned doubtfully. "Would a man who gets away with murder leave behind anything incriminating? He'd have to be a real idiot to–"

A hard thud on the floor above made them all look up.

"Isn't that around where Ryan's room is?" Ash asked quietly.

"Yes it is," Jasper answered.

They all exchanged a disbelieving glance.

"Speak of the human," Ciara said, rising to her feet. "Now, who's up for a beat down?"

"Let's move slowly," Jasper cautioned. "That man is danger-ous."

"So are we." She patted her pockets with a smirk.

"Are you still carrying around all those worms?" he cried. "Why?"

"I think today makes that clear, eh? Anyone want one?"

"Me," Quinn said eagerly.

"Me too," Ash said.

"You're a horrible influence," Jasper told her.

"I'm a *great* influence," Ciara corrected, passing a few of the fuzzy worms to each of them. Quinn's worms thrashed in their pockets before going still as they followed their friends upstairs.

The door to Ryan's room stood wide open. Inside it was ransacked, with the wardrobe empty and the furniture upturned. He was nowhere to be seen. They quickly searched over the bare room before regrouping.

The only thing they could do, they agreed, was to search the rest of the floor. It was deserted of guests and several hallways were dark where the lamps had burst. The spot where the wall had peeled away was starting to scab.

Jasper and Ciara went down one hallway while Quinn and Ash went down another. They passed the closet which he had shoved them into earlier. Quinn studied the door, clearing their throat.

"Uh… hey," they said. "Thanks for saving me earlier. You didn't have to do that."

Ash glanced at the door and shrugged. "It's okay. It was nothing."

Quinn squirmed. "It wasn't really, though. It felt important."

He looked uncomfortable. Quinn felt uncomfortable. This was weird. They didn't know why they had started talking.

"Anyway, uh… You're a good friend. That's all."

Quinn cringed at themself. But Ash smiled. "Thank you."

They both stood there for a few moments. Eventually they gave him an awkward thumbs-up.

Quinn was ashamed to admit that when Ryan burst out of the closet to tackle them, their first instinct was relief at the interruption. Horror quickly set in as they fell, frantically thrashing against his grip. Ash screamed and kicked the man in the head, causing him and Quinn to separate. Quinn rolled away from him and scrambled to their feet.

They sent a kick of their own into Ryan's side and shouted for Jasper and Ciara. Ryan caught their leg and wrenched them back down. He pinned them down with one hand and drew out a dented knife with the other. Mindless with fear, Quinn twisted to catch his attack with their shoulder rather than their neck. Ryan roared as Ash grabbed him, sinking burning-hot nails into his neck. Quinn bucked him off and dug in their pocket.

Ryan staggered to his feet and dove toward Ash. He grabbed the boy's throat and slammed him into the wall. Quinn desperately pulled the fuzzy worms from their pocket and tossed them at Ryan's back. To their horror the worms stayed limp as they tumbled off him. Just their luck.

Ryan glanced at them in confusion over his shoulder, then laughed when he saw the worms. "Enjoying my handiwork?" he teased before shifting his attention back to Ash. "You little monsters have caused me plenty of trouble. Maybe I should return the favor."

In a ginger blur Ciara rammed into him, sending him sprawling. Jasper was close behind her, sending a bolt of blue light into Ryan's chest. He stepped back to help Ash to his feet while Ciara and Ryan tumbled, trading blows with their elbows and fists.

The movement slowed as Ciara drove her knee into Ryan's chest and pinned him there. Quinn moved in and took his knife.

Suddenly Ciara went flying and Quinn was knocked back

against the wall. The knife skittered away. "An explosive spell!" Ciara warned the others as she hit the floor. "Look out!"

Ryan was already running away. Jasper dove after him and grabbed at him, tattoos glowing. Ryan's legs wobbled and gave out, but on his way down he wrenched something from his pocket and jabbed it into Jasper's thigh. Jasper cried out in pain and Ryan rolled away, stumbled uneasily to his feet, and staggered onward.

As he neared the closet Quinn was struck with an idea. They leapt at the closet door, throwing it open, and shouted, "In here!" Quickly catching on, Ciara barreled into Ryan, shoving him into the closet.

Quinn shut the door and threw their weight against it while Ash scrambled for his key to lock it. As usual, he couldn't find it. Quinn yanked theirs from its spot around their wrist and practically threw it at him. From the other side Ryan was already pounding against the keratin. Ash fumbled for a frighteningly long time with the lock and finally turned it. Quinn slumped to the floor in relief.

"Well then," Ciara said as they all caught their breath. "I suppose he can stay in there until we can recruit someone prepared to deal with those tricks of his." She turned to Jasper. "What did he do to your leg?"

Jasper gently poked the area which had been stabbed "Used some kind of dull needle, I think. It feels tingly."

A round object made of glass and metal lay on its side nearby. Quinn picked it up and examined it. A hollow needle attached to a clear bulb, the same device Delta had in her den. A small amount of silvery material sloshed around the bottom.

"Look at this," Quinn said as they walked away. "What's the

258

stuff inside?"

"It looks like life energy," Jasper said. "I guess that guest last month was wrong. I do have a soul."

Quinn gazed at the device in chilled fascination. It was hard to believe such a small thing had committed so much violence. They carefully pocketed the device.

The movement reminded them of their bare wrist and they turned to Ash. "Hey. Do you have my key?"

He nodded, dug through his pockets, then paled. "Oh– gosh. I think I dropped it."

"It's okay," they told him. "You guys go on. I'll run back for it."

Quinn turned around and went back the way they came. Sure enough, their key lay on the floor in front of the closet. They picked it up and fixed it back around their wrist, then paused, listening. No noise came from the closet. They hadn't expected Ryan to give up so soon. Maybe reality was sinking in for him. Quinn didn't really care what the murderer was thinking. Soon he wouldn't be able to hurt anyone else, and they would be lucky if they never had to think of him again. They threw one last glance at the door and walked away.

They didn't get far. Not far enough to notice Ryan waiting in a darkened hallway before he lunged at them. Not far enough to be sure their friends could hear them scream. And not far enough to escape down the staff stairs, which were around the corner, even if they could get away.

Quinn struggled against his grip on their neck. They jammed their knee into his sides, his groin, his legs, and he stumbled before quickly regaining his hold on them. His thumb dug into their throat, sending a wave of dizziness sweeping through them. Even as their vision blurred, the hatred in Ryan's eyes was terrifyingly clear.

"Why–" they wheezed. "Why?"

Ryan snorted. "Why? Do you think this is about you? I'm just cleaning up. You're in my way. That's why." He smiled. "This isn't personal, you know. It's just business."

Quinn coughed weakly. In the corner of their eye they saw the remains of a wall lamp lying on the floor. Without hesitation they used their remaining strength to throw their weight towards it. The two went down together. A few shards of glass crunched into Quinn's shoulder, but Ryan caught most of it. Distracted by shock and pain, he let go, and Quinn took off running for the staff stairs.

They barreled around the corner and threw open the door to the staircase. They darted inside and were about to run down when Ryan seized them again. Their heart sank as they twisted to face him. They were so close.

"You really are a pain," Ryan growled, shoving them against the banister. "No wonder your parents had to get rid of you." He took out another knife, one in worse shape than the last, dented at a bizarre angle. They might have laughed if the circumstances were different.

Instead tears budded in the corners of Quinn's eyes. The stairwell grumbled, steps vibrating uneasily.

"Even this place doesn't want you around," Ryan continued. "I have to agree. Maybe I should do us all a favor."

Quinn jolted with a realization. They jerked, letting the knife slash their collarbone to save their throat. Their hand dove into their pocket and emerged with the round metal and glass device which had stabbed Jasper. Ryan paused in surprise and Quinn dodged away from him, hurling the device down the stairwell.

Ryan gaped at them. He had clearly expected them to stab him. "What–"

"You're wrong," Quinn panted. "I *do* belong here. But you don't."

The device fell down and down, carrying with it the scent of its owner. Its owner, who could only know about their parents from reading their notebook and leaving his traces all over it, who wasn't known to the inn, who all along had caused those violent reactions which made Quinn feel so unwanted. Down, down to the increasingly sensitive areas of the inn, until it hit the warm earth of the basement.

At first, nothing. Quinn's stomach dropped. Had they been wrong?

Then a rumble. It started soft and quickly built into a furious roar. It spread through the stairs, which shook violently. Quinn grabbed the banister and held on tight.

Ryan tried to run for the door. It slammed shut in his face. He turned back towards Quinn, eyes blazing with horror and disgust. He lunged for them. He didn't reach them.

With a snap like a stiff joint cracking, the stairs folded in. The stairwell became one flat, very steep slope. Ryan screamed as he slid and disappeared into the darkness. Quinn breathlessly clung to the banister, feet dangling, and listened as his voice faded.

The familiar groan of the stomach opening and closing echoed upward. The stairs gently settled back into place. Another long rumble, then a pause.

Then a loud sound not unlike a burp.

- 16 -

Delta held her daughter close as the little girl shivered. When Bertram lived, Ryan had withdrawn the cure he promised, and now Brooke was doing worse than ever. Being out in the cold air and pounding rain didn't help. But there was no going back to the den, or to the inn. Ryan was at the inn, and everyone suspected her anyway. If the place was even still standing.

A beam of jaundiced light shot through the night. Delta shrank back against a tree trunk. The source of the light paused and then approached rapidly, swinging in the wind. She held her breath in terror.

Ciara trotted to a stop and waved. She carried an ancient-looking lantern in one hand. "Hark, ladies! Nasty weather tonight, eh?"

Brooke babbled weakly. Delta clutched her tighter and said nothing.

"Certainly too cold to be outside tonight," Ciara continued. "Not least with a child."

"What do you want?" Delta asked.

The vampire held up her hands. "No demands here. Just an invitation. Come back to the inn."

Delta stiffened. "What? I… I can't. We need to go somewhere else, Brooke is…"

"We know about Brooke," Ciara said gently. "And Ryan is gone. Permanently gone."

Delta stood silent, processing the news. It was hard to believe she and her daughter could really be safe. She was afraid to let her guard down. And if it was true, what would everyone think of her now that they knew? She couldn't bear the way they were going to look at her.

She shook her head. "I'm sorry. I can't go back."

Ciara tilted her head. "Your choice. I have more rounds to make, in case anyone else is caught in the storm. Good night." With a nod she ran off.

Delta settled back against the tree trunk with a sigh. She didn't know if she was doing the right thing. At every step since Brooke's accident, she had desperately hoped she was doing the right thing. It felt impossible sometimes. If she went back, she might lose her chance to get Brooke to a doctor in time. Yes, it would be warmer… and safer… and more comfortable… but she couldn't show her face there now.

Brooke shivered violently and tried to bury herself in her

mother's chest. She felt so cold to the touch, even for a riverbeast. Her tiny fingers were clumsy and stiff. Delta rubbed them anxiously to warm them.

Several minutes later Ciara ran by again. She stopped and looked the two over. "Changed your mind?"

Delta bit her lip. "No." She hoped repeating the decision would give her confidence. It did not.

Ciara shrugged. "Alright." She turned away.

"Wait! Wait." The words spilled out on a whim. Delta climbed to her feet. Ciara paused and allowed her to catch up.

Delta didn't look at her. "Lead the way."

Ciara nodded. Her lantern lit the trees in waxy yellow as they walked to the inn.

Inside the lobby was a flurry of activity. Staff and guests worked together to strip away the torn carpet, shredded wallpaper, and broken furniture, exposing the brown keratin underneath. Ciara set the lantern down on the front desk and disappeared into the swirl of motion. Delta remained by the door, uncertain what to do.

A loud cheer went up in front of the elevator. Jasper had fixed the car and it had just carried down its first passengers. Tosk, who had been helping, broke away from the group and bounded over to her.

"Delta! You're okay!" he said with a smile. "How is Brooke?" He restlessly rubbed at some rope burns along his body and tail.

Delta shifted Brooke onto her hip. "Not well. What about you?" She gestured towards his rope burns.

Tosk chittered softly. "I made a stupid mistake and paid for it. I was wrong about Fenris's involvement in all of this, and I promised I could get him locked up, but I couldn't deliver. Maybe don't visit the west end of the woods alone for a while." He stood up straighter, remembering something. "Hey, Meena is looking for you. Wait here." He sprung away.

After a few minutes Meena appeared. She approached slowly in her human form, like she didn't want to scare Delta away, holding a thick medical textbook which fluttered with sticky notes. She cut straight to the point. "How is she feeling?"

Delta struggled to control her voice. "Weaker. Groggier. She won't eat and she seems to be in a lot of pain."

Meena nodded. "Sounds familiar. I've seen a lot of patients with these symptoms." She opened the book and pulled a packet of notes from between the pages. "Look, Delta, I know this is scary. You may not trust me– that's your business. But I think I can help Brooke. At least I want to try."

Delta swallowed nervously. "How? What could you do?"

Meena led her to one of the sofas by the fire. They sat on the end untouched by the massive rip in the upholstery. Meena opened her book to a page describing the movements of life energy through the body. "This is experimental," she warned, "but it might be the only way. I believe the patients who had this revival procedure have something going wrong with their life currents. I examined some of my patients and I found the issue in one. The transfusion site was leaking. It hasn't been long since I operated, but she's already doing better."

She handed Delta the packet of notes. "Take a look. I can't make any promises, but I'll show you everything I know."

Delta hesitantly took the notes. Shuffling through them, it was

266

hard not to see the common threads running through the cases. So many patients similar to Brooke. Some who died again and some who recovered. All desperate to live. All dearly loved. Delta struggled to breathe.

"You don't have to decide now," Meena said. "Can I just take a look at her?"

Delta looked down at her daughter, overwhelmed with dread and hope. Brooke's eyes blinked up at her and crinkled in a wide smile. All along, that smile had been worth it all. It was no different now. Delta kissed the little girl's forehead, gave her a squeeze, and then carefully passed her to Meena.

Over in the lounge, Quinn and Ash swept broken glass off the floor. Frederick and the dishwasher imp sat together on the counter with a cloth napkin wrapped around their shoulders like a rescue blanket. "You missed one over there," Frederick said, pointing under a table.

Ash bent to look where Frederick was pointing, banged his head on the edge of the table, and stumbled back. Frederick cackled, legs swinging. Quinn caught Ash and steadied him before he could fall onto the debris pile. He smiled at them gratefully.

Jasper came in from the lobby and looked over the room. "Good work– hey." He grabbed Quinn's broom away. "You're supposed to be resting."

Quinn shuffled to one of the booths with a sigh. "But I feel better."

"Of course you do. Because I'm a healing genius. Now sit down."

They sat, adjusting the sigil-stenciled bandages which pressed herbs and powders against their skin. They were grateful to feel the buzz of healthy magic there. The more they learned about magic, the more vast and complicated its world felt, and they weren't sure where they fit in. Even with their notebook fixed they hadn't done a successful spell on their own yet. The thought that something could really be broken in them nagged at their mind. But they were willing to give it time.

A tremor rolled through the structure of the inn, similar to the ones when they first arrived. They exchanged concerned looks with Ash and Jasper.

"Memorial fire is all set for tomorrow," Ciara said as she came in. "Some friends and family of the victims are writing eulogies. Touching stuff. That quake is concerning, eh?"

"I'll take a look," Jasper said.

"Did you tell them how you'll redecorate this place?" she asked him.

He modestly tipped his head down. "Nope."

"Tell us!" Quinn said.

"Well, I'm keeping the gold," Jasper said. "That was Lev's favorite. It's more him than anything else. But all the red gave me a headache, so I'm replacing it."

"With!" Ciara prompted, jabbing him.

He smiled. "Blue."

"Aww," Quinn and Ash chorused.

"Shut up," Jasper laughed.

"A little of both of you," Ciara said. "Very sweet, you sentimental bastard."

The inn's frame shook again. Jasper stood. "Okay. Let's check

268

on that thing."

They all followed him down to the basement, through the workspace and into the stomach chamber. The huge organ seized and stretched in discomfort. Ciara heaved open the hatch and Ash climbed inside. After a minute he reemerged with a skull, just like the first time, but this skull looked different from the first. This one was larger and rounder. It was human. *Ryan.*

Ash held the skull out to Quinn. "Want this one too?"

Quinn took it, a chill running down their spine. Even made brittle by hours in the fire, it felt solid and heavy. They thought of the fox skull up in their room. "No," they said eventually. "I think this one belongs here."

"What should we do with it?" Ash asked, taking the skull back.

"Maybe we should bury it somewhere," Quinn suggested.

"Somewhere far away from the inn," Jasper said, wrinkling his nose.

Ash nodded. He turned to head back upstairs and promptly smacked into the hatch door, dropping the skull. It crumbled on impact with the floor.

Everyone stared at the chalky pile in silence.

"Shall I get a dustpan?" Ciara said after a long pause. The others mumbled in agreement.

When they were finished the four returned to the lobby. Under Jasper's orders Quinn sat on one of the sofas and watched the repairs continue. Across from them Meena and Delta were intently discussing something, while above their head Tosk tinkered with the remains of the chandelier. Guests treated each other's injuries and helped find each other's luggage and loved ones. Kindness flowed easily through the room.

For the first time since they found Fenris's body, Quinn relaxed. They could barely believe everything that had happened over the last several days. They felt a churning mixture of horror, sadness, pride, and relief. But an old fixture of their mental landscape wasn't there. Looking around, Quinn realized with a start that they didn't feel alone.

During the repair process, each of their needs were met without hesitation or judgment, and it felt easy to pass on the generosity. They weren't an outsider anymore but a part of a thriving ecosystem. They weren't sure they were the same person as before. That idea was both thrilling and a little frightening.

Just then a massive pill bug rolled by, unfurled itself, and wriggled its legs. One was bent at a harsh, startling angle. When the pill bug tried to put weight on the leg it pulled back in pain.

Quinn jumped to their feet. "Hey! Can I help you with that?" They grabbed the first aid kit from behind the front desk and began to wrap the bug's affected leg. "How did you hurt it? Is the inn hard to move around in for you? How do you keep from drying out?"

Maybe they hadn't changed so much after all.

ACKNOWLEDGEMENTS

Thank you…

   … to my family, for showing me what makes a home.

   … to my teachers, for believing in me. Especially you, Ms. Rabinowitz.

   … to Lucy, for helping this story take shape.

   … to my writing practice, for opening a window of hope in a dark time.

   … to Jane Kalmes, for the writing resources.

   … to my beta reader, Hailey, and my editor, Beauregard.

   … to all the authors with the courage to carve out a piece of their heart and put it on paper, for inspiring me.

   … and to you, the reader.

ABOUT THE AUTHOR

Linden Larson is a professional museum lurker, long-distance cemetery walker, and cryptid enthusiast. Their art is inspired by the deep shadows of history and mythology and the brilliant chaos of the natural world. They live in Buffalo NY with far more plants than are necessary. This is their first novel.